T0301140

Because She Looked Away

ALISON BRUCE

BECAUSE SHE LOOKED AWAY

CONSTABLE

CONSTABLE

First published in Great Britain in 2024 by Constable

1 3 5 7 9 10 8 6 4 2

A CIP catalogue record for this book
is available from the British Library.

ISBN: 978-1-47212-390-9

Typeset in Times New Roman by Hewer Text UK Ltd, Edinburgh
Printed and bound in Great Britain by Clays Ltd, Elcograf S.p.A.

Papers used by Constable are from well-managed forests and other responsible sources.

Constable
An imprint of
Little, Brown Book Group
Carmelite House
50 Victoria Embankment
London EC4Y 0DZ

An Hachette UK Company
www.hachette.co.uk

www.littlebrown.co.uk

In jail, inhuman,
coded up, lit up,
on safari and on ice . . .
. . . this book is dedicated to
Amanfi, Ben, Bex, Bhasha,
Bodalia, Charlotte, Indie,
Ken, Paul and Scott.

PROLOGUE

Twenty-four years ago

There were snippets, fragments too small to mean anything. A pause before her mother had answered that was a moment too long and a flash of a mismatch between expression and reply. And then her ever-warm hands, which had become cold and restless. They didn't clasp properly. They didn't wrap around in a comforting way. Instead, they gripped, claw-like, mechanical, as though the wiring had too much electricity flowing through it.

Her sentences grew shorter and more frequently ended with a question mark.

Ronnie supposed when she looked back on that morning and over-laid those little signs, that they had been enough to sharpen her wits. That together they had made the difference.

The memory of that day was pieced together. It had been fragments, little snippets of the picture that had been accumulated and assembled after countless hours of therapy.

Children's minds could be open to suggestion. False memories could be implanted. But she was confident that none of these images were anything but the real thing.

October the fourteenth had been cold, dismal, wet. A dirty north London day and their mother had bundled them in coats and scarves, thick layers that made their arms sit wide of their sides. Ronnie remembered the scarf, close to her mouth, getting dewy with the dampness of her breath. And the urgency as they walked, one on either side of their mother who towed them along, at not quite a run, but faster than a walk. Every few yards, Ronnie remembered scuttling forward a little, working hard to keep up, and it must have been worse for her brother George. He was three and she was five and that much taller.

It was the route they went on when they occasionally visited their grandmother in central London. Ronnie hated visiting her grandmother. She was frail and angry and never remembered who either of them was. And the visit there was always preceded with false excitement. Lots of build-up, lots of reluctance on her part. There had been none of that on this particular day. But she had known they were headed somewhere.

As an adult Ronnie had gone back many times and had retraced the steps she'd taken in the few hundred yards up to Highgate Station. The road was straight, lined with a variety of shops. Busy pavement, busy road, grubby everything and perpetually noisy.

She'd never understood what she'd expected from those visits but once, maybe twice a year for years she'd felt compelled to walk along that pavement in the hope of non-existent answers.

Her brother had begun to cry, somewhere in the last hundred yards she guessed.

Half sob, half whine. She remembered being miserably silent and wanting him just to shut up. She'd said nothing, though, and when they reached the station, her mother had maintained her tight grip on each of them. And she'd still wanted her brother to be quiet but at the same time, she'd recognised that he'd been voicing the misery that she had felt, the drudge that the day was to become.

He wailed that he wanted to go home. She stood wondering where they were going but said nothing. Apparently, they weren't long like that. The way she remembered it, they could have been standing there for hours, but apparently it was three minutes and twenty-six seconds.

Three minutes and twenty-six seconds between stepping onto the platform and their mum hauling them across it and trying to fling all three of them into the path of the 10.26 through-train.

2

And that final part she didn't remember. Could never and would never remember, she was sure of that. She only knew the outcome. That in those seconds, her little brain pieced everything together, and that she'd squirmed and fought her way from her mother's grasp.

A single sound stuck in her head.

A certain frequency that occasionally she would hear, even now, and it would send her cold. Whether it was the scream of the train, the scream of her mother, her brother, bystanders even. Or all of them rolled together. A dirty, heavy, deafening, all-encompassing squeal of something that marked the end of everything.

Her mum had called her Veronica that day. The name she used when she was angry or tense or brewing up to one of her tempers. She had never been Veronica since. Would never be. From that day onwards, she was Ronnie. And she was on her own.

CHAPTER 1

Ronnie hauled her oversized suitcase from the luggage bay of the coach. It had pulled to the kerb on a treelined road bordering a large green. She stepped back, out of the way of the other passengers as the driver reunited them with their luggage. She needed a minute to catch her breath.

Light was rapidly fading, and the pavement was damp and the grass glossy under the streetlamps. The smell of wet mud rose to meet her; fresh, natural and nothing like the air in London, which hung heavy with a cocktail of traffic and people, and their daily lives. Here the air seemed clear and empty as though she could take a deep breath and have time just to focus on her own life. The thought of it terrified her; she had never run her life that way.

Instead, she had kept her head down and worked her way through eight years of investigating serious crime with her personal life trailing behind like a tatty rag. She'd liked it like that, hadn't wanted it any other way. She had never expected to be snatched up and thrown on a different path, landing in Cambridge to live with her half-brother and their sister's child, Noah.

This was the first time she'd set foot in the place despite opportunities to visit her brother in the past. She knew no more about the city than the next person. Less in fact. Until this morning, she had thought it the home of the dreaming spires, only to discover that the title belonged to its closest rival.

4

She didn't have high expectations; as far as she could work out Cambridge was a bunch of medieval buildings sitting in a pancake of land, probably packed with rich and entitled students, little crime and a Neanderthal police force.

The passengers dispersed and the coach's hydraulics hissed as its doors shut and it pulled into the traffic. It had been obscuring her view of the opposite side of the road, and it was only then that she realised she was facing Parkside Police Station. It was a coal-coloured lump of a building which looked as though it had been prefabricated and dumped as a single block. It managed to look both out of place among the other buildings and, at the same time, completely forgettable.

I'll see you tomorrow, she thought and gave the building the smallest nod, also saying goodbye in that instant to everything she'd left in London; her hard-won career with the Met, her compact but well-ordered flat, her uncomplicated single life which allowed her to come and go as she pleased. She hoped it was all going to be worth it, not for her, but for her nephew Noah.

Noah was her half-sister Jodie's son and Jodie was dead. It would have been far harder to let him down than to give up all those other things.

There was a short line of taxis further along the road. She wheeled her case towards the nearest, stooped to speak to the driver through his open window, 'Victoria Park?'

He nodded and the journey began.

CHAPTER 2

Ronnie's half-brother Alex had bought the property in Victoria Park about two years earlier. He'd moved from north London for a new job and a new relationship – only one had worked out and he'd been saddled with a succession of lodgers as he hung on to a house he could barely afford.

Ronnie knew she should have visited before and had felt a tug of guilt about it. Now she realised, it was coming back to bite her because it meant she was moving into a house she'd never seen, not in bricks and mortar anyway.

She'd looked on Google Earth.

The road was tear-shaped, splitting part way down to make room for trees on a small green. Or maybe it had been the other way round and the trees had been there all along, and the houses had been built around them.

Either way, the bay-fronted properties at that end of the road didn't stare into each other's windows but looked out on to the grass. The houses were similar to one another, brick built, Edwardian she guessed. A few were detached, most semi-detached and Alex had one of those, the left-hand one of a pair.

She recognised the house as the taxi drove up to it. She had seen it from the inside too, on Rightmove before Alex and his ex had bought it. It had looked airy, neutral, 'modernised with original features'. Probably smelling of fresh bread and newly brewed coffee, just as the property shows recommended.

Alex opened the door before she reached it. Although neither of them took after their father with any physical characteristics, they had ended up with a similar, skinny frame and the same, easy-to-tan complexion. He leaned towards her, they briefly hugged, and she used the moment to look over his shoulder and down the hallway. It was cluttered with coats and shoes, and a couple of bikes. The only decor was a 1977 *Star Wars* poster facing the front door, with Luke Skywalker looking as though he was taking aim at her. She knew then that she might as well forget anything she'd seen on Rightmove.

'Did my stuff arrive?' she asked.

'It's all in your room.'

'And Noah?'

'Believe it or not, he went to bed.'

'So early?' It was only a few minutes past seven. Ronnie wasn't sure what time eight-year-olds went to bed but had the impression that refusing to sleep was a major childhood skill.

'Long day at school, I guess.' Alex shrugged. 'He does that sometimes. He asked if you would say goodnight to him when you arrived, but don't worry, he's already asleep.'

Alex led the way, weaving past the bikes and stepping round a couple of boxes and piles of papers that were stacked on the stairs. There were four bedrooms although the fourth was barely big enough to accommodate more than a cot. That one was going to be Ronnie's office.

Her room contained a bed, a wardrobe, and a pile of uniformly sized removal boxes filled with anything she'd thought worth keeping from her flat. She stood in the centre of the floor, momentarily feeling adrift. 'How many bathrooms?'

'Just the one and a toilet downstairs.'

She frowned, too tired to muster even a weary smile.

He folded his arms, but not in a defensive way, more as though he needed a hug. 'So, what's up?'

She answered carefully; she knew he was apprehensive about the challenges of looking after Noah. 'It's a big adjustment, I guess, after living alone I mean. Is this going to work?' she asked.

7

'It's a start.' He sobered as he processed her question properly. 'Beyond that, all we seem to have in common is that we're two anti-social people, living with a kid who's dumb enough to actually like us.'

Ronnie felt herself uncoil a little and managed that smile. 'I'll do my best.'

'Me too.' He left her without saying more. The door closed behind him, and she stood for several minutes, adjusting to the room and the silence of the house, then she slipped across the landing and into Noah's room. He was, as Alex had said, asleep. She stopped short of the bed. 'Goodnight, Noah,' she whispered, 'I'll see you tomorrow.'

She returned to her room and sat heavily on her unmade bed. More than anything she needed a few hours of restful sleep before she had to report for work. Sleep was the cure-all that settled her thoughts and added perspective but too often it eluded her. She stripped down to her T-shirt and didn't bother looking for her pyjamas, toothbrush or even clean bedding.

She lay flat on her back and stared up at the ceiling. Closing her eyes wouldn't make any difference; some kind of sleep would come in the end. But first, just like on every other night, memories flooded over her. Through her. She had tried sleeping tablets. Alcohol. Staying busy until she dropped.

It was inescapable.

She had to replay the words. See the reaction. Ride the sick feeling in her gut.

And all over again, night after night, she watched Jodie die.

CHAPTER 3

Ronnie was on edge when she woke; bad sleep often had that effect. When she'd lived alone, it hadn't mattered, she could stumble around half awake until her mood settled. But now she had other people to consider.

She was up and dressed before either Alex or Noah had come down for breakfast and was waiting for the toast to pop up when Alex walked into the kitchen.

'Is Noah still asleep?' she asked.

'Yes,' Alex checked his watch; 'I'll give him a first call in half an hour.'

'I was hoping to see him before school. Later then.'

'You could hang around for a bit or I could wake him up?'

'No, I'll see him when I'm back.' She grabbed her single slice of toast as it popped up. She left it plain and gestured towards the door, 'I want to get there early.'

'Keeping first-day nerves at bay?'

'Something like that.' She pressed her lips into a smile, 'I'm sure it will be fine.'

'But you're not looking forward to it?' he added.

She gave him a maybe-yes, maybe-no nod. 'Does anything interesting ever happen on a first day?' She folded the toast and promised to let him know how it went. She hadn't felt hungry but going to work on an empty stomach would turn the tension to irritability or a migraine by mid-morning, so it was not worth the risk.

The morning was dry and bright, the sky vast, not seen in little strips the way it was in London, glimpsed between high-rise blocks or tightly packed streets. It looked as though the weather might manage a full day without changing its mind.

She typed 'Parkside Police Station' into the maps app on her phone and listened to the walking directions through headphones. The route was a zigzag, crossing busy roads, walking the length of the quiet ones. The houses she passed were mostly bay-fronted with red and black chequerboard tiled pathways leading a few steps up to traditional panelled front doors and tiny front gardens just large enough to accommodate a small tree or leafy shrub. Not a single property looked in need of attention, and many seemed to have been extended upwards into their uniformly tiled roofs. No doubt most had been modernised but in that low-key moneyed way that didn't show. It was all so tranquil and . . . She fished for a word for the kind of people who probably lived there and realised that any description would be based on the crimes she'd dealt with where the victims lived in these kinds of homes. And in her part of London, neighbourhoods like this had been few and far between.

She turned a corner on to a busier road. Guest houses faced out across the Cam, brightly painted canal boats were moored by the towpath. She crossed the river using a narrow metal footbridge and turned along an avenue of large, evenly spaced trees. Tourist territory. Somewhere to come for a day out or even a weekend.

Feeling irritable suddenly made sense; it wasn't just the result of poor sleep. Yes, Cambridge was picturesque, but if transferring here was going to drive her career into a backwater she'd probably know by the end of the day.

It was a police officer's default position to hate the idea of change, to resist it when it arrived. She had to give it a chance, she reminded herself.

She lowered her head and increased her pace. She'd planned to arrive at Parkside station with twenty minutes to spare. In the end, she'd left the house early and walked faster than the satnav had predicted, making her a full forty-five minutes early.

There was a single officer on duty at the front desk, dealing with a student's stolen bicycle. She took the nearest seat, closed her eyes, and listened to the requests for almost endless detail.

'What was the frame size?'
'How was it locked?'
'How long have you owned it?'
'Where did you leave it?'
'What time was that?'
'Give it a chance Ronnie,' she muttered under her breath.

CHAPTER 4

Ronnie's father, who was about as empathetic as he was patient, had told her the meaning of life on many occasions. 'Life,' he would say, 'is nothing but a series of goodbyes.' The wording changed over time, and he hadn't used those words when she'd first been thrust upon him and his other family. She clearly remembered feeling tiny and miserable and broken. And the closest to empathy he had been able to muster had been to deliver a simpler version of the same message, 'Nothing lasts forever, Ronnie. Everyone loses people.'

She had been five years old, and the weight of the words had crushed her.

Maybe life really was just a series of goodbyes. Goodbye to childhood. Goodbye to innocence. Goodbye to youth, to friends who drift away and every iteration of daily life that is overwritten by the next. But she hadn't needed to know that then. And by telling her, her father proved that he shouldn't have had his first child, never mind four; his ability to nurture was close to zero.

His vacillation in choosing between his first wife and family, and his eventual second wife and their two children, had been about nothing but satisfying his own inconsistent needs. Apart from endowing all the children with the last name of Blake, he had done little to encourage any closeness between her and her half-siblings.

Because of him, she had developed her own theory about life. She had no plans to share it with Noah, but she was reminded of it as she faced Superintendent Cooper.

She'd been met in reception and wordlessly taken to his office by a police constable so young that her uniform looked more like dress-up day than a career move.

Cooper's office was small, crammed with an oversized desk, one bulbous swivel chair and two steel-framed visitor chairs, *circa* 1990. 'Take a seat.' He gestured at the chair in front of his desk, not the one next to it. A shaft of sunlight fell directly into her eyes, so she shifted her chair by about twenty degrees so that the rays hit her cheek instead. The adjustment took no time at all, but she sensed his impatience.

He was around the fifty mark. Neat featured with his beard fresh from the barber's trim. She'd seen officers maintain that look day in and day out, as though they had a micro-trim every night. She pegged Cooper as someone who would take pleasure in patrolling the corridors and checking that junior officers met his exacting standards. She wasn't prejudging anything; perhaps she would like the man, perhaps she wouldn't and perhaps it was irrelevant to the job she had to do, but everything in this first meeting from the formal seating to his flat smile and half-hearted handshake told her it was not going to be the first day she had hoped for.

'So, it's Ronnie, not Veronica. Is that correct?'

'Yes, sir.'

'Welcome to Cambridge. You come highly recommended. New resource is always a plus, especially when they are both experienced and competent.' He tilted his head back and jutted his chin as he spoke, meaning that he was looking at her through partially closed eyes. IIc paused for a few seconds before adding anything further. 'But.' The word came out like a sharp jab on the brakes, the kind that makes eyes snap open and all attention fully refocus on the road. 'Occupational health doesn't say no, but they say not yet.'

It took a second for her to register what he was saying. 'I have been back at work for the last two weeks.'

'Completing paperwork, as I understand?'

'I was handing over some cases because I was leaving, but there was no question about my fitness to work.'

'Well, we are not the Met, and you will find we have a different set of standards here.'

She bristled; it was too soon for her loyalty to the Met to fade.

His expression had switched from cool politeness to immovability. 'I spoke to our occupational health, and we agreed that without a full assessment, you are not returning to work.' There were times when negotiation with senior officers was possible, and others when any attempt would only piss them off and lead to moving one step backwards. 'They have your contact details and will be in touch to arrange an appointment. Once you have been assessed as fit to work, we can meet and start over. Right now, though, I suggest you take the opportunity to familiarise yourself with our lovely city.' He made a point of turning his gaze towards the window, although she was sure from where he was sitting that the view was of nothing but sky. 'There are twenty-five museums and galleries around Cambridge, you could start there.'

Ronnie gave a small nod but didn't reply. She didn't trust herself to open her mouth and be able to come out with anything that didn't sound either heavily sarcastic or downright rude.

He waited a few beats to see whether there was anything she did want to add and she thought the conversation was over. Without explanation he turned to his laptop, he flicked through a couple of screens and took a few seconds to read. He looked back at her. 'Have you been contacted by DI John Fenton yet?'

'I don't recognise the name. Who is he?'

'He leads the Special Investigations Team for the Eastern Region – SITfER. They're based here, they cover this region and, at times, beyond. They'd like to interview you as a witness.'

'To what?'

He ignored the question. 'Asked me to send you over as soon as we had spoken. I wasn't sure that would be appropriate, but you seem as though you would be up to it.'

'With respect, sir, I believe I am fit to work so would certainly be fit to make a statement.' She glared; she couldn't help it. She tried again, 'What does it relate to?'

'I don't have that information, but you can go up there right away. The DEAD team's on the third.'

'The DEAD team?'

'Sorry, local nickname. We all enjoy a good acronym, don't we?' A smile flashed on and off again. 'Shall I find someone to take you up there?'

Ronnie shook her head and stood as she spoke. 'Don't worry, I will find my way, thank you.'

She stepped into the corridor where the air was slightly fresher.

Life, from her experience, was a pocket full of razor blades. There were times when you dipped your hand in and pulled out the right tool to do the job, but it was just as easy to draw blood.

CHAPTER 5

'We have some questions concerning your half-sister's death.'

Ronnie blinked slow enough to see the inside of her eyelids and hope that when her eyes reopened, the scene would have reset. DI John Fenton still stared back and was waiting for an answer.

Finding the third floor had been easy enough, finding the office of the Special Investigations Team for the Eastern Region took a few seconds longer.

She had checked the signs on the first couple of doors before glancing along the corridor and spotting two that didn't match the rest. Logic told her that any department with the word *special* in the title might make a point of standing out at every opportunity. She skipped the rooms in between and went straight to the first with the dark grey frame and the paler, smoke-grey door. A recent makeover, she guessed, because grey seemed to be every decorator and car owner's favourite colour right now. The newness extended into the office, a good-sized room with four panels of tinted windows along the opposite wall and an inner office at the far end.

The space was dominated by a large circular table. There were three pairs of desks butted up to the exterior wall. Two people occupied the room. Both had their backs to her and neither turned. Ronnie walked towards them, planning to speak, when one of them made the effort to drag their attention away from their laptop. She'd only taken a couple of steps when the inner office door opened and the man she guessed to be DI John Fenton took a couple of steps across the threshold. The other two looked up then, and then straight back to their screens when they saw he wasn't looking at them.

'Ronnie Blake?' He jerked his head for her to follow and turned.

There was no preamble, no niceties about moving to Cambridge or welcoming her to Parkside. He smiled, seemed to think that was all that was needed. Ronnie guessed it had been enough for many years with many people; he had clearly once been handsome and athletic. But now he was in his forties, prematurely ageing and on the slide towards thickset and balding. A career cop for sure.

Ronnie adopted an impassive expression and followed. She had no idea what he wanted from her, but she could already feel that he was the kind of man who crushed any desire she might have to cooperate. She took the nearest chair and waited while he scanned a document on his computer screen. Then when he opened his mouth and asked about her sister, she felt something in her head slam shut. 'Jodie Blake,' he added, as though it was only lack of clarification that was preventing her from answering.

'I know who my sister is,' she replied flatly.

'Of course, and I am sorry for your loss.'

'I hope your sympathy extends to respecting my privacy?' She knew that if it did, she wouldn't be here. The details that kept her awake weren't thoughts she revisited in her fully conscious hours. Even in just her own company. She didn't plan to go there with this man.

He tilted his head as though listening, then frowned before he spoke. Perhaps it was his thinking face. 'I know your background, Ronnie. Serious crime, major and critical incidents. At what point do you afford the victims or their families the opportunity to avoid making a statement?'

'I have never avoided it. I made a full one at the time and I'm sure you have it right in front of you. I have answered every question up to now. There is nothing else I can tell you.'

She folded her hands in her lap, attempting to project composure.

'And I haven't moved to Cambridge to start going through any of it all over again. I am here to work.'

17

'I have further questions about your sister, events surrounding her death, and I'd like more details of those who knew her.'

She was torn between the urge to walk out and the desire to add sarcasm to the conversation, or better still, something caustic enough to make him back off.

She checked herself; the real problem she realised was being asked about Jodie. This meeting and being asked about her sister had blindsided her; being confrontational was not going to serve any useful purpose. It wasn't uncommon for people to rub her up the wrong way either; a proportion were idiots, and more were just rude. John Fenton was probably a bit of both, but neither on the scale she regularly encountered as a part of her daily work. She drew a slow breath, determined to sound more cooperative even if she had no intention of compromise. 'I can't explain any more than I already have. Sorry.'

He let her words settle and then moderated his tone to sound more reasonable, just as she had just done. 'Ronnie, we do need to go over the details of your witness statement.' He shifted to mirror her pose as though he had suddenly remembered that it wasn't bullishness that secured the results. The tactic should have irritated her too, but she let it slide.

'Why?' she frowned.

'We're looking for anything you might have missed. Anything that could shed more light on what happened.'

'I didn't miss anything.' But without warning it seemed as though the world tilted a fraction. Warped very slightly. 'You're a special investigations team, why are you asking?' *What did they think she'd missed?* Her stomach knotted. A wave of queasiness hit; so much for calm and in control. 'What interest is my sister to you?'

Fenton hadn't taken his eyes off her. God only knew the range of emotions that had just flashed across her failed poker face. 'Her name has come up as part of an ongoing investigation.'

'I don't believe you. Your team covers the Eastern Region, which doesn't include London. Jodie never left the place.'

'What difference would that make?' He picked up a ballpoint pen just to tap it on the desktop. Her irritation rose again, and she wanted to slap it out of his hand. 'We have local cases,' he continued, 'where the suspects are sitting in another country. You know that.'

'Yeah, well, Jodie wasn't a suspect in anything, so I smell bullshit.'

'So do I, Ronnie. You can block all you like; this conversation needs to happen.'

'Why are you called the DEAD team?'

'Where did you hear that?'

'Superintendent Cooper.'

'People should stick to our correct name.' He dropped his gaze to his laptop, typed for a few seconds, then pressed the return key with a sharp jab of his index finger. 'And I never said your sister was a suspect.'

The result of his typing appeared a couple of seconds later when the door was opened by an angular woman with hair not much longer than a buzzcut. It was hard to determine her age. If it hadn't been for her eyes she could have been anywhere between late twenties and early forties. They aged her. If she turned out to be at the younger end of the age range, then she'd seen way too much.

'Ronnie.' Fenton raised his hand, palm upwards in the direction of the door, 'Meet DC Tess Larson, she will look after you now.'

CHAPTER 6

DC Tess Larson had led them further along the third-floor corridor, to the second door with the grey-on-grey livery. Larson had punched a code into the security pad, then pressed a pass card against the sensor. Ronnie had already worked out that the team wasn't underfunded, but this room backed it up, it was plush, with state-of-the-art video-conferencing screens. Larson had pressed a remote and a projector screen slid down from the ceiling. It was the width of the narrowest wall. Another detective had been waiting for them and he'd introduced himself as DC Will Green and offered drinks. Ronnie hadn't wanted drinks; she'd wanted to go home.

Now she sat at a large table with Larson alongside her and Green diagonally opposite. The two detectives had matching laptops, high end and looking as though they'd only just been unboxed.

Larson spoke first. She seemed to have no discernible regional dialect and her tone was calm and warm. 'I'm sorry that today has taken you by surprise. I was under the impression that you'd already been contacted.'

'Who by?'

Larson glanced at the open notebook on her lap, 'I'm not sure actually. No matter.' The corners of her mouth twitched, more of an apology than a smile. 'It could have been my misunderstanding, so let me go from the start. We are the Special Investigations Team for the Eastern Region. Have you heard of us?'

'Not until today.'

'That's fine. Most people haven't.'

Picking up on some kind of invisible cue, Green took over. 'We were originally brought together for one high-profile investigation. It took us two years, and during that time this team developed a set of skills which were considered too valuable for us to disband. Since then, we have worked on any special investigation which requires a response covering multiple police forces and an advanced level of data analysis, planning and intelligence gathering.'

Ronnie had no desire to discuss her sister, but even so, she felt some of her reluctance slip away and leaned closer. 'And that's what you're working on now? A case that's bigger and more complex than a typical investigation.'

'What is a typical investigation, Ronnie?' Green shrugged.

'Too big to be handled by a single force? And connected to my sister?'

'Yes, to the first and potentially, possibly, yes to the second.' It was Larson who replied, taking over, again seamlessly. 'And that's why it's important to have the opportunity to go over what happened on the night of your sister's death, and for us to learn more about her background.'

Green had stirred Ronnie's curiosity, and it had cooled her hostility by a few degrees. Fenton had been right to hand her over to Larson and Green. 'I don't think there's anything I can add to my statement,' she told them.

'We have been over it,' Larson agreed, 'and it probably is about as comprehensive as it could be, but it reads as though it was written by a police officer, and I'd like to hear it from you, as her sister.'

Ronnie hesitated. But she understood the last comment only too well. She remembered when she'd made the statement, and she knew she'd fallen back on her police training. She'd built it on facts and chronology and making sure that her wording shut the door on any ambiguity or omission. She hadn't cried when she'd written it either; a combination of shock and training had kept her detached. And then for night after night, she'd woken in the small hours with her pillow wet from tears. Eventually replaced by the battle to get to sleep and the nightmares when she did. 'Where do you want me to start?'

21

CHAPTER 7

'Jodie was eleven months younger than me. She was my half-sister, and I have a half-brother Alex who is a couple of years older.'

Ronnie was certain that Larson and Green had all the answers in front of them, but Larson still asked the next, obvious question, 'And you all had the same father?'

'He had two families at the same time. He was married to my mother, and I remember him visiting, but he didn't live with our family.' Ronnie shifted in her chair and jumped the timeline forward, 'Jodie and I were small when we started living together; I don't remember a time when she wasn't in my life, but I do know we clashed at first.'

'Did you blame your father for your mother's death?' It was Green who had spoken, and the question jarred. Larson shot him a frustrated look.

'What does that have to do with Jodie?' Ronnie snapped, then added, 'Or Alex?'

'It's background information.'

'I think it's prying. Just stick to Jodie.' Ronnie flashed her dark gaze back first at Green, then Larson.

A detective should have control of an interview. It should be planned and managed with contingencies and options at hand to reroute and send it back on course. Ronnie guessed this was supposed to be Larson's show, but Green had thrown her off track. Larson frowned down at her paperwork and reordered some of the sheets before recovering her composure. 'I think it's important that we understand as much as possible about Jodie. Please, can we continue?'

'Sure.' Ronnie shot a warning glance at Green, but he looked as though he had no intention of interrupting again. 'Jodie and I were pretty close growing up. We had quite different personalities, but Alex bridged the gap. He was the glue for us three kids but after a while Jodie and I became close. Inseparable for a couple of years.'

'Until when?'

Ronnie considered and her gaze drifted across the room, falling on the opposite corner. The walls were the same shade of grey-tinted white, but the shadows changed that.

'Fourteen or fifteen. We all saw less of each other through secondary school; different friends, different interests, and that continued into adulthood. For a while, perhaps a year or two, Jodie and I saw each other just occasionally, but then she had Noah and wanted more support.'

'Did you see her during her pregnancy?'

'Once or twice.'

'And the father?'

'She never told me who he was.' Which was a half-truth, but a well-practised one. It sounded natural.

'I see.' Larson didn't look convinced. 'What about after Noah's birth?'

'Like I say, she never told me,'

'Perhaps she didn't know?'

'It's possible,' Ronnie conceded. 'The point is, she wanted support and I wanted to give it. And Noah brought us together again.' A natural softness had come to her voice when she spoke his name, and a smile that she couldn't help. 'When Noah arrived, Jodie and I became as close as we had ever been.'

Babies felt alien to Ronnie but the first time she'd looked at Noah, she'd seen an unmistakable resemblance to her own baby brother. It had both taken her breath away and created an unbreakable bond between her and her new nephew.

'Ronnie?' Larson's head was tilted, and her expression said she'd spoken but not been heard.

23

'Sorry, can you repeat the question?'

'What kind of mother was Jodie?'

'Emotionally, she gave him absolutely everything he needed. Organisationally? She probably wasn't the best. She would have spells of tidiness and spells of working, and others with no money. Just no consistency I suppose . . .'

'And spells of depression?'

Ronnie wasn't sure. She knew Jodie struggled, had low moods and sometimes anxiety. It was only after Jodie's death that Ronnie had realised that her sister must have struggled more than she had known. And then began the infinite and pointless loop of what-ifs and if-onlys that still kept her awake at night or followed her into sleep. 'I would have said "no", but obviously, now I'm not sure.'

'Did she talk to you about her mental health at all?'

'No. Nothing more than I've already said. And she could have talked to me.'

'So, no indication that your sister might take her own life?'

'No.' Ronnie's reply snapped back as a reflex. 'Do you think I would have known and not mentioned it in my statement? It's offensive that you've even asked.'

'Ronnie?'

'No.' Of course Ronnie understood that asking questions was Larson's job, but her own patience had hit its threshold. 'This is why I didn't want this conversation. Don't you think I've been over it time and again? Wondering if there was even the smallest window of opportunity when I could have said or done something – anything – where the outcome would have been different . . .' Ronnie broke off as her voice wavered. She took a second to regroup, to push everything from her voice apart from anger. 'I replay every second of that night. Over and over. And there's nothing. I think of the last time I saw her. Or the last time I saw Noah. Or the last time we spoke on the phone. Or the last time I was near her flat but didn't drop in . . .' She glanced across to Green and back again. They both had the same trained-to-be-empathetic expression. 'In this job we see too much at times, and perhaps it desensitises us. Maybe we're not as switched on to other people's emotions as we should be, or could be, but I cannot find one

24

moment before that night when I could have done anything to prevent what happened . . .' Again, she broke off, wondering why she didn't just leave, just as she had every right to do.

'Ronnie.' Larson's tone was firm, and she established eye contact before she continued, 'From everything we have seen, your sister's behaviour appears out of character. The coroner used the phrase "impossible to predict", and she was correct. We can't spend our lives second guessing how other people are doing, however much we care about them.'

Ronnie knew it was true, and that there would always be life-shattering events in the wings that sat beyond her control. There was nothing she could have changed about her mother's and brother's deaths, despite the ridiculous but oh-so real recurring childhood dream that she had grabbed George's hand, pulled him free and outrun that train.

'About that night, will you talk me through it?' Larson's expression was patient, her tone even.

Larson must have known how much she was asking and all Ronnie wanted was to refuse. But a sense of duty tugged at her. Larson was a fellow officer. There had to be a reason for the request. Doing as she asked might reveal it.

Finally, Ronnie nodded. 'Yes,' she replied. She closed her eyes and let the memory back in.

CHAPTER 8

The police cordon had been set up correctly. The rain formed a light mist but despite both these factors, it was still possible for Ronnie to see the woman on the parapet. Both her face and her bare legs appeared moon-white and featureless from that distance. Ronnie stared up for a few seconds, searching for something she could identify, but from where she stood it was all too abstract. She realised then that the cordon had been positioned to shield the public from having a view of the pavement rather than preventing them from seeing the top of the car park.

She recognised the officer on the cordon. PC Khan, a probationer with just a few months of independent patrol experience. He looked apprehensive and spoke quickly so that she didn't have to even slow on her way past him.

'Ma'am,' he said. 'When you turn the corner, you'll see an officer. He'll show you the stairs up.'

'Who's on the roof?' she asked.

'Galloway is with her.'

'Thank you,' she said and kept walking, and for some reason imagined that Khan had stared after her and wished her luck.

She crossed a stretch of grey flagstones that led to the entrance of the multi-storey car park. A second officer stood in the doorway, out of the weather and out of the drop zone. She made herself look up again. All that was visible from this angle were the soles of her feet.

Ronnie glanced back at the officer. She didn't recognise her, and she said nothing, just held the door open.

And what could she say really?

Ronnie took the lift, and the buttons told her that the roof was the sixth floor. Dashing up the stairs would have been the slower and incorrect option, but the journey up with the lift's slow-turning gears felt endless. She occupied herself by running through some of the fundamentals of negotiation, conscious that she was trying to use logic to block a mass of jumbled thoughts and questions. She needed to keep her head clear and remember the theory. Some threatening suicide seemed single-minded, but the negotiator's job was to find a shred of uncertainty, to build rapport and explore this ambivalence. But she feared the right words would become elusive and wondered whether this time she should do it her own way.

A knot formed in her stomach. This wasn't her speciality, not at all.

The lift creaked and then shuddered to a stop. The stainless-steel doors opened out on to a landing at the top of a stairwell. It was deserted but had the standard smell of exhaust fumes and piss.

A door with a porthole window stood between her and the roof of the car park.

'Right,' she mumbled. The word sounded orphaned, her voice unfamiliar, but she pushed firmly on the stainless-steel finger plate and the door swung wide.

She saw the two figures at once, PC Galloway in the foreground and her sister Jodie about twelve feet further beyond him. Her gaze pinned on Jodie, and she was sure she never looked away, but despite that and the rain and the lights flashing up from below, she could still read Galloway's expression – 50 per cent fear, 50 per cent relief. Relief, she guessed, because he thought that she was coming along to fix it all, or maybe because the baton of guilt and responsibility had left his hands.

Ronnie wasn't superstitious, she didn't dwell on unlucky numbers, or black cats or umbrellas open in the house. She wasn't taken in by stupid traditions, but she quickly crossed and then uncrossed her fingers in any case. Beyond that, she wasn't sure where to start, but knew she needed to act quickly. Be decisive.

27

There had once been punched metal panels around the top deck of the car park, installed to deter jumpers. Someone determined enough would still have found a way, but vandals had spray-painted some and torn down others, leaving wide gaps at several points around the top floor. Jodie sat in one of these gaps, her legs dangling over the edge. She was facing away, staring straight out. Not down, but straight out across the north London skyline. She seemed to be muttering to herself. Her head made tiny bobbing movements, almost as though she was asking herself questions and then agreeing with them.

For a split-second Ronnie wondered whether she could cross the gap between the two of them before Jodie even knew she was there, and grab hold of her and just hang on. But the thought barely had time to solidify before Jodie turned to look over her shoulder, just far enough to catch sight of Ronnie in her periphery.

'Don't.' Jodie's voice was hard edged, like a bolt slamming home.

Ronnie wasn't sure whether Jodie had seen her clearly. She might be intoxicated or in the middle of some kind of mental health episode. 'Jodie, it's me.' Ronnie needed clues. 'What's happening, Jodie?'

Jodie's chin dropped; she spoke but her words were indistinguishable as though she was muttering into her shoulder. Ronnie took a couple of cautious steps but was still at least eight feet away when Jodie's head jerked up again. She flung one arm out and held her palm towards Ronnie, gesturing for her to stop. The movement was a clumsy sweep and for one heart-stopping moment she seemed to wobble.

A pulse of fear jolted Ronnie and she instinctively lurched forward.

'Stop.' Jodie screamed the word, and Ronnie froze, raising her palms, mirroring Jodie's gesture.

'It's okay,' she breathed, 'I'll stay here.' She was about five feet from her sister now and knew she couldn't risk moving any closer. 'What can I do to help?'

Jodie had been muttering to herself, she'd swung around clumsily, but now she fixed Ronnie with a steady gaze. 'Nothing,' she replied.

Maybe there were drugs or alcohol in Jodie's system; Ronnie couldn't tell. Whatever thoughts were driving Jodie, they weren't fuelled by intoxication alone. 'You asked for me,' she said softly.

'I needed you to come.' Her sister's voice trembled. 'I wanted to tell you, this is not your fault.'

Ronnie didn't move closer but shifted her weight slightly. It startled Jodie, who sat suddenly straighter and reached to grab the edge.

'It's okay.' Ronnie spread her hands, palms to the ground. 'I'm staying back here for now.'

'It's all a mess.' Jodie's voice was raspy. 'I'm a mess.'

'All you need to do is come down and we can sort out anything, anything at all.' Ronnie's thoughts raced. Jodie could be impulsive, sometimes she trusted too readily, other times she didn't ask for help when she could have or should have. And always self-critical, dwelling on her perceived faults and then, in her eyes, trying and often failing to fix them. She would feel low then come right back up. Ronnie wasn't looking for shortcomings, just to pin down anything that might tell her why her sister was now on a ledge some eighty feet above the pavement. 'And I'm sorry I haven't been there as much as I should have been. We should have seen each other regularly. I'm not making excuses, but each week drifts into another and before I know it a couple of months have gone by.' Ronnie took a breath. 'It's not because I don't care, Jodie.'

'I know, I know.' Jodie's eyes widened, they flashed with fear and uncertainty. Her gaze wasn't steady, it flickered and darted as though searching for an answer. Finally, focusing through Ronnie and settling at a thousand yards beyond, Jodie's eyes welled with tears. 'I can't get on top of anything.'

'I can help.'

'No.' She tapped her temple then gave her head a rapid shake, as though she was trying to dislodge something, 'You can't get in here. No one can. And that's where I am all the time. In here. Running circles.' The fingers of one hand walked up the fingers of the other, up the fronts, over the backs, round again; making an endless journey. Fingers stepping over fingers.

Metronomic.

Infinite.

'How long have you been feeling like this? Jodie?'

'It goes and it comes back. You know I get down.'

29

'I do. And then you get through it. Every time. Don't forget that. Every time.'

'And then it's back again.'

'Is there anything you'd like me to do?' Ronnie asked.

Jodie refocused on Ronnie and nodded. 'I . . .' The words caught in her throat. She nodded again and whispered, 'Yes.'

'Tell me what. Whatever it is, we can fix it. I promise you. I won't let you down. And I'm so sorry if I haven't been there for you when I should've been. But there's nothing that we can't sort out. Do you hear me?'

She nodded.

Her cheeks shone with the wetness of her tears, and she began to sob, quietly at first then wracking her body with the kind of snotty, ugly crying that only really happens when control is gone.

Ronnie took a half step forward.

Jodie screamed, 'No,' with such intensity that Ronnie fell back again.

She held her breath. The last time she'd seen Jodie had been two weeks ago at Noah's birthday. It hadn't been a party as such, more like a free-for-all between Noah and a handful of his friends. Jodie, Alex and Ronnie had been the only adults present, and they had stayed on the side-lines, delivering food, and spending the rest of the time close to the kettle.

Ronnie hadn't stayed long.

She had thought Jodie seemed distant but read nothing into it. Perhaps she should have done. Perhaps this episode was brewing then. Perhaps Jodie had felt herself struggling and didn't know how to ask for help.

Had there been some sign there that she hadn't seen? An indication that Jodie was not coping, was unravelling.

Ronnie made the thoughts stop; they served no purpose. She couldn't go back and snatch up a missed opportunity. It was pointless. Instead, she spoke in the calmest voice she could muster. 'That day at Noah's party. I'm sorry I didn't stay longer. We should have talked then.'

Jodie shook her head.

'I didn't realise anything was wrong.'

'It wasn't.' Jodie whispered the words and then repeated them again more firmly, 'It wasn't, Ronnie.'

'And when you phoned me afterwards?'

'Nothing,' Jodie said. 'There *was* nothing.' She put emphasis on the second word.

'Jodie, please come down. We can fix this. You, me, Alex and Noah.' Ronnie held out her hand.

'Noah.' His name was silent on Jodie's lips.

'He needs you. He needs his mum.'

'He needs you and Alex.' Jodie closed her eyes and afterwards Ronnie remembered it as the longest moment, as enough time to bridge the few feet between them and grab Jodie and hold her back from the edge. But perhaps it was only a second because her sister's eyes snapped open before Ronnie had moved a muscle.

'Losing you would break his heart.' Ronnie half spoke, half shouted the words, the modulation awry.

'I couldn't live without him,' Jodie sobbed.

And in the next moment she was gone.

Neither Larson nor Green spoke at first; Ronnie often left a similar silence after she'd been present for the recounting of a traumatic event. A moment for the witness to regroup and a few seconds out of respect for the victim. Ronnie was grateful, and hoped it was the last time she would need to describe that night.

'Thank you,' Larson said at last. 'I appreciate how hard that must have been.' She smiled tightly. 'It was comprehensive.'

'Word for word in places,' added Green.

Larson shot him a look. If he'd planned to say anything further, he rapidly changed his mind; she had this.

'Go on,' Ronnie said.

Larson skimmed two fingers across her laptop's track pad, scrolling down the screen until she found whatever it was that she was looking for. 'According to PC Galloway there was more to your interaction with your sister.'

'Such as?'

'I will quote from his statement. "Jodie Blake was speaking quickly, but I clearly heard her say, 'He mustn't ever know.'"' Do you remember that part of the conversation?'

31

Ronnie shook her head. 'No, I don't.'

'And you replied, "He never would." Does that sound familiar?'

She wanted to say that Galloway had been mistaken, but Ronnie knew him. He was solid and had built his career on unshowy dependability. He never had time for grandstanding or embellishment, so when he said he clearly heard something, there would be no doubt. 'As I said, I don't remember.'

'So, who would your sister have been referring to?'

Ronnie hesitated. Was there more in Galloway's statement? she wondered. 'I have no idea.'

Larson looked over at Green and he picked up the questioning, 'But you replied.'

'And as I said, I don't remember.'

'And as I said, you were running almost word for word with your original statement. But missing this point makes me think you don't remember the incident quite as clearly as you think you do.'

Incident. How Ronnie hated the word. The emergency services and the media used it all the time. Serious incident. Critical incident. Major incident. In Ronnie's view, incident was too close to incidental, and there was nothing minor or insignificant here. She glared at Green, 'I remember with incredible clarity actually.'

'So, are you intentionally skipping that part? Or is your memory only unreliable in relation to certain points?'

Ronnie knew Green was deliberately goading her, hoping to make her snap at him with the answer. She replied, her words clear, slow and cold. 'If I have no recollection of that part of the conversation then it wasn't important.'

He raised an eyebrow. 'Who would Jodie have been referring to when she said "he"?'

Ronnie just had to hope there was nothing else from Galloway and replied immediately. 'Noah or Alex I guess,' she gave it a couple of seconds. She had completed enough interviews to know how to keep her body language open and engaged, how to appear thoughtful and cooperative. Finally, she shook her head. 'I'm sorry, apart from our dad, who we avoid, there is no one else.'

32

CHAPTER 9

'I didn't think you'd finish so early,' Alex said. Ronnie had met him in the Bread and Butter Café; it was a few minutes' walk from Noah's school, and Alex was waiting with coffee at a window table when she arrived.

She'd dropped her phone into her bag, glad to be finished with the satnav for the day.

'I bet you'll be pleased when you can find your way around without it.'

She didn't seem to register the comment, instead chose the seat next to him and double-checked that no one else was in earshot. It was post-lunch and pretty quiet. The closest person was a young waitress shouting instructions in Italian to the kitchen. She was slim with chestnut hair and a tattoo of a dreamcatcher on the inside of her forearm. Ronnie focused on her surroundings for the first time. The café had an old-school look, with wooden tables and chairs, the menu on a chalk board and a chrome and glass counter. There was a chiller cabinet of oranges waiting to be juiced and shelves of bags of espresso beans waiting to be ground. All that was missing was a slow fan in the ceiling and a view of the Amalfi coast. More importantly, there was no one close enough to overhear their conversation.

'How was day one?' he asked.

She eyed him thoughtfully. She hadn't decided how much to say, and this wasn't exactly the right location. On the other hand, she wanted to begin the conversation now when Noah wasn't around. In the end, she started with the word, 'Weird.'

'What kind of weird?' He lowered his voice, 'Like supernatural weird?'

'No.' She shot him a don't-joke look, which he thankfully picked up on right away. 'First I was called into Superintendent Cooper's office, and he told me I couldn't work until I'd been signed off by occupational health. I explained that I'd been on active duty until last week, but he didn't budge. Then sent me off to see this other department, called the Special Investigations Team for the Eastern Region.'

'To work for them?'

'No.' Ronnie knew her next words would raise questions she couldn't answer, but she couldn't leave it. 'It's something about Jodie.'

He became still. 'Jodie?' He searched her face for a clue.

She drew a deep breath and then, in a low voice, explained about John Fenton's team and her meeting with Larson and Green. Thankfully, she didn't need go over any details of Jodie's death; Alex had attended the inquest too.

He listened intently. He didn't interrupt, but his expression started at puzzlement and switched through a range of emotions. And of course, there was pain in his eyes. She wished she'd waited then. 'Do you want me to stop? We can pick this up at home. I . . .'

'No, no.' He shook his head. 'Go on.'

The door opened and three women entered, one pulling a stroller in after her. They looked like mums in for a quick drink before the school run. Ronnie waited for them to decide where they wanted to sit. The mum with the stroller picked a table with space to park her toddler next to her chair, and far enough from their own table that they were still out of earshot of everyone. 'I rang Dave Butterworth . . .'

'Your old boss?'

'Yes, I asked him what he knew about that team. He said he hadn't heard of them at first, but he knew them by their nickname. They're known as the DEAD team . . .'

Alex was mid-swig of coffee, and his face was partially obscured by his mug, but she saw his eyes widen. 'What does that mean?'

34

'Turns out it's an acronym for Detail, Evaluate, Act and Detain. It's what they do . . .'

'In what context?'

'They have an objective, and the team is divided into two halves. Inside and outside. The inside team gathers intelligence: background information, surveillance, financials and so on. Enough to decide on a strategy. Then the outside team goes live with it, they interface with the target until they have enough for the arrest.'

'I don't understand . . .'

Ronnie began to explain again but Alex stopped her.

'. . . what this has to do with Jodie?'

His voice rose and Ronnie glanced around to see who had noticed. 'I don't know,' she whispered.

He lowered his voice in response, but his words were sharp with urgency. 'You were there; no one else was involved, right?' The waitress and one of the mums both glanced over.

'No one else. Please keep your voice down.'

'So, who's the target, Ron?'

'I don't know.'

'You must know something.'

'Just that they deal with major investigations. But that could cover murders, manhunts, organised crime, pretty much anything requiring their skillset. And they're based in Cambridge but cover the East of England – now you know as much as me.'

Alex's demeanour switched from frustration to bemusement the moment he realised that they were in the same boat. He dropped his gaze from her to the tabletop, studying it as though he expected the woodgrain to morph into words, but this was exactly what he did when he hit a wall with a software problem, when all his energies were employed in thought and he sought the visual equivalent of white noise to help him concentrate.

Alex solved problems for a living, but he'd never been the stereotypical nerd with a disconnect from the business of being human. 'You're telling me that whatever this DEAD team is looking into has to be a serious case of some kind?'

'It looks that way, and Jodie was either a player or a victim.'

Finally, he looked at her again. 'That makes no sense,' he said. 'Why are they asking for details about her death? We both know it was suicide.'

'We do,' Ronnie agreed. But as she spoke, she felt an inexplicable stab of uneasiness. She'd been there and she knew what she'd seen; Jodie had chosen to jump. But Ronnie was equally confident that Jodie had not been herself, that her sister's thoughts had been fractured. Until this moment, Ronnie had imagined that Jodie had hidden feelings of isolation, depression and self-doubt for a long time, until they had manifested as all-consuming despair. But what if . . . and she realised she'd spoken the last thought aloud.

Alex had programmer's pallor, his complexion faded to sepia by long hours lit by a computer screen and irregular meals of beige food. Even so, he paled. 'What if what, Ronnie?'

'What if she was backed into a corner? What if the DEAD team knows why?'

CHAPTER 10

The school doors opened, and the children spilled out. They were like a bunch of puppies; most rushing to their adults as though they hadn't seen them for oh-so very long. The older children played it cool, dwindling out a couple of minutes later and barely glancing at the playground as they headed for the gate that led to the street. At most they would be eleven years old, but they'd already lost some of their youthful exuberance.

Noah was one of the last to appear. He didn't have the enthusiasm of his eight-year-old peers. He had seen a little too much of the world for that, but he beamed when he saw Alex and Ronnie waiting for him. For a precious few seconds, the weight of the day lifted from Ronnie, and she was just in the moment with her young nephew. 'Did you have a good day?'

He nodded, 'It was okay.'

'What did you do?'

He shrugged, 'I can't remember.'

Ronnie shot a look at Alex, who also shrugged. 'He always says that,' he mouthed.

They walked together in silence then. Not an unnatural silence though. Ronnie liked their company even when nobody spoke. She knew the feeling of needing to decompress at the end of a day, of letting the intensity quietly fall away, and thought it might be the same for Noah.

It took under ten minutes to reach home. Alex unlocked the door and Ronnie was hit by the smell of cooking. Alex wasn't subtle with his use of garlic and onion. It was the unidentified herbs that changed from recipe to recipe. Ronnie guessed tonight's dinner fell into the category of casserole. The Alex menu stretched to six dishes: two with rice, two with potatoes and two with pasta. Ronnie knew how to cook even fewer dishes; she would never be in demand for her culinary skills and was never going to complain about his.

Noah, with a sudden burst of energy, shed his shoes and blazer as he dashed for the kitchen.

'Cereal or toast.' Alex told her, 'Every day straight from school. One of the mums said it might be a growth spurt. Is that a thing at that age?'

'No idea.'

'Me neither.'

Ronnie changed into jeans and a T-shirt. By the time she came back down, Noah was in the living room, playing on the Xbox. He hadn't yet reached the point of loving it to the exclusion of everything else and preferred to play when Alex could join him. Ronnie settled on the sofa, planning to do nothing more than watch him play, but he froze the screen and plonked himself next to her. 'Tired?' he asked.

'A bit.'

'I was tired on my first day too, but it wasn't any longer than a normal one. It just felt like it was. I had to answer loads of questions.'

'What kind of questions?'

'About how I was feeling. Did I want someone to talk to. That kind of stuff.' He rolled his eyes. 'And it was boring. Were you bored today?'

'Not today, no.' Ronnie watched him carefully. 'They actually asked me a few questions about your mum.'

Noah looked curious, but unperturbed. 'Why?'

'I'm not sure. I think they wanted to know more about her life.'

'The people at the school asked me what she was like and if I missed her. Is that what you mean?'

'Similar,' she began, cocking her head to one side and weighing up the options. She wanted to know who, besides herself and Alex, had visited Jodie, if anyone had stayed over, whether Noah had noticed anything abnormal. But he was eight and might not know what normal was. And she could already read uncertainty in his expression. There was nothing that she wanted to ask that mattered enough to upset his fragile new life. 'People worry when someone has lost a loved one,' she told him. 'They want to make sure they're okay.'

Noah nodded. He had dark lashes and big brown eyes. He blinked, slow and heavy lidded. He managed a tight smile, then returned to his game.

Neither of them spoke again until Alex called out that it was time to eat. She held out a hand and pulled Noah to his feet. 'Are you going back again tomorrow?' he asked.

'Of course.' She was about to move towards the kitchen but sensed he wasn't ready to move.

'I told the school I had you and Alex to talk to. They said that I could tell them if I had any secrets.'

'What kind of secrets?'

'I don't know.' He frowned and screwed up his face as if forcing a thought to solidify. 'Did Mum keep secrets?'

The question was loaded, she could see that. Eight-year-old children were not equipped to deal with their small worlds being shattered without warning. *Did Mum keep secrets? And was that why she killed herself?*

And what was the secret?

And if the secret was about him, would he wonder if it was all his fault?

She couldn't help him make sense of it when she didn't understand it herself, but she understood his pain. The confusion. The bewilderment.

She squatted down so they were the same height. 'I don't know if your mum had secrets, Noah, but I will try to find out. You can ask me anything and I will always answer you. Is that okay?'

'Anything?'

'If you are ready to ask something, then you deserve an answer.'

He stared into her face for a few seconds then turned and pulled her towards the hallway. 'I'm starving,' he yelled in Alex's direction.

CHAPTER 11

Ronnie left the house before Alex and Noah woke. She had no reason to think that any of the DEAD team would arrive before 8.30, but she showed up at 7 a.m. in any case.

All she wanted was the information they were working on. She'd mulled over a few approaches, options that might give her reasonable odds of persuading them to cooperate. She had enough experience of victims, witnesses and suspects to be able to pull a few strategies out of the bag. But she ruled out strategies that required her to be helpful, cooperative, determined or vulnerable; she really wasn't in the mood.

Her approach needed to be either justifiable outrage or don't-insult-my-intelligence.

By the time she'd spent an hour and a half pacing the small waiting area, the two options had snarled together in a single angry knot. She was about to ask the front desk to call the DEAD office for a third time when a young DC opened the internal door. He was lean and over six feet tall, black with a smattering of freckles.

'Thank you for coming back in,' he said.

Ronnie had already worked out that the Cambridge accent drew in elements of estuary English, a rural Fenland dialect and a trace of something a bit more upmarket. She could tell that he was 100 per cent a Londoner.

'Henry. Malachi Henry.' He blinked, then added, 'I have to say the whole thing otherwise people think Henry's my first name. And it's not.'

'Clearly.'

He blinked again.

'I'm not here because anybody's called me in,' she corrected him. 'I want to speak to DI Fenton. I was just dragged in yesterday and I'm not impressed by it.'

'Well, he's not in yet, he's probably doing the school run. But it was DC Horvat and DS Reynolds who wanted to speak to you and they're upstairs now. I can take you.'

There was no sign that he'd picked up on her frustration and he didn't attempt to lead her further into the building. He just waited for her response with an expression of practised patience.

'Give me their names again.'

'DC Horvat and DS Reynolds.'

'I see. And why do they want me?'

'Probably best you hear it from them.'

'Because you can't tell me or because you don't know?'

He shrugged. 'I know the route from here up to their office,' he said, sounding resigned rather than cocky. 'Do you want me to take you or not?'

She glared, but let him lead the way.

Ronnie found herself back in the same plush interview suite, this time with two detectives she hadn't met before. In their own way, each looked as though they stayed out of the light, but beyond that Horvat and Reynolds were probably as visually mismatched as it was possible to be. DC Dimitri Horvat introduced himself first; he was a bony, sallow-skinned and nocturnal looking man of about thirty; his jeans and T-shirt were faded and crumpled, but not as a style choice. He probably slept in them regularly. And then he introduced DS Jenna Reynolds. She wore black trousers and a pale blue open-necked shirt, both pristine. She was slightly older than her colleague with auburn hair and the creamy complexion of someone who either avoided the sun or wore a make-up range that included the word flawless.

41

Ronnie touched her own cheek, trying to remember whether she'd bothered with foundation this morning. DS Reynolds had sharp green eyes that seemed to study Ronnie's every move. 'I'm guessing,' Ronnie said, 'you two are on the inside team and Larson and Green are on the outside and then Fenton is the boss.'

Ronnie knew that in a setup like this, the inside team were the ones who collated the information, who mined for data, their unseen shadows pre-empting an operation. Whereas, the outside team were the public face, the delivery team, or the executioners of the plan.

Ronnie put this to Reynolds, who swayed her head as though she was approximately right. 'Near enough,' she replied. 'I'm the only DS so I cover when Fenton's not around.' She raised an eyebrow at Horvat, and he returned a knowing look.

Ronnie smiled and broke the short silence, 'That's a small team.'

Horvat cut in. 'Five is big enough for the kind of cases we work.' His English was heavily accented, and she guessed his first language was from one of the Balkan states.

'And if you want any more help from me, you'll need to tell me what kind of case this is. I was blindsided yesterday by a line of questioning that I didn't expect, and it wasn't fair. I'm no stranger to serious investigations.'

Horvat replied with a crooked smile.

'We are well aware of your reputation. You work alone, you guard your caseload, you don't help others and they don't help you. And I quote: "Ronnie Blake is only a team player when she chooses to be. She knows how to be empathetic and equally knows how to be detached but she treats every case as though it is hers and hers alone."'

The words had come from her last performance review. Horvat had not only had access to it, but he had also taken the time to memorise the quote.

'By your playbook,' he said, 'we wouldn't tell you anything. You'd be keeping your colleagues in the dark.'

'Not quite,' she replied. 'I'd turn on the light just enough to point them in the direction I wanted to go. I'd share enough to get results, not what you're doing here. So, tell me what you're investigating. Tell me why you want to know about my sister's death and why the hell you've got information about my service record.'

DC Horvat began to speak but DS Reynolds stopped him with a small shake of her head. 'It's okay, Dimitri,' she said. 'I'm not meaning to word this insensitively but it's fair to say that your sister's death has derailed your career, at least temporarily. Whatever you were working on is now in someone else's pile.'

Ronnie had years of experience practising the art of giving away little or nothing whenever possible, but she felt her colour drain a little and then quickly return with a hot flush in her cheeks. She picked apart what Reynolds had said, acknowledging the facts, and sure enough, she couldn't deny that the DS was correct; Ronnie's cases had been reallocated and she was here. She would not have planned either. 'What's your point?' she replied.

'Who has gained now your career has stalled, Ronnie? That's what we want to know.'

Ronnie narrowed her eyes and considered the current conversation. It was on a different track to yesterday's. They were trying to lift the lid on something, she was sure, and were trying it from a couple of different angles. First Larson and Green, now Horvat and Reynolds. 'You're just fishing. You're all looking for an answer and I don't have it. You've brought me into your flash interview suite, but if it's that much of a big deal, where's Fenton?' She leaned forward a little. 'Tell him he can get in here and ask me these questions himself.' Then added faux sweetly, 'If you don't mind.'

Reynolds glared but said nothing. Horvat's gaze shifted towards the door and a couple of seconds later it opened.

DI John Fenton dismissed Reynolds and Horvat and chose the seat closest to Ronnie.

'Why the subterfuge?' she asked.

His response was blunt, 'Do you think there is any possibility your sister was murdered?'

She shook her head but stopped short of a reactive denial. Jodie murdered? It felt unlikely, but she paused and felt her world tremble, then shudder and tilt as though it might slide away from her.

Jodie's final, imploring expression had been burned into her memory. Ronnie saw it in her sleep. She'd tried to pin a description to it, tried to distil it down to its base elements. She'd rewound through their pasts. She knew how her sister wore remorse, guilt, love, hate, frustration, and had run through these and countless more trying to find the cocktail of emotions she'd seen at that moment.

Yes, there had been fear and desperation, resignation and apology. But she had been unable to decipher the overriding message that Jodie had been trying to convey.

She did not want to accept what Fenton was proposing, but in that moment, she finally understood Jodie. Her last silent request had been to give Ronnie the responsibility. Jodie's eyes were asking, *Do you know what you need to do?*

But Ronnie had never replied with even a slight nod or acknowledgement.

'I don't see how she could have been murdered. But I can understand that something pushed her to it and, to my eyes, that's no different.'

The door opened then, and DC Henry came in with cups of tea. He tried to hand a mug to Ronnie, but she shook her head, so he put it on the table next to her with a spoon and a couple of sachets of sugar to one side.

'I don't understand what you think I know,' she continued.

'Honestly,' Fenton said, 'we are in the dark. All we've had is a couple of names and one was your sister's.'

'You've had a couple of names? What does that mean? Some kind of tip off?'

'Something like that.'

'And whose was the other?'

He shook his head. 'No, that's not information available to anybody outside our team until we know what we're dealing with.'

'What else did you get?'

'Just the names.'

Ronnie scowled.

'What makes you think you need to look at Jodie's death or at my career?'

'It's a hypothesis, a working hypothesis.'

'Don't give me that bullshit. You're not investigating this,' she waved her arm at the wider room, 'based on a couple of names and nothing more.'

He pressed his lips tight and shook his head. 'There really is nothing else I can tell you. I'm sorry.'

Ronnie stood, filled with anger that had nowhere to go. 'I'm done here.'

CHAPTER 12

Fenton opened the door to the outer office and addressed DC Henry.

'Malachi, show Detective Blake from the building. Offer her a lift home.'

He gestured for Ronnie to pass through the doorway before him. 'We will be in touch if we need any further help.'

The young DC looked flustered and scrambled to grab his keys and his phone. Ronnie passed him on the way to the door.

'Don't worry,' she said, 'I can find my own way out.'

He muttered something she didn't catch. She kept walking but he caught up with her at the end of the corridor.

'No one's immune from shock,' were his opening words.

She shot him a side-eyed glance. 'And what's that supposed to mean?'

'Well, from what I know, you turned up expecting to work, not to be involved in something that's so personal. You weren't expecting to be on the other side of the fence, were you? It's not going to be easy, is it? Being on the receiving end, I mean, when you're used to being in the driving seat.'

Ronnie wanted to blank him and keep walking, but he was earnest and seemingly happy to risk being told where he could put his unsolicited sympathy. 'And I suppose yours is the voice of experience, you being what, eighteen or something?'

'Twenty-four actually. And you're right, I am new.'

'And now you work with that lot? Number six.'

'I'm sorry?'

'I thought there were five in the team . . .'

'Oh, I see.'

He didn't elaborate, but she caught a flash of disappointment in his expression and suddenly felt a little sorry for him. 'So what's your role? More than driving people home and making tea, I hope?'

'I'm waiting to see,' he smiled tightly. 'What's your address?'

Ronnie had already discovered that walking in Cambridge was different to London. Even when the place bustled, there was a stillness that hung in the air. In Cambridge walking was so much more than an inconvenience bolted on to each end of a tube journey. 'I'm happy to walk,' she told him.

'And I'm happy to drive,' he countered. 'It will be worth it.'

She eyed him. 'Why?'

He shrugged. 'It just will.'

So, she gave in and told him her address.

He waited until they were in his car before he tapped the details into his phone. He glanced once at the map and then switched the satnav off again. 'Easy,' he said and smiled at her. 'Seatbelt?'

He was either thick-skinned or knew how to take bad-tempered people in his stride. He claimed he wasn't sure what his role would be and yet he had been taken into a supposedly specialist team. There had to be more to him. 'Where were you before?'

'Over at Wembley, but I transferred up here a few months ago. I'm good at recognising people, so I used to watch the crowds arriving at Wembley Stadium for sports' events and concerts, trying to spot known troublemakers. It's a thing I do but I'm hoping to spread my wings a bit.'

'Does Cambridge even have a football team?'

'Of course. But I'm just kind of hanging around the DEAD team and waiting for something new to happen.'

The traffic moved slowly. Ronnie's gaze fell on the car in front. When she'd been a new detective, she'd been given cases, too many too quickly probably, but she'd felt on the periphery of the team and in a way that had never changed. She'd stuck at it through determination, not because of any particular support or encouragement she'd received from the department, but she had felt as though each case solved shored up her position and made her less expendable.

It seemed as though Malachi wasn't even being given that opportunity. He was just waiting.

'I'm sorry I've been rude to you,' she said. 'It will get better. Just keep your head down and get a few results under your belt and you'll be fine.'

'Thanks,' he said. 'I'd already made up my mind to stick it out but I appreciate it.'

And then they drove the rest of the way in silence. She'd never been one for small talk and made a point of diverting her gaze through her side window to discourage any coming from him. It was a short drive and he pulled up to her house without double checking the address.

She opened the door and turned to thank him, but before she could speak, he said, 'Nigel Beckett.'

'Who's he?'

But he simply repeated the name and fixed her with an expression that told her she should take it and go.

CHAPTER 13

Nigel Beckett.
Nigel Beckett.
Nigel Beckett.
Ronnie repeated the name until she was inside and had written it down. She had no access to police systems, but she did have access to the electoral register, company directorships, county court judgements and databases of other open access information. She started with the obvious and googled him on her phone and then switched to her laptop. A name alone wasn't much to go on and the first search returned 1.4 million results.

She added *UK* and narrowed it down to 166,000.

'Great,' she muttered.

She scanned down the first few pages in any case, quite sure that anything recent and newsworthy would come somewhere near the top. But all she saw were company directors, doctors, financial advisors, middle managers, all people with profile pages that cropped up near the top of the list.

She clicked on *images* instead.

The average Nigel Beckett, it seemed, enjoyed being photographed in his work shirt and multicoloured tie and was generally over fifty. She couldn't imagine that any of them had even the slightest connection to her sister.

The thought made her try *Nigel Beckett Jodie Blake* in the same search. Next, she tried *Nigel Beckett Enfield* then *Nigel Beckett suicide.*

49

Alex was working from home and she could hear the steady tap of his fingers on the keyboard, the occasional creak of his office chair. She wasn't going to disturb him but she tried to use his logic. He talked about searches in terms of mathematics. Logarithmic searches and binary finds. Perhaps they were the same thing, she wasn't sure, but the theory that he'd explained to her involved taking the whole pool of information, the 1.4 million in this case, and homing in.

Her logic was entirely the other way round. She closed her eyes for a second.

Start close to home.

Her eyes sprang open, and her fingers touched the keys the moment the idea entered her head.

She searched again, *Nigel Beckett police.*

She hit return and in 0.21 seconds, there it was.

CHAPTER 14

Husband of senior Cambridgeshire officer convicted of fraud.

It only took three more searches to discover that his wife, ex-Detective Inspector Linda Beckett, now lived in Kirton, a small village south of Boston, Lincolnshire.

Ronnie borrowed Alex's ten-year-old Ford and headed north from Cambridge. It took twenty minutes to leave the city behind her, then she drove for sixty miles, through probably the flattest, emptiest countryside she'd ever seen.

Kirton itself seemed like a village that had sprung up in the middle of nowhere. Beckett's bungalow was a red-brick semi on Horseshoe Lane. Small and bland, presented in that neutral way that estate agents recommend. The front garden was gravelled and there was no car parked outside.

Ronnie had considered calling first but she liked to see people's faces when she first met them, to catch those micro expressions that flash in and out of people's eyes, or the involuntary twitch of a facial muscle that comes in the moment before they have time to be guarded. Any sign that gives away a little too much.

Ronnie parked in the road and knocked at the door. She didn't have to wait long. It was opened by Linda Beckett. She recognised her straight away from the stock image that had come up on Google. There, she'd been in her uniform, standing in front of a Cambridgeshire Constabulary insignia. She'd looked vigorous, competent, driven.

The woman before her looked like Linda Beckett's tired twin. She leaned heavily on a cane.

'DS Ronnie Blake.'

'Show me your warrant card.'

Ronnie produced a driving licence instead. 'I'm not on duty right now. I'm signed off, actually.'

'Hold it up,' she instructed, then asked Ronnie to turn it over. There was a slight slur in her voice. 'What do you want?'

Ronnie hadn't planned exactly what she was going to say beyond sticking to the bare facts.

'My sister died six weeks ago, but now there's some kind of investigation. I really don't know what. However, your husband's name was given to me as a tip off, some kind of connection.'

'What connection?'

'I don't know. That's why I'm here.'

Linda Beckett wore light make-up, imperfectly applied. She studied Ronnie, her eyes bright beneath unevenly mascaraed lashes. 'So you've taken it upon yourself?' She snorted. 'I used to think everything was possible with the right levels of resilience and determination. I'm not so sure now, but you'd better come in.'

She moved slowly along the hallway, only pausing to point out the kitchen. 'If you want a drink, you're welcome, but you'll need to make it yourself.' She spoke as she shuffled, Ronnie barely catching her words. 'I can do it, but let's just say I'm better with cold drinks and no, I'm not thirsty, thank you.'

She faced Ronnie as they reached the doorway at the end of the hall.

'I had a stroke,' Linda Beckett told her.

Ronnie had guessed as much. 'How long ago?'

'Summer, last year. Apparently, I'm doing well.'

She had led them to a square lounge, with a settee and two high-backed armchairs arranged in a curve and all facing the window, which looked on to the street outside. A small television set was positioned to one side, with a spray of family photos on the wall above it. Most showed the same young woman at various stages of her life: school uniform, prom and university graduation. Finally in a group with an auburn-haired man and two young boys.

'Your daughter?'

'Monica and her family.' Her speech was slow, the same speed as a child just learning to read and carefully picking over each word.

There were none of Linda's husband.

'I can sit in my chair and see everything I need to. I can read on my Kindle and have my books read to me when my eyes get tired.'

The rest of the room was sparsely furnished with just a coffee table and a small bookcase.

'Apparently, I'm benefiting from being bloody-minded. Bloody-minded people either do much worse or much better, depending on whether they're being bloody-minded towards the treatment or bloody-minded towards the cause. I'm told my odds were better because I was only fifty-one. But I was fit, healthy, with minimal drinking and no smoking. So, the most likely cause was stress and that hasn't gone anywhere. Ask me what you like but if you make me keel over with another one, it's on you.'

There was a glint of dark humour in her eyes. Police humour. Morgue humour. It was all the same.

'I'll do my best,' Ronnie said.

Ronnie told Linda Beckett about her sister's death and her own move to Cambridge, her first interactions with the DEAD team and finally Malachi's tip off. She referred to the DEAD team by their proper name, the Special Investigations Team for the Eastern Region.

Linda Beckett was sitting straight in her chair. Her left hand was in her lap while her right leaned on the armrest, taking most of the weight. At the mention of Fenton and his team, the fingers of her right hand began to strum the armrest like a small Mexican wave. 'So, the DEAD team are involved, are they?'

Ronnie nodded. 'It seems so, but I don't know who or what they're after.'

'Who, not what. They chase one person. They research, they prep and then they go in. It seems to me that they are looking for a link between your sister and my husband. I think you should put the kettle on. This might take more than five minutes.'

CHAPTER 15

Linda Beckett drank sweet rhubarb tea, brewed first, then with a splash of cold water added to take the worst of the heat out of it. She held it in her good hand, with her fingers wrapped around the body of the mug.

Ronnie sat in the chair closest to Linda, her elbows on her knees with her mug of coffee cradled in her hands.

They had progressed to first names as the kettle boiled.

'They gave you Nigel's name, not mine, so it would make sense if the link to your sister related to his crime.'

'It would, but I don't see how. I don't think her social circle was very big and her work was mostly picking up short-term temporary contracts. It gave her a level of flexibility around school holidays.'

'She had children?'

'Yes, just one son. He's eight now, so she was pretty young. Our dad kicked her out. I was living in a shared house at the time and my brother still lived at home, so she ended up being in a hostel and then eventually got a flat. It's not exactly the way to kick off a career, so she always picked up bits of work where she could. She seemed to get by.'

'What was that?' Linda asked.

'What?'

'Your expression? Your voice faltered and I saw something.'

'It was nothing. I just realised how many assumptions I made about her being okay and the fact that I really didn't know very much about her life at all. I saw them pretty often and I'm very close to my nephew. But, the details of Jodie's life . . .' Ronnie flashed her palms at the ceiling, 'I know the names of a couple of casual friends. I met one or two more at her funeral, but I don't think there was anybody particularly close. She led a simple life as far as I can work out.'

'It sounds lonely to me, Ronnie.'

Ronnie's coffee was too strong and too bitter, and she'd been avoiding it since the first taste. But now she brought the mug up to her mouth, using it to stall her answer.

Ronnie didn't have many friends, didn't have much of a support network herself, but loneliness was never something she considered. But then again, she was a very different person to Jodie. She lowered her mug again.

'Actually, I don't really know.' Ronnie paused to change direction. 'She worked locally so unless your husband visited Enfield, I think the connection must either be online or through a third party. Were you in court for your husband's trial?'

'Good switch of topic and yes, every day. I went as a wife. I wanted to be there as a wife. But there were times when I could only see it through the eyes of a police officer. I looked at myself then and I just thought I'd been naive and gullible. He gambled sometimes. A bit on the lottery, a few quid on a football match. I thought that was it. I had no idea there was this massive black hole in our finances.'

'When did you first find out?'

'On the morning of his arrest, shockingly. I had no indication before then. He worked in the purchasing department for Lloyd and Wright. They're a big house builder in north Cambridgeshire. Their contracts are spread across this area of the country, from north Cambridgeshire up to mid-Lincolnshire. The company had started in the seventies and grown from there. Nigel joined them straight from school and they had complete trust in him. I had complete trust in him.'

Linda blinked and neither of them acknowledged the tears that welled and then subsided.

'What happened to the money?'

'Gone. Most of it gone. Our home computer was taken away, but he hadn't been gambling online. He'd used a local bookie who had a shop close to Nigel's Peterborough office, and Nigel had lost just under twenty thousand there. You can't gamble with a credit card, so he'd used that to pay the bills, and the money for the bills went on the horses. Then there had been a new credit card to pay the first, and then a loan secured against the house. You can imagine the spiral?'

'I can,' Ronnie agreed.

'I knew none of it. He was convicted of embezzling over a hundred thousand pounds, but apart from the twenty thousand he'd gambled, and the brutal amount of interest on the credit cards, I never worked out where the rest went. He wouldn't, or couldn't explain, and before you ask, no, he wasn't taking trips to London.

'Once the secrets started coming out, I was looking everywhere for answers, going through his phone, trying to find evidence of a mistress or a secret love child. But there was nothing. He wasn't who I thought he was, but he wasn't an entirely different person either. It left over eighty thousand pounds unaccounted for and now there's a possible connection to your sister. It makes no sense.'

The information didn't seem to fit, but Ronnie was sure it was part of the same picture. 'Only because we don't have enough information yet.' Ronnie mused, then added, 'There will be an answer and I'd like to see him.'

Linda didn't look surprised.

CHAPTER 16

Nigel Beckett was being held in HMP Lincoln, a category B prison which, from the outside with its brick walls, stone jambs, mullions, castellations and Gothic arches looked more like a private school.

Prison visits needed to be booked ahead of time, but it seemed that Linda Beckett still had the odd favour she could pull in.

In just under two hours from leaving Linda, Ronnie found herself face-to-face with him. He was like one of those kids at school, the ones who get bullied constantly but barely flinch any more. He didn't face her properly. Instead, he sat at a thirty-degree angle, as if about to leave.

Ronnie introduced herself, then she said, 'I'm looking for a link between you stealing over a hundred thousand pounds and the death of a young mum in London. Her name was Jodie Blake. Does that mean anything to you?'

He shook his head, 'No.'

'She lived in Enfield, north London.'

Again, he shook his head. He was a faded man, hair, skin, eyes, all from the same greyscale chart. He was gaunt, leaving his eye sockets too prominent and too much loose skin around his jowls.

'How about the bookie? The one you paid off, was there more you owed him?'

For the first time there was a flicker of interest and he turned to study her straight on. 'Baz? No. Nothing was his fault. He took the bets I wanted him to take, no more than that, and there was nothing else due.' His focus on Ronnie suddenly sharpened, and he narrowed his eyes almost to a squint. 'I spoke to Linda. I know the woman you're referring to is your sister and I'm sorry for your loss. But please . . . please leave my family out of it. You have no idea what Linda has lost because of this.' He tipped his face towards the ceiling. 'Not just her job and her health. She moved house, paid back my old employer . . .'

Ronnie leaned forward, her voice low. 'That doesn't explain enough. What happened to the money that disappeared? If it wasn't paid to the bookie, did you have another gambling debt? Or is it something else?'

'It's in the past. Just leave it alone. I agreed to see you because Linda asked me to. Please, promise me you will stop. My family has suffered enough.'

Neither of them made any attempt to leave but Ronnie knew she didn't have long. The man was an enigma, clearly unsuited to prison life. He looked desperate but he didn't sound it. His voice had become increasingly resolute, his message was clear.

Leave my family alone.

So clear, in fact, that it made Ronnie wonder. She silently picked over the conversation while Nigel Beckett watched. Something had jarred and it took her a couple of minutes to work out what it was.

'When I brought up the subject of your debt with the bookie, it piqued your interest.'

'Did it?'

'Yes, why was that?'

'You tell me.' He blinked his sunken eyes and waited.

'Because I thought the bookie was important when he's not. The gambling itself isn't either, but you could tell that I had no idea that both were irrelevant.'

His nod was as close to imperceptible as she could imagine. 'It's not connected,' he agreed.

'And I proved to you that I'm a complete outsider in this, an outsider who knows what it's like to lose a close family member.'

His lips parted and she thought for a moment he was going to speak again, but his fingers knotted and unknotted in his lap, and he remained silent.

She leaned closer, her voice low and urgent: 'Whatever it is, isn't over. I don't understand yet, but my sister died six weeks ago and I'm not going to let this drop.'

He stood then. 'Tell Linda I'm thinking of her.'

'Trust me,' she said.

He paused before turning away. 'Tell Linda . . .' He emphasised the first two words and then finished the rest of the sentence with slow deliberation '. . . Tell her she reflects all the good things in the world.'

He nodded to the guard and then he was gone.

CHAPTER 17

'Thank you for arranging the meeting. Your husband couldn't or wouldn't give me any more information, but once he understood that my sister's death could be connected, he became visibly shaken. I don't want to alarm you, but I think he believes your family could be in danger.'

Linda frowned, shaking her head slowly. 'I don't see how.'

Ronnie had driven straight back to Linda's after leaving HMP Lincoln. The wind had picked up and the dry air was blowing dust across the roads. The land was flat and open. The fields had been harvested and the land was bedding down, getting ready to wait out the winter.

In London, she hadn't seen the countryside from one month to the next. The seasons had still been apparent in London, but more evident in the way the weather hit the pavements than by seeing nature at work.

She imagined that winter would be bleak in these flat lands and winter in prison bleaker still.

She thought back to her conversation with Nigel Beckett and wondered how he would cope. He didn't seem like a strong man, but maybe his streak of stubbornness would see him through.

Ronnie had eventually pulled up outside Linda's house. She had phoned ahead and an unlocked door and a sandwich were both waiting for her.

'I guessed you wouldn't have eaten.'

'You're right, thank you.'

Ronnie chose the same chair and pulled it a little closer to Linda. 'Communication between you and your husband must be difficult?'

Linda shrugged, then nodded. 'I don't even know what our relationship is any more. Doomed probably.' Again, she shrugged. 'I think we are sailing in marriage guidance uncharted territory.'

That made sense. If Nigel felt that his family were under threat and if he thought he was being watched, he couldn't risk phone calls to his wife, even if they were on speaking terms.

'He didn't have much to say to me at first,' Ronnie began, 'but then there was this shift in conversation and the change of expression. You know, the one where somebody wants to be sure that you understand that a comment is significant.'

'The loaded look? Yes, I've seen it many times. I can't imagine, though, what he might have been trying to tell you.'

'I didn't make notes, so this is from memory. I put forward the theory that perhaps my sister had been under some kind of threat, and I could tell that resonated with him. Any idea why?'

'Prison makes some people paranoid. I'm not dismissing it, but I can't see.'

'He said something about reflecting good things, I can't remember the whole sentence. He was talking about you.' Ronnie closed her eyes and tried to squeeze the precise memory into consciousness.

Ronnie opened her eyes again just in time to see Linda's good hand slide up her body and press itself over her mouth. It was her turn to close her eyes and Ronnie waited as Linda took heavy breaths and tried to regain her composure. It took thirty seconds, but it felt like longer.

'It's a Maya Angelou quote,' Linda told her when she finally spoke. 'The full quote is "Precious jewel, you glow, you shine, reflecting all the good things in the world".'

Ronnie had no idea of its significance, but it was clear from Linda's stricken expression that she knew exactly what her husband had been trying to convey.

'I spoke on behalf of the police force at the funeral of one of our colleagues. She was a young officer, just twenty-four when she died. Drugged and strangled in her own home. She worked in my team and the case is still open. Kirsten McLeod. Do you remember the case?'

There are some names that don't get forgotten. Cases where the names of victims or killers become household. Innocent people plucked from happy obscurity by complete disappearance, or by a murder so shocking or puzzling that it breaks into the public consciousness. Or the guilty whose crimes take up column inch after morbid column inch.

And for a police officer, the names of fallen colleagues.

Ronnie had never met Kirsten McLeod, but she had still followed the case as it progressed, in the same way that she might have done if Kirsten had been a cousin or a former classmate.

'I read what appeared in the papers.'

Linda nodded slowly, 'She'd joined up straight after sixth form. She'd worked with me from the time she completed independent patrol status. She was keen, not overly ambitious, just steady. Turned up every day, did what she needed to do. Then one morning, she didn't show up. No warning, no sign that she was ill, so we sent a car around for a welfare check.'

Linda's speech slowed more than before, and she frequently broke off between sentences. Collating her thoughts each time before continuing.

'Kirsten lived in a downstairs flat. It was a house which had been subdivided, an older style property. The neighbours were a retired couple in their sixties. They hadn't seen her. Hadn't been aware of anything untoward. But Kirsten's car was still parked in her space and when the officers called her mobile, they could hear it ringing from inside the building.'

Linda's gaze drifted away and worked its way up the wall of family photos before returning to Ronnie. 'She was dead in the bath.'

Everything Linda had told her so far matched with what Ronnie knew from the press coverage, but she could tell from Linda's expression that there was more she wanted to share.

'There have been so many times,' Linda continued, 'when I've thought, *I've seen it all now*. But this was something else. Not the ferocity of the crime but the weirdness of it. Kirsten had been drugged and she was naked when she was found. There was some evidence of sexual assault, but nothing conclusive.'

Linda paused and Ronnie could see her reach and struggle with one particular memory, as though its contents still caused bewilderment.

'They heard the water running as soon as they went inside. The bathroom door was shut but unlocked and she was there, sitting up at the tap end of the bath, under the running shower. It was turned to cold. It was November so the flat was chilly too. One of the officers described her as appearing blue and marbled from cold. There were no signs of life.'

'Why the running water?' The question to herself as much as to Linda.

'One theory was that he was forensically aware. Washing down the body was more likely to destroy trace evidence. Interfering with the body's temperature would also mask the time of death.'

Ronnie closed her eyes and pictured Kirsten McLeod sitting upright in her bath, her chin on her chest and the shower water flattening her hair across her skin.

Tied upright with the tap pressing into her spine.

That wasn't what Linda had just said. Not quite. But another similar image had flashed into Ronnie's head. She had to take a slow, steady breath before she spoke.

'You said she was sitting up. How? Surely, she would have slid down in a wet bath?'

But Linda's next comment was, 'She was manually strangled, with equal pressure on both sides of her neck. Based on that, the conclusion was that she'd been killed and then placed in the bath, positioned sitting upright, and it was after then that the shower was turned on.'

Ronnie forced her voice to stay even.

'Yes, but how did a limp body not just slide down the bath?'

'She was tied upright. Rope under her arms and around her chest. Tied to the taps so tightly that they left dents in her back. And her hands between her legs and tied to her ankles.'

63

'So similar,' Ronnie muttered.

'To what?' Linda asked, then reached towards Ronnie, touching her lightly with her good hand. 'Are you okay?'

Ronnie nodded but it was a lie. She was far from okay.

For years, and against her better judgement, she'd carried a secret for her sister. Jodie had told her, Ronnie guessed, because she needed to tell someone, but had pared back the details to make sure Ronnie could do nothing beyond listen. Jodie hadn't allowed Ronnie any scope to act like a police officer, just as a sister. And in the years from then she'd never encountered any possible link. Until now.

Fenton had two names – Nigel Beckett and Jodie Blake.

He might not know how they were connected, but she did.

And she planned to start with Malachi.

CHAPTER 18

Ronnie drove hard back towards Cambridge, pushing Alex's old car until the engine whined. The roads were flat and straight, and she ate up the miles, cutting through the landscape of stripped fields and threadbare trees.

In the space of just a few minutes, everything had changed for her. She'd been stumbling in the dark and then it was as though a switch had been thrown with such abruptness that she'd been stopped in her tracks and stood, frozen and blinking, until her brain caught up.

She overtook two cars and the tractor they loitered behind in a single manoeuvre. She swore under her breath and darted back to her side of the road. It was a single carriageway road, but she was tipping over seventy for most of it, touching eighty once or twice. She glanced at the dashboard clock.

17:35

Still rush hour, but most of the traffic was coming in the other direction, heading back out into the sticks.

She wasn't a fan of making snap judgements about people, but she was a fan of making quick ones. The two things were different.

Snap judgements didn't weigh the evidence. Letting her subconscious absorb the facts and come to a fast decision was something else. First impressions were based on the culmination of experience, the subconscious processing faster than the conscious mind, and she knew that her first impressions often turned out to be correct.

Her first impression of Malachi had been of a young officer who was keen to get things right, the sort that would turn up early and leave late, and she wanted to get back and catch him before he walked away from Parkside Police Station. Before he headed off to who knows where and she'd be stuck waiting until the morning, festering, even more unable to sleep than usual.

She continued against the flow of the rush hour and made it to the edge of the city by ten to six. The traffic became heavier, and she cursed again, then pulled the wheel to one side and drove along the bus lane. It would be worth the fine.

It took her most of the way to Parkside station and she pulled into the kerb across the road. She allowed herself thirty minutes to wait for him.

The time was almost up when he appeared. Ronnie left the car on the double yellows. She could have a ticket for that one as well, for all she cared. She strode across the road towards him and spotted the moment he spotted her. There was the smallest stiffening of his shoulders and he slowed for a couple of strides.

'Nigel Beckett,' she shouted at him. 'Why did you give me his name?'

Malachi diverted towards her, intercepting her in the middle of the road. He ushered her back towards her car. The light was fading, and they were caught in the headlights of the vehicles.

'I wanted to help,' he said.

'Bullshit. Why that name, Malachi?'

'It's just a name they're working on at the moment. I thought it would help.'

'So you said.'

She unlocked the car. 'Get in. We're going somewhere to talk.'

'But I only live up there,' he said.

'Fine. I'll walk with you and when I get a parking ticket you can pay it.'

He got in then and she swung the car through the traffic and straight over at the lights. The road was different to other roads she'd seen in Cambridge. This was more like a London suburb. Crowded Victorian terraces turned into shops, a mix of cafés and supermarkets specialising in produce from various parts of the world, old-style pubs still boasting real ales and homecooked food and, in between all of those, an array of independent shops.

He pointed to a small café, still open even though it was early evening.

'We'll go in there,' he said.

She parked in a side street, and they said nothing until they were inside the 5 Blends Coffee House and seated at a corner table.

'Malachi Henry, number six on a team of five. So, what exactly is it you do?'

'Whatever anyone tells me to.' He frowned. 'I don't mean that as though I can't think for myself. I just don't have specific responsibilities as yet.'

'Right. So, you're the gopher in the team, you're the new starter. You're floating around, you don't really know what your position is. And yet you give me that name. Why?'

'You weren't being told anything and I thought it was wrong.'

'So why did you pick Nigel Beckett? How did you know that there was a connection between him and me?'

He shrugged. 'I knew the boss had his name and your sister's. I didn't know what else I could tell you.'

'I don't know whether you have the ability to pull off a good lie, Malachi, but the script isn't doing you any favours.'

'I don't know what—'

'Yes, you do. You're new to the team and keen to settle in. From what I can see there's some serious investment going into that team, and I guess you had to be good to get the nod. Are you really going to risk that by passing a confidential name to a benched officer? I don't think so.'

Malachi studied her for a moment or two, weighing her up, or so she thought.

A few more seconds passed before he caved. 'I was told to tell you,' he said quietly.

'Who told you?'

Malachi hesitated, as though he planned to clam up again.

Ronnie wasn't prepared to wait for him and rapped on the table in irritation. 'Was it Fenton?' she snapped.

Malachi nodded. 'He was sent a list of names. I don't know how many but it included your sister and Beckett. I don't know any more. He told me to tip you off with Nigel's name.'

'What were his exact words?'

'Give her the name, see what she digs up.'

'Malachi, do you know the name Kirsten McLeod?'

'Of course.'

'Is the DEAD team involved in the investigation?'

'I don't think so.' Malachi looked suddenly defeated. 'I'm supposed to be on the team and how much do I know?'

She and Malachi were two capable people and yet both were in the dark. 'Why couldn't they just tell me what's going on?' she growled. 'I'm a police officer, for fuck's sake.' And at that moment, Ronnie began to feel angry for both of them.

Malachi glanced around but the words had been under her breath, and nobody had heard.

'I'll see him in the morning,' she said. 'Unless of course you know his home address?'

Malachi mistook the last comment for humour, and he dropped his guard. His smile was brief and boyish. He even had dimples and the thought flashed through Ronnie's mind that a hardened criminal might not take him seriously. His smile faded when he realised she wasn't joking.

'I don't know,' he said, 'except I know two of his kids go to school in Trumpington and he comes in from that direction. And how many Fentons can there be?'

She nodded. She crossed to the counter and bought a ready-made sandwich. Cheese salad on brown bread and a bottle of iced tea. 'Do you want anything?'

He shook his head. 'My aunt makes my dinner. She's expecting me home. She only lives around the corner.'

He waited until she had paid then held the door while the two of them stepped on to the pavement.

'I'm sorry I wasn't straight with you. I could have explained the list.'

'That's not what you were told to do, was it?'

'No, but it doesn't make it right. He should have trusted you.'

Ronnie didn't reply. But she couldn't disagree either. Fenton should have either been open, or told her nothing.

'He doesn't know the connection,' Malachi continued, 'so how did he know you wouldn't get hurt, or inadvertently interfere with an investigation? I don't think he thought it through.'

'You're right.' It was an astute observation, especially from such a relatively inexperienced detective. Fenton should have known better. 'What a twat,' Ronnie muttered, and Malachi risked half a smile. 'That's a technical term,' she told him and tapped her food bag.

'See you tomorrow,' he said.

And Ronnie guessed she probably would.

CHAPTER 19

Ronnie paid for subscriptions every month to multiple open-source databases. The kind that held publicly available information, collated in an accessible and fast-to-retrieve format.

She had John Fenton's address within a couple of minutes. He lived with his second wife and their two children in Trumpington, on the south side of the city, three miles in the opposite direction to home.

She sent Alex a quick text.

Don't wait for me. See you later.

And set the satnav. She followed the directions and skirted around the centre of the city before turning away into a road lined with three- and four-storey town houses. The ones that weren't private residences seemed to be private schools.

Eventually, the larger houses petered out and the development became more mixed. It was as though Cambridge had crept towards the village of Trumpington and swallowed it years ago.

John Fenton's house had been built in the 1970s. It had big windows and was the same shape as a cuckoo clock, but without any of the adornment. There were two cars parked on the driveway. She parked across the back of both, blocking them in and slammed her own door, hoping he would hear. She rapped just as sharply on the chrome knocker.

She waited a few seconds then reached out to bang again, but heard him call, 'Hang on,' from the other side. His expression darkened as soon as he saw her.

'What are you doing here?'

'I want to talk to you.'

'Yeah, well I'm not at work right now, am I?'

But then he glanced over his shoulder, muttered something she didn't catch and when he turned back to her, he pulled the door wider.

'Come in,' he said.

He took her through to a study that was part office, part man-cave. There was a photo on the wall showing a group of young police officers, no doubt his passing-out photo, and he was one of the fresh-faced constables.

There were two scarves, Cambridge United Football Club, and a photograph of him in football kit, standing with a couple of mates. But there were also family photos, a bigger display than Linda Beckett's with birthday groups and Christmas dinners. The lower part of one wall was covered with scribbled drawings of unidentified animals with gangly limbs and misshapen heads.

She waved at the wall, 'Nice, but I'm not in the mood to be softened up by a demonstration of your . . .' she made air quotes even though she hated them, ' "human" side.'

He crossed back to the door and pushed it shut. 'Jess is upstairs with the kids so keep this quiet. I don't want them disturbed.' He waved her to a chair and leaned back against his desk. 'I know you're upset.'

He was about to add something else, but she glared hard enough to stop him. If the words *calm down* had been uttered, she would have given up trying to hold back.

'You were given a list which included my sister and Nigel Beckett. Who by?'

'We don't know.'

'How many names were on it?'

'Three in total.'

'And was the third name Kirsten McLeod?'

He looked startled. 'No.'

'Then who?' she asked.

'I'm not discussing the details.'

'But you instructed DC Henry to drop Nigel Beckett's name so I could find the connection to my sister.'

He shrugged.

'You wanted me to work it out. You expected me to come back with the answer.'

'Pretty much.' He tilted his head, leaned forward a little and made his tone even. 'What do you know?'

'I'm not some halfwit who's going to just share information, just because you're ready to listen.' She was sorry she'd sat in the chair. 'Your face might be two foot above mine, but I'm not in any way looking up to you. This is going to be a two-way exchange.'

'Two things, Ronnie. First, you are disproportionately angry—'

'You don't know what's disproportionate until you hear what I have to say.'

'And second, I can't involve you in this.'

'In which case I never found a connection.' The man was an idiot if he thought she would just reveal everything. 'Tell me what you're working on. Tell me how my sister is involved.'

'I don't know the connection to Jodie—' he began.

'You know something, even if you don't have all the details.'

'But,' he continued, doggedly sticking with his patient, even tone, 'I think the information you have might lead us to discover what happened to Jodie. That is in everybody's best interest, isn't it?'

'Well unfortunately, I didn't find a connection. Nothing at all. Nothing I can give you, unless I know what's going on.' She now had information that might advance the investigation into a murdered police officer. There was no way she was going to keep that to herself, but he didn't know her, and she had to at least try to call his bluff.

He leaned back in his chair and studied her for a few seconds. 'You can't work with us on this.'

'Officially no, but as a minimum you can tell me what I need to know.' She shrugged and held his gaze, 'Your choice.'

And in the end, he caved. 'What's going to keep you happy?'

Happy wasn't the aim, but she let that slide. 'If someone gave me three names and nothing else, I wouldn't waste time on it. There must have been more. I need to know.'

He stretched his hands out, spreading his fingers on the desk and exhaled.

'Okay,' he said, 'I'll tell you.'

CHAPTER 20

Within fifteen minutes Fenton and Ronnie were seated in an unoccupied corner at the Lord Byron pub. It didn't look as though it had changed much since the locals had been villagers, the beer had been delivered by dray and the only woman to set foot inside the place was the barmaid.

The decor was all dark wood and low ceilings. They sat across from one another, coffees in between.

'Why are we here?' she asked.

'This won't be a conversation for home, and I can't take you to the station. I'll take the flack.'

'What flack?'

'From the missus. This isn't like popping down the local with Dimitri, if you get my drift.'

Ronnie glanced at him coldly.

'You can assure your wife it really is.' She had no intention of losing control of any element of the conversation. 'Now,' she said, 'you go first.'

'Operation Byron is our longest standing open case.'

'Byron?' she queried.

He shot a glance across the bar. 'Yes, it is me that gets to choose the names. Op Byron is investigating a very clever little extortion racket. The victims are picked carefully, they're not celebrities, not politicians, they're just your normal Joe in the street and they're selected because they have a secret. Typically, an affair, or something dubious at work that they're trying to keep from their partner. Or a secret that needs to be kept from reaching the public domain. They've been blackmailed for a manageable amount of money, the kind of sum that will hurt but can be raised without too much difficulty. We found several cases and there are a few links, but it could be the tip of the iceberg.'

'And people won't report it to the police if it will cost their personal lives more than the amount of money they have to pay.'

'Exactly. The victims we have identified have been because of luck or chance, and it has been untraceable sums of money that they've handed over in every case.'

'How long has this been going on?'

'Around three years, we think, but obviously we don't know if there were earlier cases.'

'And why does it sit with your team? You cover the Eastern Region, right? Are you saying the victims are all from the same area?'

Fenton chuckled. 'What you should know about our team, Ronnie, is that we only nominally cover the Eastern Region. It keeps us independent of the local force but everything we do links back to Cambridge. Always. We will travel the country if necessary, but it all starts from here.' He tapped the tabletop with his index finger.

Ronnie stared at the table then back to Fenton. 'You're kidding me?'

'No. As you know, we're a small team and so there may be cases that we hand over to other partners, for example to the National Crime Agency. But Cambridge is unique.'

Ronnie felt sceptical and it must have showed.

'It isn't just grand architecture and selfie opportunities, you know.' He leaned across his half-drunk coffee and spoke in a low voice. 'Some of the best minds in the world are educated here. They teach here, they work here. Biomedical development, genetic modification, AI, the biggest concentration of museums in the country, priceless artefacts, it goes on and on. There are international players. And money is everywhere. Why wouldn't Cambridge have the crime to go with it?'

'You make it sound more influential than London.'

'And sometimes it is.' He rested his elbow on the table. 'I can tell you look at me and think I'm a bit of a twat . . .'

'It had crossed my mind.'

He ignored her. 'But I'm passionate about this team and its potential. You've met them all, haven't you?'

'I have,' she confirmed.

'Red's my number two . . .'

'You mean DS Jenna Reynolds?'

'I do,' he confirmed.

'And I supposed that's because of her hair colour?' Ronnie felt irritated on the other woman's behalf. 'Do you give nicknames to all your team?'

'Back in the day we all had nicknames. Jenna and I came into this team together, and then we built it from there. We keep Dimitri from going down virtual rabbit holes, and Tess and Will out of danger, and now we have to try to work out what to do with the other lad.'

'Malachi.'

'Yeah, Malachi. We're a solid team and we've worked on other cases, all successfully, but each time we come back to Byron and don't seem to make any more progress. Until a couple of weeks ago, out of the blue, we get a list of three names under the heading, *Operation Byron.*' He reached for the remainder of his coffee, although it had to have gone cold by now. 'Your sister, Nigel Beckett, and Dr Zoe Richardson.

'On the face of it, they didn't look connected. Beckett, he'd taken way more than the twenty grand he needed to pay off his gambling debts. He wouldn't talk, but the missing money was a valid link and the Beckett family had connections to Cambridge. Linda Beckett spent her career down here, so I thought maybe, just maybe . . . And then Dr Richardson, she worked for the university, had a house here in the city. She seemed a closer match, but I kept puzzling over your sister.

'We all did. Your connection to Cambridge isn't strong. How come your brother lives here?'

'He studied for his master's here.'

And as she said it, Ronnie realised Jodie had studied at Cambridge

75

too, except she had never made it to the end of the first semester. Jodie had not taken to university life. She'd been isolated, homesick. She had come home and wanted to put it behind her. Jodie's failure to achieve everything she might have done had been a taboo subject. And it was after that when everything had started to go so horribly wrong for her.

'Ronnie?'

She focused back on Fenton.

'Sorry, yes . . . he came back a couple of years ago. He applied for a position with a software company, and he's been here ever since.'

'As I said, we couldn't see the connection to your sister, so I decided to drop one of the names and see if you could work it out. Now your turn. Tell me what you know.'

'One question first. Why pick Nigel Beckett and not this Dr Zoe Richardson?'

'Simply because you could speak to Nigel and Linda Beckett, but Dr Richardson is dead.'

CHAPTER 21

Ronnie's second meeting with Linda Beckett had shaken her to the core.

She'd been involved in plenty of serious cases. Brutal murders, things she didn't particularly want to recall. But none of them had been this close to home.

She'd driven back to Cambridge with a burning sense of urgency. It was an instinctive rush to action, only tempered when she realised that Fenton might take the information and close the door on her if she gave away too much too soon.

'I appreciate you sharing as much as you did with me,' she began. 'I want you to know that what I'm going to tell you, I would have told you anyway.'

He nodded. 'Malachi called me, said you were agitated. I figured you'd discovered something, and I also figured that if I shared some information about the case, that you might make another connection or two.'

She had, but she couldn't share everything quite yet.

She watched carefully for his reaction, to find out whether he already knew. 'The connection isn't Nigel Beckett. It's Kirsten McLeod.'

Fenton was instantly still and looked momentarily confused. He rested his forehead in his palm and she could almost see his mind working over her words, redrawing a view of the case which only existed in his mind's eye. He was still frowning when he looked back at her, 'Go on.'

He hadn't known, she was sure of it. In one way she was glad, but somehow it made it harder to start telling him. As she fished around for the next sentence, she felt her mouth dry and a cold tightness grip her. There was no one else in the bar and she knew she couldn't be overheard, but she couldn't just spell it out either. 'Walk with me,' she said, and he followed her outside. It had started to rain and she was glad. It insulated them from the rest of the world.

'How much do you know of Kirsten McLeod's murder? Do you know more than appeared in the press?'

'I do,' he said.

'The way she was found. It's very specific. Do you know all the details?'

'I believe so.'

They turned the corner on to the main road. There was more road noise, but still no pedestrians and she felt safe to keep talking. 'My sister had been on a couple of dates with a guy. He turned nasty on the third. They'd both had a few to drink and something small turned into something big. I'd say you know how it is, but not in this case.'

Ronnie watched the pavement in front of her. She didn't need to look at Fenton for confirmation that he was listening, and he didn't need to prompt her each time she fell silent.

'She woke up in the morning, naked and alone in her flat. She was in the bath, tied to the taps with rope around the tap unit, pulled tight under her arms so that she was in a sitting position. The shower was on, flooding her with chilly water.'

The light from the streetlamps made chrysanthemum-shaped blooms on the wet pavement.

'She said she wasn't aware of any of it until she was suddenly awake and overwhelmed with everything at once. She couldn't call out. There was a gag in her mouth, and I suppose that part is different. But then Kirsten McLeod was dead at that point. Jodie said she knew she'd been raped straight away. On top of that, she had rope burns under her arms and across her body, and bruises on her spine from the tap.

'She worked herself free and managed to turn off the water, pulled a towel on top of herself. She said she lay in the bath then, drifting in and out of consciousness.

'She knew she'd been drugged.

'Eventually, she crawled into bed. Her flatmate had been away for the weekend. Came back and found her on Monday. Jodie was ill by then but just claimed it was the flu.'

He didn't speak until the silence was long enough for him to be sure he wasn't interrupting her. 'When was this?' he asked.

She shook her head. 'Years ago.'

'What happened when you found out?'

'I wanted her to report it, but she wouldn't. She said it was too late. Said it had happened months before.'

Ronnie stopped then. She dug her hands in her pockets and looked down at the pavement. She couldn't quite meet Fenton's gaze.

'It was one of the few times we fell out. The attack was so extreme, so unique that I said that it might have happened before, or it would happen again, and her coming forward might make a difference.

'She said I was trying to guilt trip her. Of course, I didn't mean it that way. I just didn't want her to think she wouldn't be taken seriously. The attack was so specific and not like anything I'd come across before. I figured that if somebody was going to assault someone like that, it wouldn't be a one-off because it would be part of some kind of compulsion. I told her there could be another case that would corroborate what she'd been through.'

Emotion welled in Ronnie faster than she expected. Yes, it had been years ago, but it suddenly felt so recent, so relevant. Jodie had put that time of her life so firmly in her past that Ronnie hadn't for a moment connected it to her sister's death, and she hadn't connected the attack to Cambridge until today. 'I wasn't trying to force her.'

Fenton reached out and placed his hand gently on her upper arm.

'Do you know who it was?'

Ronnie shook her head.

'I saw Jodie what must have been a few days after the attack. Caught sight of some of the bruising. She made up some excuse about falling on to her back and that was it. It didn't come up again until months later. It was then she told me everything. She referred to him as Dan. I don't know whether that was his name or a name he went by or just a name she used because she didn't want to tell me more. But you can't tell me what happened to Kirsten McLeod is just a coincidence.'

'No. It won't be. I'll need a statement from you. Come in tomorrow.'

She agreed she would. She left Trumpington for home, relieved he hadn't asked her if she'd told him everything. She hadn't, but the rest would need to wait.

CHAPTER 22

It was just after eleven when Ronnie arrived home. Her clothes were damp, her hair was wet, and the house sounded quiet.

She was greeted, as always, by Luke Skywalker staring at her from the other end of the hall. She thought at first that she was the only one awake but when she opened the door to the sitting room, Alex was on the sofa, working by the light of his computer screen. His features were a ghostly combination of reflected blue-white light and deep shadow. She flicked the switch for the overhead light. 'Sorry it's so late.'

'Don't worry,' he said. 'I got your message. I told Noah.'

'How is he?'

'Asleep. How are you? Tired?'

'Just mentally.' She gave a tight and apologetic smile. 'We need to talk.'

'Ah, the catchphrase of every girlfriend I've ever dated.'

'I'm going to say goodnight to him first.'

'He dropped off hours ago.'

'It doesn't matter.'

Alex was right. Noah was in the deepest sleep, breathing heavily with his face red and hot, his thick hair tousled. She placed a hand on his cheek.

'Love you,' she whispered, then closed the door quietly behind her. Alex was in the same chair, but the laptop was folded shut on the table. Two cans of Pepsi Max had appeared next to it. She scooped up the closest and dropped into the chair.

'What happened to no caffeine before bed?'

'You don't look like you're going to sleep anyway.' He shrugged. 'You've got that wired brain thing going on, I can see it on your face. Anything you can talk about?'

'Unfortunately, yes.'

Luckily, Alex already knew about Jodie's assault. Not every detail, but thankfully Jodie had given Ronnie permission to tell him at the time.

'And now there's another case, Alex. The details are so similar it has to be the same man.'

'How much did you tell Fenton?'

'Not everything, but I need to. I wanted to speak to you first, though.'

'No, we discussed this, we agreed. It's not fair on Noah.'

'It was different then, Alex. We were doing what Jodie wanted, but we were also making a mistake. Somebody who commits crimes like that doesn't just do it once. He's killed somebody.'

'I don't want Noah put through anything else.'

'It will be a cheek swab. He'll just think he's going to the doctor's, nothing more. And eventually we have to tell him, Alex.'

Alex was good at problem solving, just not with the kind of problems that involved humans. Half of Noah's DNA belonged to the man who had raped Jodie. And the evidence pointed to him being the killer of Kirsten McLeod. Keeping that to themselves was no longer an option. But morally, at least, she needed Alex's blessing. He already looked immovable.

'There are two things you need to know, Alex. The police were given Jodie's name because somebody else knows that Noah's father and the murderer are the same person. That leaves Noah exposed. Keeping the information to ourselves won't stop it coming out because it already has.'

She let that settle. She could see her brother working through the logic.

'And secondly?' he asked.

'I realised tonight that the attack happened here in Cambridge, not in London.'

'You said . . .'

'I know. That's what she told me.'

'She said she left uni because she hated it,' he reminded her.

'I know what she said. That she'd come back to London a few weeks earlier and crashed out with a friend because she was too embarrassed to let everybody know that she hadn't coped with uni life.' Ronnie put the can back on the table and then pushed it away. 'Alex, that only made sense up to a point. She'd worked so hard to get that place and you and I were too busy with our own lives to do anything apart from take what she said at face value.'

He had listened and his face seemed to pale and become heavy with shadows and this time it was nothing to do with the light from his laptop. 'You're right,' he said. 'It's different now. I'm just scared for Noah.'

Ronnie managed a tight smile. 'So am I.'

CHAPTER 23

Ronnie's father played an almost non-existent part in her adult life. She hadn't seen him since Jodie's funeral and, as far as she was aware, he hadn't attempted to make contact with Alex or Noah, never mind her. But she spent much of the night awake, considering nature versus nurture and the power of genetics.

When she'd first been taken in by her father and his wife, Alex and Jodie had baffled her. Alex with his fully functioning left side of the brain, the logic, the reasoning, the love of science. And then Jodie, just as bright but imaginative and creative, and Ronnie, somewhere between the two, plodding, it always felt. Her own mother had made sure that she was clean and tidy and fed. Their mother expected top of the class and nothing less. It had been a big adjustment.

Ronnie had been drawn to the police early. It was a world neither her father or stepmother understood and that was part of the appeal. And she couldn't imagine Alex on any other path beyond a top university and a job somewhere in the tech sector. Jodie's path had never been clear like that. Her passions were more transient, swinging between her own ambitions and those of her parents. She'd wanted to be a journalist, then a travel writer, and after that, a screenwriter. In the end, she'd applied for and been accepted on to an undergraduate degree in English literature. It was at St Eldith's, one of Cambridge's smaller colleges. She said her plan was to go from there to the university's Homerton College to train to be a teacher.

Ronnie let the information slide past her at the time. There were good odds that Jodie's plans wouldn't last, especially as Ronnie was sure that Jodie's choices were more to please other people than to please Jodie herself.

Ronnie woke in the small hours, her thoughts a continuation of those that she'd fallen asleep to. She'd been a fairly new officer when Jodie had left for Cambridge. She'd been striving to prove her place in the team, fighting to keep from being buried under an ever-mounting workload, putting in extra hours, trying to find ways to be more efficient, just concentrating on her own little bubble.

Ronnie's stepmother had posted a photo on her Facebook page. Jodie, standing at the entrance to her new college, the wrought-iron gates open behind her, supported by sober stone columns topped with carved urns. Behind her, two bowed stone steps worn with age, leading to an ancient arch. It should have been a film set, not a real place.

Ronnie reached for her phone on the bedside table and scrolled through her stepmother's Facebook page until she found the photo. She took a screenshot then zoomed in and studied her sister's expression. Part pride, part trepidation, she decided. It was a sunny photo, honey-tinted from the autumn light.

Ronnie glanced at the window; it was dark outside and damp and everything that that photo wasn't.

But right then, Ronnie knew that St Eldith's was the place she needed to be.

CHAPTER 24

Ronnie understood that it was grief that had overtaken her. She didn't fight it.

She pulled on warm clothes and walked away from the house. Cambridge in the small hours was unnaturally still. The streetlamps glowed but virtually every house was in darkness, and she did not see a single vehicle from Victoria Park to the centre of town.

For the whole way it was just the sound of her footsteps and the sound of her breathing. But when she neared the centre and heard the bells of the great St Mary's clock, she knew she was close to St Eldith's. She finally found the entrance in the photo. She stood at the locked gate, stared through the railings at the bolted wooden door.

In the nine intervening years nothing had changed. Fenton had talked about the investment, the innovation, the new money. She turned away and walked through the city until dawn, reading the blue tourist plaques on the walls, understanding the people and achievements that had passed before. Grand buildings had been constructed without computer-aided design, without the benefit of modern mathematics and power tools.

She was close to completing a full circuit when she came across the blue plaque for Watson and Crick, recognising their achievements in understanding the structure of DNA, work that had made a global impact and was undoubtedly about to change her world too. A student would have to be thick-skinned not to be simultaneously inspired and humbled by everybody who had achieved before them.

She waited at the gates of St Eldith's College. They were opened by the porter on the first of the seven chimes of the church clock.

She stepped across the two worn steps, just as Jodie must have done, and whispered under her breath, 'I miss you.'

CHAPTER 25

If a child was ready to ask a question, then they deserved to have an answer. Ronnie had thought it had been a sound principle. It had seemed like a solid way to build trust, openness too. And if a child understood enough to ask the question, wasn't it usually the case that the answer wouldn't be beyond their grasp?

But now she realised it was flawed. Fenton had called in a favour and arranged for the DNA swabs to be done at a private health clinic in Hills Road. He'd wanted swabs from both Alex and Noah because Alex was Jodie's full brother, while Jodie and Ronnie had only been half siblings.

Alex had agreed, but only because of his sense of duty, and they'd picked up Noah from school at lunchtime. Alex was quieter than usual. He understood why it was important, but he wasn't happy. They were just entering the clinic building, when Noah looked up at Alex and asked, 'Why is it we need these tests?'

Alex shot a look at Ronnie then smiled at his nephew.

'I think Auntie Ronnie can explain it better than I can.'

And so, when it came down to it, Noah had asked the question and Ronnie hadn't been able to give a proper answer.

They were in and out of the clinic in just under fifteen minutes. They left the building together. Ronnie's phone rang before she'd even stepped on to the pavement of Hills Road. She didn't recognise the number but answered in any case.

'Can you send them home without you?'

It was Fenton. She glanced in both directions but couldn't see him. She pressed *end* and dropped the phone back in her pocket.

'How about a family lunch, then a boys' trip to Forbidden Planet?'

'We don't need Forbidden Planet to have a good time, do we, Noah?'

Noah beamed up at him. 'Oh yes we do!'

And from there they walked together just a few feet ahead of her, debating Marvel versus DC and then the colours of lightsabres and, finally, who should win in a fight between Batman and Superman. She didn't catch the answer, but it involved laughter and the two of them shouting 'Martha! Martha!'

She had a lot to learn, and she was thankful for Alex and the way he never held on to an argument once it was in the past. They stopped at Signorelli's Deli, Noah and Alex devouring lunch in just about the shortest time possible, then clearing off without her. She returned the call to Fenton then.

'Where are you?' he said.

She checked the nearest road sign, 'Burleigh Street?'

'Five minutes tops,' he told her, then met her in the reception of Parkside Police Station and walked her up to his office.

'The DNA results will take a couple of days. We fast-tracked them and it goes without saying that everything's confidential. Even if there's a trial, Noah's identity will not be revealed.'

She wouldn't have expected anything less, but it was still a comfort to hear him say so.

'Well, I appreciate the update, but you could have told me that over the phone.'

'Well, there's something else. More favours I've called in, if you like. I've spoken to a few people, Superintendent Cooper, your old boss, occupational health. I've arranged for you to be temporarily seconded to my team. Not to work on anything directly connected with your sister, but since Op Byron is our only active investigation, that's a slight fudge . . . a massive fudge.

'To be honest, I have to pull every kind of nonsense to keep this team running. Each success buys us a few more months but, right now, our only case is the only one we haven't resolved. I'll be briefing the team in a few minutes. I just need to know if you're up for this?'

In truth, Ronnie was up for anything that would take her out of detective limbo. She wasn't going to turn him down, but she wasn't sure what to make of him either. He was more complex and self-aware than she'd first given him credit for.

But there was also something of the chancer about him. She wasn't sure if he was trustworthy. But at that very moment, it wasn't important.

She reached forward and offered him her hand to shake. 'Yes. I'm in.'

CHAPTER 26

Fenton gathered them together in the room with the hi-tech roll-down screen and the rest of the state-of-the-art equipment. He'd given it the imaginative title of Room A.

She realised it was the first time she'd seen them all together and it underlined what an eclectic bunch they were. Malachi had already made a round of teas and coffees and was clearly surprised when she entered the room. He disappeared and returned with an extra mug for her, and he'd remembered how she took her coffee.

The tables were positioned into a loose horseshoe with Dimitri at one end of the arc and Will at the other. If they were seated in any kind of order, Ronnie reckoned it had to be ascending order of gregariousness or descending order of IQ. Perhaps that was a little harsh, but she felt it was about right to be sitting somewhere in the middle, where there were two empty seats, one for her and the other for Malachi, she guessed.

Fenton stood in front of them. Despite the room brimming with digital equipment, he had only sheets of paper and a thin file to work from. He began to speak and her already changing view of him shifted again. Everything from his posture, the tone of his voice, had suddenly become sharper, more focused.

'To begin, I'd like to formally welcome Ronnie to the team. She is on secondment to us for a few weeks, less if we can deal with this quickly. As you are all aware, a significant connection has now been made between our case and the investigation into the murder of

Kirsten McLeod. This morning, I met with the SIO on that team, DCI Beetham. At this point our investigation is not merging with theirs. However, we will be maintaining close contact with one another.'

Tess raised a hand then and Fenton paused to let her speak.

'We don't have absolute proof that our Byron guy is Kirsten McLeod's killer do we, sir?'

Fenton nodded. 'You are correct and that is the main reason we have decided to keep two separate but parallel investigations running and, with that in mind, DCI Beetham has agreed that I can share the following with you. The main line of our enquiries is that the murder of Kirsten McLeod is linked to a series of serious sexual assaults. All the victims have suffered a prolonged and traumatic experience, any of which could have resulted in their deaths. We're working on the hypothesis that Kirsten McLeod was assaulted in the same way. But as the result either of putting up a fight or some other element, the assault culminated in her murder. There have been three similar assaults since Kirsten McLeod's attack but, fortunately, the women in each instance have survived.

'Significant information regarding this case has been withheld from the media for three reasons. To prevent public alarm, to prevent copy-cat attacks and, finally, to ensure that new reports and evidence we receive can be compared to information that is not in the public domain. It is on this basis that we conclude that the further information we have received this week, regarding a previously unknown assault of a woman nine years ago, becomes the first known case in the series.'

There was movement in the room, and Fenton paused and looked up from the notes. Dimitri had his hand half raised.

'Are the rape cases in the Cambridge area?'

'The cases go further afield, Dimitri. They've provided me with a map, and I will pin that up when I've finished, but essentially, the furthest is about sixty-five miles away, with the centre point of the pattern being the city of Cambridge. This briefing contains some rather, in my opinion, obvious comments about the profile of the perpetrator. For example,' he read from the page again, 'due to the timings and location of the assaults, it would appear that the perpetrator either doesn't work or has a flexible work schedule, which may include travel.'

Jenna shook her head in disapproval. 'That probably leaves fifty per cent of the adult male population.'

'It would,' Fenton agreed, 'if it wasn't for this final point.' He shot a look in Ronnie's direction. 'A new development means that we are waiting on the results of some new DNA samples. With the resulting profile, we will have strong enough evidence to look for familial connections, which might identify the perpetrator.'

Fenton stopped reading and rattled the sheet.

'DCI Beetham then goes on to stress all the usual about confidential nature of the investigation. You all know the score. Read this, digest it. I will be the single point of contact for any liaison that needs to go between our team and the DCI.

'You two,' he turned his attention to Ronnie and Malachi. He scooped up a folder from the table. It was A4 sized and thin enough to appear empty. 'Dr Zoe Richardson, deceased. The third name on the list. It's down to you two to try and work out what the connection is between her and the rest of this case.'

'Why would Dr Richardson be linked to the blackmail investigation when my sister wasn't?'

'Keep an open mind. The tip off links it to Operation Byron. I can't authorise you to go anywhere in relation to someone else's case.'

Ronnie wanted to know more about the wider investigation but, before she had a chance to speak, Fenton held up his hand to stop her. 'You're working on this, Ronnie. You, Malachi. Nothing else.'

She snatched up the folder. It felt as empty as it looked.

'It's just her obituary,' Malachi whispered. 'There was more online than there is in there. She had articles published on repeat victimisation, adverse childhood experiences. Her specialist area was the social impact of crime.'

'And you read them, I suppose?'

'Doesn't mean I understood them, though. They were on the dry side. She was an academic at one of the smaller colleges. Have you heard of St Eldith's?'

A burst of adrenaline shot through her. 'I have and I even know where it is.'

CHAPTER 27

Malachi was right about the contents of the file. Nothing but the brief obituary.

It included an unflattering photograph of Dr Richardson; the kind that gets taken at a seminar or official dinner. She wore a suit complete with lanyard and smiled stiffly at the camera. Her steel-grey hair was clipped back, giving prominence to her strong jawline and diamond-shaped face.

She had passed away on 12 June 2019. Five years ago, then. She'd been just fifty-four years old and had died in Cambridge. Left behind her second husband, an academic named Colin Knox, and her two sons from her previous marriage, Matthew (thirty-three) and Owen (thirty).

She had been a course leader at St Eldith's College, lecturing in her specialist area of criminal psychology and offender rehabilitation.

As an obituary, it was poor. A paint-by-numbers profile with the details harvested from the university who's who pages or the back of a book cover.

Ronnie handed Malachi the file.

'Is there somewhere you can leave this? I don't exactly have a desk, do I?'

Malachi removed the single sheet, folded it in four and slipped it into his pocket.

'In case you want to read it later,' he said, and left the empty folder on the table. 'I have her publications and other information about her on my laptop. Where do you think we should start?'

The first thing Ronnie had done on her arrival at Parkside that morning was to give Fenton a full statement. At least, he believed it was full. The one thing she had left out was her suspicion that Jodie had been attacked in Cambridge. If she was being honest with herself, it wasn't even a suspicion. She was certain that it had happened that way. Nothing else made sense to her now and she should have gone back. She should have turned round and explained that to Fenton.

'Will you walk to St Eldith's with me?'

'Why?' Malachi asked. 'The boss said you don't like company and I'd have to work hard not to get ditched.'

She tapped him on the elbow. 'Come on, let's get walking. Perhaps I'm turning over a new leaf. Or maybe I just want to pump you for information? You pick.'

'I'm going to put my money on all of the above.'

'Optimism, realism and diplomacy all in one sentence. I'm impressed, Malachi.'

They took the stairs. There didn't seem to be anybody around, but she kept her voice low anyway.

'There were a couple of things about my sister that I never told Fenton. Don't ask me why, I just didn't. One didn't seem relevant until a minute ago and that was that my sister was briefly, very briefly, a student at St Eldith's. She didn't even make it through her first semester. It barely registered with me at the time. It felt as though she was excited to be going and the next thing she was back home again. But the more I think about it, it only makes sense that the assault happened here as well.'

Malachi reached the bottom of the stairs and held the door for her. There was a hint of mischief in his expression.

'If you had told Fenton, we wouldn't be going over there now.' Then his face fell. 'I'm so sorry. That was really tactless of me.'

'Don't worry. I agree with you. I'm glad we've got this opportunity.'

Outside, the wind had increased and the temperature had dropped. They needed to take a relatively short walk across Parker's Piece.

Ronnie zipped up her jacket and they strode out, heads down in the wind.

'Who do you want to speak to first?' Malachi asked.

'We'll start with Colin Knox, and I'd like to see the accommodation. Although I suppose it may have completely changed since my sister was here.'

Malachi disagreed. 'It might have expanded, but it won't have changed. The room your sister occupied probably has the same furniture, the same paint on the walls, and even the same bedder. It's brains and technology that run quickly round here, not much else.'

'Is that true?'

'Often, not always,' he conceded.

'And what's a bedder anyway?'

She barely caught his words before they were whipped away. 'You really are new to town.'

CHAPTER 28

Colin Knox's study was on the ground floor and faced on to the quadrangle. It was opposite the entrance and through the tiny diamond panes in the leaded mullion windows, he could view everyone who arrived. Some days he barely gave a glance, but others, like today, when it felt as though there was change in the air, his eyes were constantly drawn to the window.

He recognised the young black detective immediately. On his previous visit, he had asked questions solely about Zoe. Most had been general, one or two had been more obscure and, the whole time, Colin had felt that the detective was like a man poking a pile of firewood with a stick, waiting for the rat to run out.

Undoubtedly ready to pounce.

So, it was no surprise that he was back again, although it hadn't been a surprise when he'd come the first time. So much connected with Zoe and her death had felt like unfinished business. He shut his laptop, gathered the loose papers on his desk into a single pile, then he retrieved a framed six-by-four photo of Zoe from the drawer below.

For such a long time, it had been his favourite photograph of her. He'd been the one who had taken it. He'd come into her study and found her reading in her bay window. She'd been wearing a red rollneck sweater with the sleeves pushed up above her elbows. She'd lowered the book to her lap and the sun coming off the window had bounced off the pages. The effect had been to illuminate her, and she'd

97

stared into the camera, her eyes bright and clear, a question paused on her lips. He could pinpoint that as the exact moment when his feelings for her had changed. It wasn't an exaggeration to think of it as an epiphany, a great revelation. The revelations that had come later had been less profound. They'd chipped away at what he thought he had until looking at that picture brought with it as much distaste and frustration as it had once brought joy.

He hadn't yet decided what line he would take with the police, and he wasn't sure what line they would take with him. But if they were expecting a grieving partner, that was exactly what they were going to get. He wasn't sure whether the truth actually mattered any more.

CHAPTER 29

The grounds of St Eldith's were protected from the wind. There was a stillness in the air and their footsteps echoed on the stone paving. It felt far removed from the Cambridge they'd just left.

'So, you met with Colin Knox?' she asked.

'Yes, once briefly, just to establish some basic details and to ask him whether he knew why his partner's name might have come up on an anonymous note sent to the police.'

'And what did he say?'

'He had no idea. He assured us that her financial affairs had been in order and, at that point, we had no further questions for him.'

Malachi remembered the route to Knox's office and led the way, taking them through low arches and doorways where he needed to duck his head, before turning into a narrow corridor that looked more likely to lead to a chapel than to somebody's office.

Colin Knox, as it turned out, was a professor. His title and name were mounted on the door on a piece of dark wood about the size of a six-inch ruler. Ronnie rapped on the door and a man's deep voice instructed them to enter. Perhaps because the doorways had been low and the corridors narrow with tight turns, she had expected Knox's study to be modest in size.

Instead, it was what she would have described as a private library. His antique oak desk was expansive. A pair of ox-blood leather

Chesterfield armchairs were positioned in a reading nook and the rest of the room was lined with bookshelves.

He directed them to a couple of chairs that looked as though they had come from a pre-war primary school. They were positioned at one end of his desk, and he swivelled his chair ninety degrees to face them. 'How can I help you both?'

'We're following up on my last visit,' Malachi began. 'Further information has come to light, and we have some more specific questions.'

Knox, Ronnie knew, was fifty-nine years old. He was fairly average height with fairly average looks. His clothes and his personal grooming were both tidy, but with no evidence that he tried too hard. He seemed extremely comfortable with himself. Urbane was the word that popped into her head, and she imagined that he was generally considered more attractive than the sum of his constituent parts.

'I'm happy to answer anything I can,' he said. His left hand was touching his desktop, the tips of his fingers close to a small rectangular photo frame. He took a second to glance at the picture of Zoe Richardson. Ronnie found it a little too much, but perhaps she was just cynical.

Malachi remained impassive, his voice even. 'We are investigating the possibility that Dr Richardson could have been the victim of blackmail. Are you aware of any information that could have been held and used against her?'

Knox shook his head. 'No, absolutely not.'

'Could she have been worried that something would be revealed to you?'

Knox frowned and seemed to be searching the ceiling for the answer. Then he brought his attention back to Malachi. 'I'm not sure how to answer that. I think I knew Zoe very well. We worked together; we spent a lot of time together. We weren't cohabiting in the end. We stayed over with each other, but I still had my house, and she still had hers. So, we weren't as intertwined as some couples are. There could have been things I didn't know.'

Ronnie had suggested that Malachi should lead with the questions primarily because this was his second meeting with Knox, and it made sense for him to continue what he had already started. 'Dr Richardson's recorded cause of death as cirrhosis of the liver caused by acute alcoholism. Were you aware of her drinking issues?'

'I was aware that she drank too much, even that she was alcoholic, but I had no idea of the severity of it. I didn't know it would kill her.'

Malachi was making notes of the conversation but was asking questions from memory.

'According to my notes, you and Dr Richardson were living together until ten months before her death. Was the relationship over?' There was no immediate response, but Malachi let the question hang in the air.

Knox clasped the back of his neck and massaged the top of his spine for a few seconds. His eyes were closed, and pain was etched on his face. 'Addictions turn people into liars,' he said at last. 'They say whatever they need to, to achieve what they want. That's a major personality change for somebody who was previously studious and earnest and morally responsible. And then, on the other hand, we're told that it's an illness. Her alcoholism turned her into somebody needy and manipulative.'

He swung his hand in the direction of the picture. 'From everything you can see in that photo, to somebody I didn't recognise. I had to live with the guilt, and just leave for my own sanity. But we were never over. No.'

Without warning, he flipped the picture on to its face.

'But the alcoholism wasn't a secret and wouldn't have brought her down. People knew she drank.' He swallowed and his voice tightened, 'Perhaps you should be asking what changed? What made her go from social drinking to killing herself in the space of a few years? How about that for a question?'

Knox had become emotional very quickly; that happened when grief started to find its way out of the cracks in a fragile exterior. It also happened when witnesses were full of shit. The jury was out.

Malachi lowered his voice, and Knox stilled at the change in tone, 'On August the third, 2018, the police were called to a domestic incident at your property. Was it domestic violence that drove her to drink, Professor?'

Knox deflated instantly. 'She hit me. I never touched her. But it was just the drink which caused it, there was no malice from either of us. That was the moment I think our relationship truly cracked.'

'She had two broken fingers.'

'She told me she fell.'

Malachi paused with his pen over the pad. 'Was it into a door by any chance?'

Ronnie should have stopped him at that dig, but her attention, which had landed on the facedown photo, slid further across the desk and she found herself staring at the spine of a book. She cut across the increasingly terse exchange. 'What do you teach?' she asked Knox.

Knox looked startled. Probably shocked that she had to ask the question. 'English literature.'

'And how long have you been here?'

'This is my twelfth year. Why?'

'Do you remember if you taught a student named Jodie Blake?'

Ronnie couldn't begin to guess the number of students that must have passed through St Eldith's in twelve years. Few would remain in any lecturer's memory, but he recognised Jodie's name in an instant.

CHAPTER 30

The information had come from Professor Knox in a reluctant trickle until Jodie's name came into play. Until then, it felt as though he had been selective with what he was prepared to share. But now he didn't seem to have a strategy for holding back and was in the midst of such a stream of consciousness that Ronnie doubted that there was any filter between his brain and his mouth.

Malachi made notes and did his best not to interrupt.

'Jodie Blake was here on a scholarship. We only have a couple each year and they have to be very strong applicants. For every-one we take, there must be a hundred that we don't. So, I expected her to be top notch before I'd even met her, and I was not disappointed.

'First-year students often come expecting everything to be laid out for them. They haven't yet developed the inquisitive mindset or the ability to study independently. But she already understood theories such as formalism and postmodernism. She was familiar with Polti's thirty-six situations and made a very strong argument that *Jane Eyre* was not written as a role model for fortitude but as a cautionary tale. *Stay in your place. Be careful what you wish for.*'

He filled his lungs at the memory, closing his eyes and inhaling as though he was listening to the sweetest music.

It lasted two or three seconds, then his attention snapped back to Ronnie and Malachi. 'I have a habit,' he announced. 'A bad habit.'

But it was said with a puff of the chest and a *how-clever-am-I* smirk.

'At the start of every year, at the end of week one, I take a list of the names in the year and highlight against each whether they're going to drop out and when, or for the ones I think will stay until the end, I note what degree classification I think they'll achieve. Then I seal it in an envelope and don't look until their final week. The results are often eerily accurate and I'm not telling you this in a *how-clever-am-I* type way.'

Ronnie wanted to interrupt and say, *Oh, but you are.* But she stayed quiet.

Malachi outdid her. 'Of course you're not,' he said, injecting a sliver of sarcasm so subtle that the esteemed English professor barely hesitated before moving on.

'What,' Ronnie asked, 'was your prediction for Jodie Blake?'

'I thought it would be an easy first, as long as she persevered with the course.'

'Did you think she wouldn't?'

He considered the question. 'The confident, gregarious scholarship students tend to do well. The ones that feel like outsiders don't. I didn't see her mix with anybody at first. It was just in the last week or so. She sat with another girl. Erm . . .' He paused to rummage through his memory, trying to pull out a name. 'Philippa something. Unremarkable student but bright enough to latch on to Jodie. I'm sure Student Services can find the details. If you want them, that is?'

Malachi nodded. 'Thank you. Now, can you tell me what you know about Jodie Blake's departure?'

'Jodie had been missing from a couple of my lectures and supervision sessions. It's not uncommon for students to skip out. They're supposed to be adults, after all, their choice. But then Zoe stopped me in the corridor, said that something had happened and Jodie was ill. I guessed freshers' flu or similar; I didn't realise that she was as ill as she was. I assumed she'd be back at some point, but I never saw her again. I don't remember all our alumni, never mind the students who have left early, but she had something.'

He tapped his first two fingers against his lips, like a man at a crossroads trying to decide which way to turn. 'Then I heard rumours and Zoe heard them too. The words *fresher visitation* started flying around.'

'Hazing?' Malachi asked.

'Yes, that's what we thought, and Zoe took it upon herself to investigate. She was worried that there was a toxic culture forming among the students. She reached out to Jodie; I know that much. But couldn't get anywhere. If she discovered more than that, she never told me, and by the time Jodie's cohort graduated, the rumours had all but gone.'

Up to that point, Knox's account had tallied with the sparse details Jodie had shared with Ronnie.

'We'd like to speak to her roommate as well,' she said. 'Is that also information we can get from Student Services?'

He shook his head. 'She had no roommate. The accommodation for our female students consists of single rooms and private bathrooms. What you need is her bedder.'

CHAPTER 31

A bedder turned out to be the affectionate term for a bed maker and it dated back to the time when male students required something akin to a daily maid. They met Tina Runham at the Housekeeping office, a windowless room which was literally a broom cupboard apart from a metal-legged table serving as a desk. Above it were key hooks and a corkboard plastered with Post-it notes. Tina had held the job for thirty-eight years and mentioned this more than once in the first couple of minutes.

It reminded Ronnie of police officers. They tended to introduce themselves by rank, force, years in the job. People in prison did the same. Perhaps it was a sign of being institutionalised.

'I joined straight from school,' Tina said again. Her face was deeply lined and the skin on her hands shiny and cracked. She could have been mistaken for a woman ten years older.

'I remember that day so clearly. I'd change the bedding over once a week, still do. And I try to pick a time when the students are scheduled for lectures. We'd never go in without knocking first but it's more efficient if I know that I'm calling at a time when they're likely to be out. I don't want to work around them; the rooms are compact, you might say.'

'Do you remember which one was hers?' Ronnie asked.

'I do. Of course I do.'

Tina reached to the key hooks. Every key was brass, rudimentary looking, and each was attached to its own wooden fob, hand-painted with the number of the room. Jodie's had been number 22.

'The last room on the left,' Tina told them and led them deeper into the heart of the college.

'It's much easier to show you than to explain,' she told them as she stopped outside Room 22. 'I had my housekeeping trolley with me. I would have knocked . . . and don't worry, I know it's empty today.'

She held up the key. 'All the keys are a bit basic, so even if a student slept through my knock, the chances are they would have locked their door from the inside. Every room has one of those hook-and-eye catches for security. So, I knocked. There was no reply, so I entered the room backwards pulling the trolley behind me.'

Tina opened the door on to a room so small that it reminded Ronnie of a cabin on a ship.

Daylight slipped in through a narrow window and the only concession to the twentieth century seemed to be a four-column radiator under the window and, to the twenty-first century, the partitioning of part of the room to make a bathroom. Tina stood in front of its closed door.

'So, you see,' she said, 'I came in and turned and I couldn't miss her, lying on the bed. She was completely still. Her eyes were open, she was staring towards me. Almost jumped out of my skin, and for a second . . .' She clasped her hand to her mouth. 'For a second, I actually thought she was dead. I reached over and pressed my hand against her forehead.'

Tina was animated when she spoke and gestured to illustrate everything that she was saying.

'She groaned a little. And I can't tell you how relieved I was. Poor girl was burning up and she wanted water. I wanted to call for help but she was adamant. Weak, but adamant.

'She wanted help sitting up, so I put my arm around her and that was the first time I realised that she was naked under the covers. She didn't seem to care and as she leaned on me, I saw her back. She was bruised . . . really bruised. She said she'd slipped in the bath. And maybe she did.'

Tina reached behind her and opened the bathroom door. The

sanitaryware looked at least a hundred years old; grand white porcelain with copper fittings. Tina reached over and patted the curved spout of the bath tap. 'Imagine the bruise that would leave. A curve, a crescent; am I right?'

They both nodded.

'She had more than I can count. That's not falling over in the bath; that would be a single impact. This was many.'

'Did she say anything else?'

'I made her a hot drink and sat with her for a while. I knew it was serious and I asked if she wanted to speak to anyone, but she flatly refused.'

The tub was shorter than average, but very deep. Ronnie imagined Jodie trapped in this windowless room, not knowing when she would be found, the cold running water blocking every sound from the outside world.

'What do you think happened to her, Tina?'

'Funny, that's what Dr Zoe asked me. She had rooms in the college for a time and I heard she used to walk the corridors at night. Then a couple of years later, I put the same question to her that she put to me, but I knew straight away that I'd said the wrong thing.

'She looked blank, like she'd never heard of Jodie. I started to explain, but she raised her voice. Put up a hand like this and said "I don't want to hear it." She looked so angry, and I didn't want to make a scene so I kind of apologised and said I was mistaken. Never had a proper conversation with her after that.'

CHAPTER 32

As soon as they left St Eldith's College, Malachi pulled Ronnie to one side.

'We need to talk.'

'I know what you're going to say.'

'This is all wrong. The one thing you're not supposed to be involved in is anything to do with your sister.'

'Fenton knew what he was doing. There are three names on the list and one of them is Jodie's and he sends us to speak to the third name. He knew there was going to be a connection; he told us to find one.'

He shook his head. 'No, you shouldn't be listening to that about your own sister. It's damaging.'

Ronnie swallowed. She didn't have an answer for that one.

He pointed ahead to the Cambridge University Arms Hotel. 'We'll go in there. We'll get coffee. We'll talk this out.'

He was out of line. He was the DC; she was the DS. 'It's not for you to make the plans, Malachi.'

'I disagree. You're the one in a compromised situation, I'm the one being dragged into it. I'm supposed to be one of the new wave of independent-thinking, decision-making police officers. If buying you a coffee and talking to you for twenty minutes is a misuse of my initiative, then I can't be expected to come through in a real emergency, can I?'

Again, Ronnie didn't have a comeback; he was right. Besides, she knew that she needed to find some way to decompress before she returned to Parkside.

The hotel bar was quiet. It had the look of a Victorian gentlemen's club with velvet armchairs, muted lighting and a fire burning in half of a floor-to-ceiling fireplace. Malachi chose a quiet corner, one with a large picture window looking out over Parker's Piece, and where the nearest customers were about twenty feet away.

They had a clear view of Parkside Police Station. 'What do you do over there most days, Malachi?'

He replied with a crooked smile. 'I'm like a research assistant, running errands and waiting to be given things to do. Sometimes I'm like the waiter or the taxi driver that everybody talks in front of, and nobody notices. I'm storing it all.' He tapped his temple. He didn't say it in a boastful way, just matter of fact. 'That must have been hard back there. Are you okay?'

He was an unusual combination; reticent in one remark, outspoken in the next.

'I couldn't stop thinking about how scared and isolated Jodie must have felt. And I know it's too late to fix that, but I kept wishing that she'd called me . . . Or wishing that she felt she could.'

'That, as my aunt would say, is the path to madness. You need to stop.'

He wasn't wrong. She didn't know how to reply, but he understood to drop the subject and left Ronnie to pick the next. 'You said the other day you do facial identification. What did that involve?'

'Yeah, I'm just good at remembering stuff, so I looked for faces in crowds. I was with the crowd-control team for a while. We spent much of the time monitoring football matches; we'd receive photographs of troublemakers from one match and the aim was to spot them at the next. It gave me a real buzz when I identified someone, but in between times it was the most boring job.' He rolled his eyes. 'Even milling around that office is more exciting.'

'Have you said that to Fenton?'

'Absolutely not. My mum would kill me if I was sent back to London. Where we come from, kids don't join the police. My family

110

was getting a load of flack because people on the estate knew I'd been employed by the Met. So, my aunt – great aunt actually – lives up here and Mum decided that I ought to move.'

'Malachi, you're twenty-four. Why are you still doing what your mum wants you to do? And going to live with a boring old aunt?'

'Oh God, she's not boring,' he laughed, 'and she makes the best cakes.'

The drinks arrived. Ronnie sighed and said, 'Well, that's all right then.'

Malachi had ordered cappuccino for her, complete with cocoa powder. His was a hot chocolate with fresh cream and a flake.

'I feel like I'm your aunt right now, Malachi. I mean, hot chocolate?'

He cocked his head at the window. 'It's practically winter out there. Besides, I personally think chocolate is the ultimate foodstuff.'

'Oh, stop now,' she said, but underneath it all she was appreciative of the break, glad that he'd brought them in here. Even, she realised, pleased to have his company. 'You're okay, Malachi.'

She said it as though it was a grudging compliment, but she meant it.

He looked disproportionately pleased.

'And you're okay. Fenton said you'd be a pain in the arse.'

The cup was to her lips as he said it. Another second and she would have choked on the contents.

'Now you're crossing the line, Malachi.'

'No, he crossed the line. You can't shoot me for being honest.'

'So, I'm a pain in the arse?'

'He heard that you're stubborn, not a team player, you can't keep regular hours.'

'I can't disagree with any of that.' Ronnie laughed, and it actually felt good, she realised, to cut herself a little slack for a few minutes. She wasn't sure that Malachi was a kindred spirit exactly, but her gut told her that she could trust him. 'We should get back in a minute.'

'Fenton says he wants you around until we work out the link between Jodie and Dr Richardson. We could go back with what we have, but I think we can do more.'

111

She leaned back in her chair and half closed her eyes. 'So, what would you do next, Malachi?'

'This is another initiative test, isn't it?'

'Something like that.'

She waited. She watched him rewind through the day. It took longer than she expected, but then again, an answer was easy if you knew what it was, and she'd been around the block a few more times than he had.

She could read in his expression the moment when he saw the answer. 'Why the hell did that take me so long?' He pulled out the folded obituary and opened it onto the coffee table. 'We need to speak to her sons.'

CHAPTER 33

Ronnie had asked Malachi to return to Parkside without her, and to find out what he could about Matthew and Owen Richardson. She had needed an hour or so of her own space, her own thinking time, and it was no reflection on Malachi; it would have been the same if she had been with anybody else.

She had spent the next hour making a new circuit of the city centre and, of course, in the daylight and with busy streets, it took on a completely different feel. She'd followed the flow of the pedestrians, paying no attention to her route, oblivious to the cold, her thoughts purely on her sister.

Ronnie could feel Jodie's isolation, and if Jodie had felt able to tell anyone about the assault when it had first occurred, it certainly hadn't been Ronnie. And even when she had confided in Ronnie, it hadn't all been true. Jodie hadn't been attacked in a London flat, that was clear. Ronnie wondered about the rest. The fight with a fledgeling boyfriend, and the amnesia.

Maybe Jodie had remembered and for one brutal, vivid, burning instant, she pictured Jodie's terror-filled eyes, jammed open with fear. Jodie freezing every detail into her mind. Jodie reliving mute memories that she had never been able to articulate.

And when she had eventually told Ronnie part of the truth, she had pushed Jodie to make a statement. Probably asking her to do the impossible.

113

Ronnie, like always back then, had been a police officer first and a sister second.

Her phone rang as she stood on the opposite pavement to the time-eater clock watching the giant locust crawl on the top of its golden face. Scraping through the seconds with its brittle legs. Relentless.

It was Malachi. 'Did you find addresses for both of them?' she asked him.

'Yes, a work address for Matthew and a home address for Owen. But . . .' He squeezed in the 'but' before she could speak.

'What?'

'I'm not giving them to you.' He was calling from outside and she heard a car door closing. 'I'm sorry, but I'm going. It can't be you who speaks to them.'

'What the hell, Malachi?'

'And Fenton wants to see you,' he said quickly, then hung up.

She stared across at the clockwork locust, wishing she could snap off its persistent little legs.

CHAPTER 34

Malachi had weighed up the situation. He knew that he had been risking Ronnie's ire, but Fenton's disapproval held more threat.

He didn't want to be transferred back to the Met.

He'd settled into Cambridge almost immediately and it had
surprised him. He had expected to find it too small and too elite, and
in terms of population and land area, yes, it was small, but it was also
incredibly complex, like an intricately cut gem, with each facet
reflecting something different and with so many different angles that
it was impossible to see them all at once.

True, it was still comparatively new to him, but he already felt that
he never wanted to live anywhere else. And therefore, risking Ronnie's
anger concerned him far less than it might have done.

He reminded himself yet again that his refusal to give her the
details of Matthew and Owen Richardson was for her own good and
for the good of the investigation. His logic was sound and when she
stopped to consider that, he was sure that she would see it too. At
least, he hoped so.

Malachi was sure that Fenton's intention had never been to give
Ronnie a free rein, and on his return to Parkside he'd made a point of
telling Fenton as much. Fenton had sat back in his chair, steepled his
fingers, and listened without interruption.

The first reaction to his comments had been an awful, nerve-jarring
silence. 'You're correct, Malachi,' Fenton finally responded. 'Any

part of this investigation could link to her sister, but any connection to St Eldith's is now too close. You can interview them.'

Malachi was more than capable, but he had still hesitated. It would be the first time he had been given any responsibility to work independently outside their office. 'And what about Ronnie?'

'Send her back here.' Fenton then shooed him away. 'You've shown initiative, Malachi. Now get out there and use it.'

Malachi chose to visit Matthew Richardson first. He worked as the contracts manager for a company called MRH Ltd. Malachi Googled it. The H stood for hydraulics and the company had been established in Cambridge in 2003 by his father, Michael Richardson. That and an address on the north side of the city was all he found.

Malachi parked up and walked towards MRH. The office building looked flashy, but as anonymous as the company name sounded. It stood eight grey steps up from the road in a black glass cuboid, which reflected the sky and made it impossible to know whether the building was occupied.

He pushed the heavy doors and entered the reception area. It was narrow but ran deep into the building. The desk by the door was manned by a security guard and Malachi realised that MRH was one of a list of companies renting floor space in the building.

The guard asked for Malachi's name, but not for the reason for his visit, then directed him towards an L-shaped seating area, comprising two low-level and uncomfortable-looking settees positioned at ninety degrees to one another. Perhaps all the budget had been splashed on the exterior.

Malachi didn't have long to wait; the lift doors opened a couple of minutes later. Matthew Richardson bore a strong resemblance to his mother. Similar complexion and the same deep-set brown eyes. He smiled when he saw Malachi but not in recognition, more likely ready to politely turn down a request for an interview.

'DC Malachi Henry,' he said, and offered a hand, which Matthew shook. 'I'd like to ask you a few questions about your mother and the time you lived at Saint Eldith's.'

He looked mystified. 'That was a long time ago.'

'How long?' he asked.

116

Matthew ran a hand through his hair, pushing his fingertips into his scalp. 'From memory, until a couple of years before Mum's death.'

'And for how long before that?'

'The college offered short-term accommodation after our parents' divorce, but then arranged for us to stay on. Being in the heart of the city suited all of us, but Mum in particular. St Eldith's was her passion.'

'And when was your parents' divorce?'

He squinted and spoke slowly as he worked through the calculation. 'I think I was fifteen, from memory, coming towards the end of the first year of my GCSEs. How bad is that for parental timing?' He said it with no hint of even dark humour. 'And then I think we moved in the summer holidays, so that would be 2007.'

Malachi took a couple of steps backwards and sat on one of the two uncomfortable sofas. Matthew followed suit and sat at the other end, angling himself to face Malachi. 'I'm not clear what you would like to know from me.'

'The police received some information that there may be a connection between your mother, an ongoing investigation and a former student named Jodie Blake.' Malachi wondered whether Colin Knox would have already told him of their earlier visit. 'Jodie studied English literature at St Eldith's. She was there briefly nine years ago. Do you remember her?'

He could immediately tell that the answer was yes, but the urge was to say no. In the end, Matthew's answer fell between the two. 'I think I might. I mean, I'd probably have to see a photo.'

Ronnie had shown Malachi a photo of Jodie standing at the gates of St Eldith's and had shared it with him. He held up his phone. Facially, Matthew had it under control, but the flesh around his throat reddened, livid against his white shirt. But he didn't glance at the photo and glance away as though it made him uncomfortable; instead he stared much longer than that, as though the image stirred a deeper memory, and it was playing out somewhere behind his eyes. 'Yes,' he said. 'I remember her. I didn't really—'

Malachi cut in before he completed whatever denial was about to come out of his mouth. 'I believe you went on a date with her.'

It threw Richardson off balance. The red rose close to his earlobes, and he fell over the start of his sentence before settling on, 'Not really.'

That reply was usually a concession to the truth, but this wasn't a formal interview and Malachi needed to keep it conversational. 'How did you meet her?'

'She had English supervisions with my stepdad, and my mum always took an interest in the first-year students, particularly the girls.' He rubbed his palms on his trousers. 'They would be in halls on the same site as us and she was always worried about them not settling in. I'd bumped into Jodie a couple of times, and we ended up hanging out one afternoon, just walking around the shops. No big deal.'

'Was that a date?'

'No, definitely not.'

There was, of course, no way of knowing whether Jodie's recollection would have been the same.

'Living on site like that, it must have been a great way to meet people.'

Matthew nodded. 'I guess.'

'For you?'

He shrugged. 'I'd been studying at uni. I didn't have much to do with the under grads.'

'Did you know any of the male students? Jodie went on multiple dates with the same person. Any idea who that might have been?'

His neck flushed again and there was the rub of irritation in his voice. 'Why don't you ask her?'

Malachi kept his tone even. 'Because she's dead.'

Matthew Richardson said nothing, just blinked.

'Six weeks ago,' Malachi added, guessing it was the answer to one of the questions Matthew was suddenly unable to articulate. 'So, I can't ask her, and I can't ask your mum, but somehow the two of them are connected.'

Matthew's eyes darkened and a moment later his demeanour changed. The difference was abrupt and absolute. He rose to his feet and stood over Malachi, a little too close. 'I'm not discussing this out here. We will go to my office.'

Matthew Richardson pushed through a door that led from reception to a short corridor and turned immediately right into the boardroom. He gestured for Malachi to sit at one of the chairs nearest the door, then made a point of circling round the long desk to sit directly opposite.

The boardroom lighting was dull and yellowed. The view through the part-obscured windows, monochrome. Matthew Richardson was still dreary by comparison. All signs of the genial public-facing salesman had vanished and had been replaced by a grim and grey expression.

Malachi didn't care. What really mattered was still being in a room with him. As long as there was communication, there was a chance to gain something.

'Why are you coming in here with this now?' Matthew's tone was low, his voice heavy. 'I'm sorry to hear of Jodie's death, of course I am. But my mum was ill, and it was all Colin, Owen and I could do to keep it together. Did you know she died of alcoholism?'

Malachi nodded. 'Yes, I am aware.'

'We were supporting Mum as she fell apart, but also protecting each other. I don't know what the connection was between my mum and Jodie. But I'll tell you how I see it. Sometime back then, something occurred which triggered a reaction.

'I don't think Mum enjoyed alcohol. I don't think her drinking habit just deepened. I think she used alcohol as self-medication to block out whatever was going on in her head.' He tapped his temple. 'Was that connected to Jodie? I don't know. But it was certainly Colin and me, and to some extent Owen, who bore the brunt of it.' He scowled. 'And that's nothing against Owen. He cleared off to uni. I studied here in Cambridge. I never got the break from it the way he did.'

'How was your relationship with them?'

'Okay, I suppose. Not brilliant. Colin was just Colin. He sided with my mother, always, until eventually he couldn't deny that she had a drinking problem any longer and their relationship became strained. And Owen just breezes through life, not touched by anything.' Matthew shrugged. 'We're all still in contact, but I see less of them than I used to.'

It occurred to Malachi that he was less than ten years younger than Richardson and wondered whether it was normal that all vestiges of youth could disappear so soon. It seemed more likely that Richardson had completely skipped being young.

'What do you think happened to Jodie Blake then, Mr Richardson?'

Richardson considered the question before replying. 'Nothing, absolutely nothing. Some girls don't get the attention they think they deserve, and they make things up.'

'What things? What do you mean exactly?'

Richardson shrugged and fixed Malachi with a stubborn expression.

'Whatever suits them. It's how women are, isn't it?'

CHAPTER 35

There had been no up-to-date address for Owen Richardson and Matthew had suddenly changed his tune and claimed he currently had no means of contacting him. Malachi had tracked Owen down by chasing through his social media and passing his phone number to several likely contacts. Eventually, Owen had called him and agreed to meet him on the corner of Mill Road and Cavendish Road.

Mill Road stretched from the junction nearest Parkside Police Station through to the suburb of Cherry Hinton. Local navigation referred to 'this side' of the railway line and 'the other'. It was the common terminology, no matter where you were located. From Parkside, the meet-up point was on the other side of the bridge, far enough to warrant driving, even though parking was always a challenge.

Malachi reached Cavendish Road with a couple of minutes to spare. A man of about thirty, in jeans, trainers and a dark green hoodie stood on the corner. Malachi raised his hand as he turned in, and by the time he had manoeuvred into the only available parking space, the man had caught up with him and was standing, hands in pockets, watching him park. 'I guess you get a free pass for a resident's bay?' Owen grinned broadly and beat Malachi to the introductions. There was the tinge of an accent when he spoke but too faint for Malachi to identify. 'I'm living above the café at the moment. Easier to meet you outside, though, than to expect you to find the entrance.'

He walked them back towards Mill Road and a flat-roofed, pre-war row of shops known as the Broadway. Owen took them to the back of the property and up a short metal fire escape. The afternoon light was fading, and he flicked a light switch as he opened the door. 'Welcome to my squat,' he said, and a single naked bulb lit up a bare room with threadbare orange carpet and large-print mustard and brown paper, barely clinging to the walls. He walked backwards a couple of steps as he spoke to Malachi. 'It's not really a squat, by the way, and it's warmer through here.'

The room he took them was at the front of the property, and the furnishings consisted of a camp bed, sleeping bag, two camping chairs and a rucksack in the corner. 'I've got cans if you want one. Coke or 7UP?'

Malachi declined. 'Okay if I sit on this one?'

'Help yourself,' Owen said and pulled the second chair a little closer.

Malachi nodded at the backpack. 'I take more than that away for the weekend. Is this your permanent home?'

'No, I'm doing a favour for a friend. Free accommodation, such as it is, in return for decorating. I'm pretty shit at most things but I know my way around a pot of paint and a roll of wallpaper. Matty rang me, said you'd be calling.' There was a vitality to Owen that his brother didn't possess, but it had slipped as soon as he mentioned Matthew, as though something suddenly weighed him down. 'He said you want to talk about our mum.'

Malachi felt irritated but not surprised at Matthew's lack of cooperation.

'Is that all he said?'

'Our mum and St Eldith's.' His voice grew softer still. 'There was never one without the other. You're welcome to ask me, but I probably won't be able to tell you much. Matty and our stepdad Colin, they were there more than I was. I'm afraid I wasn't around for much of it.'

'Matthew told me you were at university.'

Owen fixed Malachi with a dead-eye stare. 'Really, that's what he said? I don't have the brains or the motivation for a degree. Matthew should have studied politics instead of literature. He always picks the

122

angle that sounds better, and in politician speak, I'm afraid he was mistaken. I cleared off and backpacked round Australia and New Zealand. I planned to stay until my visa ran out but, eventually, I realised it was time for me to come back.'

'Why?'

He shrugged. 'You know when you go to a house party and it peaks at eleven, but you stay till one? Well, it just felt like eleven-thirty, if you get me?'

Malachi nodded, that made complete sense. 'And when was this?'

'Three or four months before she died.' The comment must have been joined by a sudden, bitter memory; there was an unexpected catch in his voice and his forehead puckered as he spoke. 'My mother wasn't the same woman at all. Clichéd, I know. Physically, she lost weight, she was all skin and bone. She said she'd been weak, she kept saying it.'

'What do you think she meant by that?'

'I assumed she meant the drinking, not being able to give up alcohol and I asked her, if I stayed, if there was something I could do to help her give up. But she said . . . wait a second . . . I know this word for word . . . I can still hear her say it.' He closed his eyes and buried his face in the palm of his hand. 'Alcohol is what I do to stop me thinking about what I didn't.'

'What do you think she meant by that?'

'No idea.' There was a sigh mixed with the words.

When he opened his eyes, Malachi was ready with the next question. 'Do you remember a student named Jodie Blake?'

His voice lifted again, glad, Malachi guessed, to move away from the subject of his mother. 'Of course. She caused a lot of trouble considering she didn't even make it through Michaelmas term.'

'Go on.'

'She was a bit lost when she first arrived. One of those girls that gets on better with lads than she does with other women. And she was trying a bit too hard, you know, trying to be liked, trying to fit in.

'I'd seen it so many times there. They get into cliques so fast, there's always a bit of shuffling round, but if you haven't managed it in those first few weeks, you could spend the rest of the term sitting

123

on your own, waiting for enough people to fall out so it all shuffles around again.

'But of course, she was never there long enough for that. This one particular week, I just kept crossing paths with her. It turned into a bit of a joke, you know, *you again*, and so on. And I don't exactly know how it came about, but we ended up going to the cinema, the Arts Picturehouse. I had a couple of free tickets, and we smuggled in crisps and cans of drink. I can't remember the film. It was subtitled.'

'So, it was a date?'

Owen rocked his head from side to side, in a *maybe yes, maybe no* gesture.

'I don't think either of us thought so at the time. It certainly wasn't planned that way; it was just the way the evening worked out. I bumped into her a couple of times after that and neither of us said anything about it, but Matty didn't see it that way.' A small wince.

'Did you ask him about her?'

'I did.'

'And I'm guessing he didn't say much?'

Malachi ignored the question. 'I'm more interested right now in what you have to say.'

Owen rose from the chair, pulled a couple more cans of 7UP from his rucksack and dropped one into Malachi's lap. He then went and stood by the window, looking down on the steady stream of traffic flowing out of town. 'Would it surprise you if I said that Matty and I are the same? I'm here, living like this, scraping together every penny I can so that I can afford to be here for good. And there he is trying to keep up appearances, trying to keep our dad's old business afloat when it's leaking money in every direction. And there will be a point where we both end up in the same place, at the same time, older, wiser, and only just keeping our heads above water.' He leaned back, his spine against the corner of the wall and the window reveal. 'The big difference is that he still lives under the shadow of what happened back then, and I refuse to.'

'In relation to your mother, or Jodie Blake?'

'Same thing if you ask me. And no, I don't know what happened to Jodie. I just know the police weren't involved, but my mother

124

was, and was convinced that it was only through luck that she didn't die.'

Owen paused, but Malachi could see that he had no need to prompt him to continue.

'Matty met her a week or so after the cinema trip. I was a flirt. He was nothing like that. It was a big thing for him to connect with her. He told me about her after the first date and I should have said something then, but I didn't.

'He found out on the night of the third date. The first I knew that anything was wrong was when he came banging on my bedroom door. He was drunk and that made it worse. He was . . . I think the term is bellicose?'

He looked to Malachi for confirmation, who nodded.

'I don't even remember what he said now, I can just remember him jabbing at me with his finger and shouting with his face right up to mine.' Owen returned to the chair next to Malachi. 'I could have gone to see if she was okay, but I didn't. Worse than that, it didn't even cross my mind, and the next thing I knew, Mum was involved. She got Jodie out of there as fast as she could. And I never worked out whether she was protecting her son or her college.'

'What do you think happened, Owen?'

'I've said what I know. I'll leave you to do the speculating.'

CHAPTER 36

Malachi and Fenton had been right to keep Ronnie away from anyone connected to St Eldith's, but she had still been angry at the situation. Fenton recognised it as soon as she walked into his office. 'As soon as you found any connection to your sister, you should have pulled out.'

'I know.'

'So, what's your problem, Ronnie?'

Her right to be annoyed was absolutely zero, but that wasn't making her feel any better. 'I want to be involved.'

'You need to trust us to progress anything related to your sister.' He scowled. 'What's that look?'

'The blackmail is your case. My sister's assault belongs to DCI Beetham's team, so how can you say now I need to trust you?'

'We're going to accumulate as much evidence as we can before I hand over any information. I will keep you in the loop. It's clearly linked to the PC McLeod murder enquiry; the MO is almost identical, and this could be a significant breakthrough for them.'

'What information have you given them so far?'

'Beetham is up to date, and the enquiry into Jodie's assault will end up with them.'

Ronnie wasn't stupid; she knew that hoping for a rape conviction when no crime had been recorded, without evidence and when the victim was dead, would be close to impossible, even if they had a suspect, which they didn't. It was the injustice and a fear of failing her sister that was fuelling her. 'When? And will I be able to speak with the DCI?'

'They will want a statement from you, if nothing more.' He leaned back and studied her face for a few seconds, then rocked forward to place his elbows on his desk. 'You can work on Operation Byron. There's no proven link to your sister yet.'

She stared at him. 'You're splitting hairs. Your team is following up on Jodie, Zoe Richardson and Nigel Beckett because you received a note that linked them all to Operation Byron. Nigel Beckett stole more money than has been traced, no doubt because the blackmailer threatened him, and there's suspicion that Dr Richardson was blackmailed too.'

'But no proven links,' Fenton said stubbornly. 'Although, as soon as one is confirmed, I'm sure the cases will merge, and Beetham's investigation will swallow ours.' He sucked air in through his gritted teeth.

'And you don't want that?'

'I want whatever captures the bastard. But I'll be disappointed if it isn't us.' Fenton forced a smile.

It looked uncomfortable.

Then he left his desk and crossed to the door leading to the main office. 'I have a talented team, but you have the advantage of fresh eyes. If you want to stay involved in this, pay attention.' He grabbed the handle but used it to hold the door shut. 'Jenna will brief you, she's the only DS and knows each of the cases. Ask Dimitri when you want all fact and no opinion. Will and Tess know the victims like the other two know the data.' He pulled the door wide and stepped through. 'Listen up everyone, Ronnie's finished her tour of St Eldith's, now get her up to speed on Operation Byron.'

Jenna printed a list and handed it to Ronnie. There were just five columns: date, full name, case number and amount; the final column was a single letter with no heading above it and each row had either the letter S or C against it.

'C is a confirmed case and S is suspected.'

There were eleven rows but only three of them had a C marked against them.

'Having so few confirmed cases has made it difficult,' Jenna told her. 'The confirmed cases were reported to Cambridgeshire Constabulary and handed over to our team when they were all found to be linked, and Operation Byron was born.'

'And how about the suspected cases?'

'We've compiled that information from a number of sources. The most common is when one partner, business or romantic – we've had both – suddenly notices that money is missing. They raise the issue and, in the face of a blank denial from their other half, insurers or the police or both get involved. Spend some time with Tess and Will. They've been the points of contact for the victims in the confirmed cases and, Dimitri, can you give Ronnie access to the case files?'

He had his back to them and briefly turned his head and spoke over his shoulder. 'I did it already.'

'In that case,' Jenna said, 'I think you have everything you need, at least for now.'

Tess and Will's desks were on the opposite side of the room. Jenna called across to them. 'Ronnie's all yours.'

Will made a point of looking at the clock. 'I think we'll start in the morning,' he said.

Tess pulled a Post-it note from the block on her desk. She didn't move from her chair but held it out towards Ronnie. It was an address in Hills Road.

'Eight a.m. tomorrow,' Tess told her. 'We'll start with Robert Douglas. Meet me there. He knows we're coming.'

CHAPTER 37

Gleneagles was a detached house. Victorian, gable-ended with an in-and-out drive and trees protecting it from the road. A home like this would have once had servants' quarters with their own staircase bells to summon them, a cellar, and enough bedrooms for an oversized Victorian brood.

Ronnie checked Rightmove. This part of town was littered with private schools. A more modest version in need of updating was the only one for sale and offers were invited in excess of £1.6 million.

But it was Jenna who arrived, instead of Tess. She drove a one-year-old Mercedes, black, the paintwork so glossy that it looked as though she had driven straight from the car wash. She swung through the gates on to the cobbled driveway and stepped out wearing a pristine trouser suit. She tweaked the cuffs to pull the arm straight and gave her jacket a quick but unnecessary brush down with the backs of her fingers.

Ronnie was glad she'd left Alex's old Ford at home, but the walk had left her looking crumpled by comparison with her colleague.

'No car?' Jenna asked, skipping any other morning greeting.

'No Tess?' Ronnie responded as she stepped forward to ring the bell.

'I thought this should have been a visit with Fenton; he wasn't around so I called it.'

'Makes sense. I don't have a car yet, so I was hoping for a lift back to Parkside.'

Jenna nodded. 'I'd stay carless if I were you. I don't live far from the station, so I don't have the parking problem. I'm lucky I guess.' She took a step closer to the door and peered at the leaded glass, looking for movement from the other side. 'Did you read the case notes?'

'I did.' And as Ronnie answered, the door opened.

Robert Douglas was bearded and shaggy haired. Ronnie knew from the notes that he was fifty-eight years old, but it would have been hard to tell with so much of his face obscured. He wore glasses too and they darkened slightly against the outdoor light. A liver and white English pointer stood at his heel.

'Come in then,' he said in an accent unmistakably Scottish. He was of average height and build and there was nothing imposing about his appearance, but he used his voice with authority.

Ronnie had noticed that Cambridge rather liked its oak panelling and was expecting more of the same, but the inside of the house favoured white woodwork, and walls painted in light, bright colours. He led them through to the back of the house into an orangery that overlooked the garden. Four chairs were tucked away at a breakfast table, and he invited them to sit.

'Go to bed, Rufus,' he told the pointer, who obediently flopped into a beanbag to one side of the external door. Jenna made the introductions and then handed over to Ronnie.

'I know the key points of the case, Mr Douglas, but I have some questions which I could probably answer by reading more, but I'd like to hear them in your own words.'

'To hear whether I give the same story twice?'

She shook her head and smiled. She could already see that he had a straightforward way about him. 'No, it's more to pick up on things that words alone don't convey.'

'My emails are often misconstrued. I've learned to type what I say, then go back to the start and add something polite to kick it off. Val and I were similar like that. Bark worse than bite, or so I would have said. But once, maybe twice a year, she would lose her temper. Proper red-mist stuff. It nearly finished us off in the early years and then

130

again in the later ones. We had a spell of accepting we were in it for good in the middle, but of course then when retirement looms, you start to question whether you are with the person you want to spend the next twenty years with, because it's going to be a damn sight different when it's just the two of you knocking around the house together without work to mask it. I'm semi-retired, by the way, I can't quite take the plunge. I think I'll carry on like that.'

She'd read that Douglas was a company director but couldn't remember reading any other details of the business. 'What do you do?'

'My company installs air conditioning. It's been a growth business.' He raised a hand palm up at the ceiling. 'The weather is moving in our direction. Once it was established, it gave us a good life, a good income, this house. My wife, meanwhile, managed a nursery. Daycare, not plants. It might have been different if her business had been all about nurturing trees and being the patron of a nature-supporting charity.'

It could have sounded as though he was drifting off topic, but Ronnie had already mapped the path he was taking and knew that it was working its way back round to his wife.

'Instead, she was the patron of a local charity to support children who had witnessed or been victims of domestic violence and that, in turn, had come about because she'd made a success of the children's nursery. It's called Play Steps. It still runs. Her staff bought it from me after she passed. It was her baby, excuse the pun, not mine. That's one half of the picture.'

He placed his right hand on the table in front of him and spread out the fingers, then did the same with the left, positioning it with his thumbs almost touching, one hand mirroring the other.

'I find it difficult to reconcile what she did with the woman I knew. But at the same time, I have no doubt it's true. As I said, her loss of temper was rare, but unforgettable.'

He slid his right hand away and stared down at the left, as though it represented everything that had gone wrong. 'I know you've read the facts of the incident, but I want you to know how it unfolded from my point of view. There were two boys, Ethan Laird, who was nine,

131

and Harris Lee, known as Harry, who was just eight. They were out on their bikes, chasing around after each other like kids do. They were down on the side road off Brooklands Avenue. Harry went flying into the road and Val slammed the brakes on. Ethan couldn't stop in time and hit the front side of her car, the passenger side. They would have been shocked and I guess she was shocked too.

'She leaped from her car and pulled Harry on to his feet. Bundled him onto the pavement, then hurled the bike after him. The bike hit Ethan, so she'd injured both boys. Then she drove off. There was no CCTV. No adults witnessed it. Harry had a fractured wrist. Ethan needed several stitches just above his eye. Any normal person would have jumped out of the car, and probably shouted at them, but no harm would have been done. Everybody would have been shaken and the boys would have had a learning experience.

'She never told me about it at the time, but the incident made the local paper, then the national paper. As it was, it turned into this manhunt. I never saw a scratch on the car and there was never a hint that anything had bothered Val. I will never know whether she felt any real remorse for what happened.'

Throughout, Mr Douglas's head had hung; he had continued to stare at his hand on the tabletop.

'How did you find out what she'd done?'

'Because of Rufus.' The dog opened an eye at the sound of his name. 'You know how they are when they're puppies. He went for the post. We eventually put a cage on the letterbox until he grew out of it at least, but I hadn't got round to it at that point. He was fine if we were in, but if he was home alone, we'd come back and find the post obliterated. And that's how I saw a bank statement for a loan I knew nothing about.'

'And you challenged her?'

He shook his head.

'Not straight away. I didn't want the confrontation at first and I certainly didn't connect missing money with what had happened to those boys. That was later. She'd borrowed an extra twenty thousand pounds and the first thing I did was try to work out where it had gone. I wondered if Play Steps was in financial trouble. In the end, I had no choice but to raise it with her. I suppose the rage was predictable. Hoping to avoid it was what had held me back. She shouted, asked what I was accusing her of, and I told her I didn't know. We had this nasty, spiteful row and I threatened her with legal action if she attempted to increase any of our debt. I didn't even know if that was possible – probably not. But in the heat of the moment, it was enough for her to buckle.

'And after all of that, she thought I would be understanding. But imagine it from the point of view of those two boys. That's what I couldn't get beyond. I felt that the difference between Val being held responsible for what she'd done, compared to her getting away scot-free, might be enough to colour the lives of those two boys one way or another.'

'And that's when you decided to go to the police?'

He nodded.

'She'd told nobody what she'd done. The money was paid across the internet, and she was sure the blackmailer wouldn't be caught. She was interviewed under caution about the attack on Harry and Ethan, and although her name hadn't been released at that point, the press interest started up again. I'm sure she would have been charged and she hadn't slept for days with the worry of it. But she died first. I woke up in the morning and she was dead on the floor. She'd had a huge heart attack. The blackmailer had contacted me the same morning, sent me one of those disappearing WhatsApp messages. I reported it straight away. They were wasting their time. It was secrets that had got us into the mess in the first place.'

Robert Douglas looked drained by the time he'd finished speaking but also composed. He seemed at peace with the decisions he'd made, despite the repercussions.

CHAPTER 38

In the end, Ronnie declined the lift in Jenna's showroom-ready Mercedes. Stepping from a freshly decorated house into a vehicle where the new car smell hadn't come from a can felt too much like risking sensory overload.

She called Malachi instead. He pulled up to the kerb ten minutes later, driving a high-mileage pool car and wearing jeans and a hoodie.

'I'm buying you breakfast,' she told him. 'Or did you eat already?'

'Two breakfasts are never a problem,' he grinned. 'Did you have somewhere in mind?'

'How would I?'

'Good point.'

In what felt like no time at all, he had located a café, parked up, got them a table and chosen his breakfast order – full English with extra toast. He filled her in with details about his visits to Matthew and Owen Richardson, concluding with their varying descriptions of the time they spent with Jodie. 'Owen claimed Matthew had briefly dated Jodie, but Matthew played it down, said it was nothing and they both denied any sexual contact.'

'And what rang true?'

'Difficult to say. But there was a clear mismatch between their stories, so at least one of them has it wrong. On the face of it, they are nothing alike,' he concluded. 'But Owen said that they're the same, and I could understand what he meant.'

'Fractured but still bonded at the same time?' she queried.

He harpooned a piece of bacon but paused before eating it. 'But isn't that how families are supposed to be when things go wrong?'

She didn't feel as though she was qualified to reply, but he didn't wait for one either.

'For both of them and their stepfather, Colin Knox, there's a common acknowledgement that what happened to Jodie and the repercussions were the start of the problems for Zoe Richardson.'

'And putting that all aside for a minute, Malachi, talk to me about the blackmail and what you've picked up while you've been with the DEAD team.'

'Most of the time I've just been a bystander.'

She reached across and stole half a hash brown, picking it up with her fingers. 'Sorry, it was calling to me. And I don't think you've been a bystander; I think you've been a spectator.'

Malachi manoeuvred his remaining hash brown to his side of the plate before he replied. 'First off,' he said, 'I thought it was a weird case to come to the DEAD team. Everything else they've worked on has been time critical – kidnapping, surveillance, a couple of escaped prisoners, that kind of thing. This case arrived here before I did, but I wonder whether it got dumped on them because nobody else wanted it. The blackmail cases on the list aren't getting any fresher either. No new ones have been added. Perhaps they've run out of opportunities?'

Ronnie shook her head. 'Could be any number of reasons: change in MO, victims keeping quiet . . . who knows?'

'Have you had a good look at them?'

'Jenna talked me through the list. A few confirmed cases and the rest suspected. Dimitri gave me access. I concentrated on the confirmed cases. Jenna just took me to meet Robert Douglas.'

Malachi slid his phone towards him and unlocked the screen. He spun it round so that it was the right way up for Ronnie and showed her a short spreadsheet.

'These are all the confirmed and suspected cases put together in one report. I've added an extra column for the date payment was first handed over. Now, watch what happens,' he said, 'when I sort it in date order based on that column.'

He clicked the screen and it refreshed with the confirmed cases appearing as three of the top five.

'What do you notice?' he said and leaned forward, watching eagerly as she scanned the information. She'd always been told to follow the money, so she looked at that column first. Nothing jumped out at her, and she switched to the dates column because, of course, he'd added that detail for a reason.

'There's a gap,' she said. The first five stood apart from the others with almost two years in between. 'What do you think it means? Are some cases missing from the list?'

He shook his head. 'That's not the way I read it. Think about it.'

He took the last slice of toast from his side plate, buttered it, and used it to wipe up the last of his breakfast.

'You're one of those people that can eat whatever you want and not put on weight, aren't you?'

He nodded.

'I hate you,' she said. He shrugged, then when he'd finished, he finally pushed the plate to one side.

'Perhaps there are two perpetrators, and the first batch is the result of one person's blackmail and the rest are somebody else's?' It was an answer, but she didn't buy it. 'Come on, what's your theory?'

'Well, both your ideas are possible . . .' He paused for effect, and she wanted to shout at him. 'Maybe,' he continued, 'there's only one, and that person took a break.'

'Prison perhaps,' she considered. It was possible. 'Or illness?'

'Who knows? Perhaps they were raking in so much from the first five . . .'

'Have you shared this with Fenton?'

'Yeah, I shared it with the whole team, and Fenton wasn't convinced. And once Dimitri pointed out that there could be multiple reasons and,' Malachi paused, mimicking Dimitri's monotone, 'almost infinite variables, it was kind of forgotten about.'

But he leaned forward again, becoming more intense. 'The gap in the dates is still sitting there, whether anybody's interested or not. It

136

might seem tiny, Ronnie, but it would tell us something about the perpetrator. And there's one more thing. What happens at the start of the gap between the cases, Ronnie?'

There had been a lot for Ronnie to absorb in a very short space of time. She'd written down the key dates in an attempt to memorise them all.

Malachi said, 'The gap between the reported cases was from October 2021 to July 2023 and in November 2021, just three weeks after the last of the first five cases, Kirstin McLeod had been murdered. Of course, it could be a coincidence.'

But there was challenge in his expression and she met it with her own. 'Operation Byron is still wide open. What harm can we do by checking it out?'

Malachi's response was instant. He may as well have punched the air.

'Thank you so much. Where are we going to start?'

She tapped his phone screen with her fingertip.

'Case number five.'

'I like case five,' Malachi told her.

Ronnie thought she knew why. It had stood out from all the other cases because it was the only one showing the amount paid as £0.00. There had been a failed blackmail attempt reported by the wife of the intended victim. Ronnie hoped that a failed crime might be at least as informative as a successful one. They weren't going to be following the money after all, but the A14 out of town to Newmarket.

'How far is it?' she asked.

'Fifteen miles, so half an hour at most.'

CHAPTER 39

Fenton had told Ronnie that Will and Tess knew the blackmail victims better than anyone else on the team. Perhaps that was mostly the case, but it didn't apply to Mrs Charley De Santis. The aborted blackmail attempt had been low on everyone's priority list. The intended victim, her ex-husband Enzo De Santis, hadn't even been the one to report the threat to the police and hadn't been interested in cooperating either. The scant details had waited on file like an odd shoe that no one wanted to claim.

Even when Malachi had queried its possible significance, his interest had been met with indifference and he was part way through being passed from one member of the team to the next when he'd given up and skipped straight to Fenton. He'd sold it to him as an opportunity to double-check the details, saving the bother for anyone else in the team. Fenton had seen no reason not to agree. Malachi's initial visit hadn't borne fruit, but he was pleased to have the opportunity to return with Ronnie.

Malachi took a sharp left from the main road immediately after a sign welcoming them to NEWMARKET – HISTORIC HEADQUARTERS OF HORSERACING, followed by a right into a pillared gateway and a tree-lined driveway. The name carved into the stonework read CORMAC HALLORAN RACING in the place of an estate name. Ronnie caught glimpses of the house between the evergreens. It was three storeys high and about five times wider than it was tall. 'That's impressive.'

Malachi nodded. 'And you haven't seen the best bit.' The driveway split before they reached the house. Malachi turned to the right but pointed left. 'Caretaker's cottage and six-vehicle car garage that way.' Their car passed through another stone arch and alongside post-and-rail fenced paddocks. He pointed again, 'And there are the stables, like a horse hotel and spa.'

But he hadn't turned towards the house and didn't turn towards the stables either. His expression was expectant. If the house and the stables weren't the best bit . . . and then he made one more turn and she knew. 'Mrs De Santis lives there?'

In front of them was a pair of farm cottages with pebble-dashed walls, black paintwork and fifty-year-old aluminium replacement windows. The houses shared a small front lawn, and to the side of the left-hand of the pair was a swing set and a push-along car. Everything was clean and tidy, but the glossy-magazine lifestyle clearly didn't reach this end of the estate. Ronnie nodded, 'This is the best bit, isn't it?'

'I think so, because it shows the blackmailer didn't know they couldn't pay.'

'Who did you tell about this? Did you come out here on your own?'

'I did, and I explained when I got back, but it was taken as confirmation that this case didn't matter. But it's the reason I think it does.'

'Because the blackmailer got it wrong.'

'Exactly.'

She and Malachi had drawn similar conclusions and had understood what the other was thinking several times now. It was becoming unnerving. She preferred it when no one knew what was going on in her head.

She knocked and saw the shadow of a figure behind the frosted glass. A moment before it opened, Malachi whispered, 'My sister knows what I'm thinking too.'

For fuck's sake, Malachi. And it was only the appearance of Mrs De Santis that stopped Ronnie from spluttering it out loud.

Mrs Charley De Santis was twenty-eight years old. She wore skinny jeans and a fitted turtleneck sweater. Her dark hair tumbled across one shoulder. She didn't appear to be wearing make-up, but everything about her seemed to glow. Ronnie was sure that if she tried anything similar, she would be offered a hairbrush and asked if she was running a temperature.

Mrs 'call me Charley' De Santis opened the door wide. 'Through there.' She waved them into the front room where a little boy of about three was curled asleep in a chair. They sat at either end of the settee and Charley perched on the edge of the chair, close to her son. 'This is Ben, he's a bit nocturnal. Stays up most of the night, then conks out in the morning. Hang on,' she said, left the room and then returned with three mugs, a jug and a bowl of sugar on a tray. 'No teabags so it's coffee or nothing. Help yourselves.'

'Aren't we going to wake him?' Ronnie asked.

'Who knows,' Charley replied. 'Do you have kids?' she asked.

Malachi clearly thought the question was for Ronnie, Ronnie stared back at him, but Charley didn't wait for an answer. 'My eldest, Dom, is six, so at school right now, but when he was smaller, I used to get stressed about each phase. Then I realised that each one passes, and when it does you lose the good stuff as well as the bad. It changed my mindset.' When she smiled, she lit up. 'So, who's the hopeless blackmailer then?'

'I'm afraid we don't know yet.' Ronnie said, 'I'm new to the team and taking a fresh look at some of the enquiries. I know you've already made a statement, and you spoke to DC Henry, but I have a few questions too.'

'Of course.' Everything about the woman radiated energy. Lots of it.

'To begin, why was it you rather than your former husband who contacted the police?' Ronnie asked.

'That's simple. Because he thought I was the blackmailer.'

Ronnie frowned, 'Why?'

Malachi settled back with his coffee.

'He had a message saying that he had to pay twenty thousand pounds if he didn't want me to find out about his affair. There we were with two small kids and living in a tied cottage. We had no assets. Someone was having a laugh.' Charley lowered her voice and leaned closer. 'Except they weren't, and I would have been devastated if that's how I'd found out. But you see, I'd found out almost two weeks before. I'd had that feeling, the one when you know but you're telling yourself that you're mistaken?'

Ronnie nodded. She did know.

'He was a driver for the boss, Mr Cormac Halloran, which meant some evening work, but he was coming in later than usual. Bad tempered each time, too, like everything I said was stupid.'

'What kind of driver?'

'You know, personal driver, like a chauffeur. Anyway,' she continued, 'I'm up in the middle of the night with one of the kids and his phone is beside the bed. I needed to know.' She sighed. 'I hesitated, but if he was sleeping with one of the staff, was I supposed to feel that I was crossing the line by looking at his phone? I don't think so.' Ben stirred and she reached out to smooth his hair. He settled at once. 'It was one of the trainee grooms, Bethany Wiley. I was angry, gutted that our homelife was being trashed. I don't think the affair had been going on for long, but our marriage had to be over. I phoned a solicitor in the morning. Then, when I confronted Enzo, he suddenly realised the problem; we all worked here and me for the longest.'

'What job do you do?'

'I was in the yard until the first pregnancy, but then I took over booking travel, arranging transport for the horses, overseas and UK. It works, I know the staff, the horses and the events. I work around the kids – no one works regular hours in a yard. Did you know it's the world's most northerly siesta?'

'I didn't. And I still don't know why he thought you were the blackmailer either.'

'Because I told him I wanted a divorce and he begged me to give him a few weeks to "sort something out", whatever that meant. I didn't question it, don't ask me why. But when the blackmail demand came through, he completely lost it. Accused me of manipulating him and trying to play mind games. He said I was the only one who knew about the affair.' She rolled her eyes, 'I said, "you forgot about Bethany", and he kicked off again. I went to Mr Halloran and went to the police. Enzo and Bethany ...' She made a sweeping gesture.

141

'Gone. Mr Halloran sent them packing. It is me and my boys now, and that's fine.'

'Does he still see them?'

'Every other weekend, in theory, but he's often busy with driving jobs, so I don't make plans.' She glanced at Ben, and finally fell silent for a few seconds. 'He split up with her a few months ago, and wanted to come back. I don't know what was more insulting, him wrecking everything in the first place or thinking I'd go for it a second time. He said I should for the sake of the kids. I said that was the number-one reason I wouldn't.'

CHAPTER 40

'Interesting woman,' Ronnie mused as they drove back to Parkside.

'She's determined.'

'Yes, and running on empty. She's pushing herself the whole way.' Ronnie could have added that she had been like that and knew the signs. Instead, she said, 'I wanted to tell her to stop, or at least slow down. People really do screw each other up.' She glanced over at him, wondering who he was apart from a detective. 'Are you in a relationship, Malachi?'

They were at the edge of Cambridge then, within sight of the airport, and he negotiated a roundabout before he replied, 'No, I haven't met anyone here, but it's not good timing either. My last girlfriend was in London, she was training as a paramedic, that ended a while ago, but I haven't been in a rush to get into anything else, especially as I don't know where I'll be. Anyway, I'm hoping to stay in Cambridge, but I'm still not sure.'

'Because of the job?'

'Until this week I felt like a spare part and kept thinking the DI would end my secondment. I don't feel I've been busy enough to justify my place in the team. I suppose I could transfer to Cambridgeshire Constabulary; they're crying out for detectives.'

'Like all forces.'

'Exactly, but I still feel I can make a difference in the DEAD team. We'll see.'

'So, in answer to my question, you don't have a girlfriend and it's Fenton's fault.'

He laughed. 'Put like that, I might be overthinking it. Not that I've met anyone . . .' He looked across at Ronnie. 'Just an observation, but you didn't know what to say when Charley De Santis asked if you have kids.'

It was true, the question had blindsided her, and it wouldn't be the last time she faced it. 'I'm Noah's aunt, Jodie's his mum, not me, so it feels wrong to call him mine, but wrong to say I don't have kids either. And I'm not going to give strangers the full explanation, am I?'

'Now you are the one who's overthinking it.'

'How?'

'Just say, "I have an awesome nephew and we're really close."'

'I don't think *awesome* is in my vocabulary, but I get your point,' she conceded. 'And where are you going?'

'Hot chocolate stop,' he said as he swung into McDonald's drive-through. 'Can I get you a drink?'

'I'm okay, thanks.' She closed her eyes while they queued and waited for Malachi to complete the familiar process of ordering, paying and collecting. She would talk to him again once he was done.

Welcome to McDonald's, can I take your order?

Is that everything?

Drive to the first window.

Thank you. Have a good day.

No surprises. No deviations. Just a process designed and refined.

Like an MO.

Malachi secured the hot chocolate in the drinks' holder. 'It'll be the perfect temperature by the time we reach Parkside.'

'I need you to do something for me when we get there.'

'Okay.'

'I want to know how our blackmailer made the mistake with Enzo De Santis. Mrs De Santis sounded certain that she found out about the affair when it was very new. That means there's a window of just a few weeks when they could have been caught out. I need you to find out where they went, who they saw.'

'Enzo De Santis thought nobody knew.'

144

'We both know somebody did and De Santis is clearly not the quickest horse in the stable.'

'We have no grounds to ask for his financials and he probably paid cash.'

'And he probably took her somewhere meant to impress. You have been wanting something more challenging, so find Bethany and ask her.'

CHAPTER 41

DI John Fenton didn't like to fail.

He'd been a quiet child, not ready to stand out until he was sure he knew how to do so without showing himself up. Failure and embarrassment had been his childhood demons. His recurring childhood nightmare had seen him on the track at the school sports day with heavy legs that would not coordinate; limbs weighed down and unable to move. The harder he tried to move his legs, the more they disobeyed him. Other kids flew, he stumbled with the air knocked from his lungs.

His dreams were so real that they haunted his teens, pulsing adrenalin through him as though it had been a physical memory. Maybe it was a normal part of growing up. He never shared his experience, and no one shared theirs with him. It had felt shameful somehow.

He changed schools at sixteen and wiped the slate clean. No one knew him and they made assumptions. Assumed he was sporting because he happened to be tall with broad shoulders; he never told them it was thanks to his weekend job moving turf for a landscape gardener. They assumed he was smart because his grades were good without seeming to try, but he never admitted how many extra hours went in just to ensure a pass.

By eighteen, the hated childhood version of himself had been left behind, but the memory of leaden limbs and the feeling of shame had never gone. His failures since had been few, but painful.

146

Operation Byron was at risk. He knew it. He was certain the team did as well.

'Fuck.' He screwed his eyes shut, balled his hands into fists and banged his knuckles together. 'Fuck, fuck, fuck.'

'Done?' Ronnie stood in the half-open doorway. 'Or do you need a little longer?'

'It was a private moment.'

'Really? You surprise me.' She closed the door and pulled a chair round to his side of the desk, 'I think *fuck, fuck, fuck* should be your team motto right now.'

'What do you know? You've been here five minutes . . .'

'Is that from a page-a-day calendar of inspirational quotes?'

'You're out of line,' he growled.

'Because someone needs to be. I wanted to talk to you, but I walk in and you're in the middle of forty fucks; it just tells me that all is not well. You need to listen to someone, and it might as well be me.'

'Do you always speak to people like this?'

'Frequently. Apparently, it helps with focus. Ask my old boss, Butterworth.'

There had been a flash of this attitude when she'd turned up at his house, but this was on another level. Fenton was tempted to have her escorted out, but it would have been a knee jerk, and he knew it. 'He said I'd find out what you were like once you'd settled in. Your temperament's not ideal.'

She shrugged. 'When something becomes clear, I will say so.'

Ronnie was a striking woman. There was no doubt that she turned heads and he doubted she was aware of it. But up close and determined, she was . . . he trawled his mind for the right word and settled on 'fearsome'. He leaned back in his chair and interlocked his hands, steepling the index fingers. 'Go on.'

'Number one. You gave me a rundown of the team, you mentioned all of them except Malachi. He's being sidelined, but he's asking the right questions, and nobody listens. We just went to visit Mrs De Santis.'

It took Fenton a moment to register the name and Ronnie jumped on it. 'The blackmail attempt where nothing was paid. Remember it now?'

'Of course.'

'That was written off by everyone except Malachi.'

Fenton had already decided that he would be responding in his own time. 'Okay. Number two?'

She glared. 'Number two. Malachi wonders why the DEAD team were even given Operation Byron, and I agree with him, it's not a good fit. Not only that, it sounds like it's been on the backburner while you've had other time-sensitive investigations on your caseload, so you've been doing nothing but tread water with it.' She drew a breath, long enough for him to respond if he planned to.

Then she continued, 'And finally, you had three names on that list, and they link Operation Byron to a rape and murder investigation. Where is DCI Beetham's team? You said you wanted it solved by the DEAD team. Are you holding back information, trying to keep it for yourself?'

Throwing her out still appealed, but not failing with the investigation appealed more. Her attitude was part frustration, part passion and more than a suggestion that he was doing a bad job with Operation Byron.

He wasn't going to let it hurt his personal pride; it was better to let Ronnie try to fix it with him than the whole world seeing it fail if she was right.

He measured his response, divorcing her points from her delivery. 'Our first case was a huge success, and we had the infrastructure to continue, so we were put on to other work rather than being disbanded. We thought we'd expand, and I took Malachi then, but it's all gone quiet.'

'Why?'

'There are cuts all over. Chiefs are reluctant to hand us cases if it leads to further reductions in resourcing for their own teams. Everyone is hanging on to what they have. We're only as good as our latest results, and Operation Byron isn't a good calling card for us. No one wanted it. It's a dud. Then Malachi became an extra we didn't really need.'

'And that's how he feels.'

'I'll speak to him,' he softened his voice, 'and that's not just a stock response, Ronnie. And to your last point. My forty fucks, as you

148

called them, were in response to a call from DCI Beetham. Operation Byron isn't just struggling, it's a speck in the ocean compared to the Kirsten McLeod enquiry.

'I told you yesterday; DCI Beetham is up to date but now he wants to meet. I don't know what progress he expects us to have made in twenty-four hours . . . I have nothing.'

'Perhaps he has an update for you?' There was a shift in her expression.

'It's not the DNA, not yet.'

'When are you going?' she asked.

Fenton checked the time, 'I need to be there by two, I'll leave in ten. I can't take you. It wouldn't be—'

'You said he would want a statement from me. Why not now?'

'You could do that from here.'

'I want to meet him. Take Malachi too, give him a chance to feel he's not wasting his time.'

Fenton didn't like to fail and, it was clear to him, neither did Ronnie Blake. 'Just you,' he said at last.

CHAPTER 42

Cambridgeshire Constabulary Headquarters was in Huntingdon. While Ronnie was in Cambridge it felt as though the city was at the heart of the county, but it was actually located in the south and it was Huntingdon that was most centrally positioned, making it the most suitable site for the HQ.

DCI Beetham had met them in the lobby. He had either retired and returned or had refused to leave in the first place. He was an avuncular-looking man, and a thinker, she guessed, from the way his answers sounded measured.

Fenton had introduced her. 'I came because I know you want a statement from me,' she said.

'The statement you gave to SITfER was a start, but you're right, we do have some more questions. And so,' he'd widened his attention to both of them, 'I'm going to send DI Fenton up to the third floor and start with a one-to-one with you. How does that sound?'

It clearly hadn't been a question.

And now Ronnie sat across from DCI Beetham in a small, square interview room and the warmth of his welcome had faded. Their first few exchanges had triggered a game of verbal battleships. She wasn't quite sure why, or whether either of them had any idea what the other wanted. She decided to let it unfold at his pace.

'You find yourself in rather a unique position, don't you, DS Blake? You've managed to provide us with crucial information, but it leaves you in a situation where you are excluded from working on the case.'

'Hypothetically it's even more complicated than that. The only report on the assault on my sister comes from me. And it is therefore hearsay. Theoretically, couldn't I retract the statement, and then there would be no problem with me working on the investigation?'

'Apart from your integrity being rather compromised?' he said.

'True, which means that my current approach is more honest, and yet it leaves me in a more stressful and restricted position.'

'Even so, I understand that you and DI Fenton have been stretching the limits of what you should and shouldn't be doing,' he said.

'The link to Operation Byron is unconfirmed, isn't it? It's a lead, nothing more. DI Fenton arranged for my secondment; I believe I'm being of use.'

DCI Beetham said nothing.

Silence never bothered Ronnie, but this had not been the reception she was expecting. She had thought that the most likely outcome would be giving a statement and learning nothing in return. Her best shot, or so she had thought, would have been meeting Beetham and trying to push him for answers. But he wanted something from her, and a statement wouldn't suffice.

She asked for a drink of water, which he provided in an orange plastic beaker. She was down to the last swig before she worked it out.

She slammed the empty upturned cup down on the table. It made a hollow sound and a few water droplets sprang outwards. He looked at her sharply at the same time as she said, 'Do you think I made up Jodie's assault?'

'Did you?' His reply was a reflex, not calculated at all.

'Of course not,' she batted back. 'And no, I didn't send the list of names either. I'd never heard of the DEAD team or Operation Byron. And how would I have known what happened to Kirsten McLeod?'

He shrugged. 'Linda Beckett told you. I know she did.'

Ronnie slowed, 'That's true, but after the note was delivered to Fenton.' Getting angry wouldn't help, but it was unthinkable that she had fabricated Jodie's assault. 'I didn't make anything up,' she told him, and tried to keep her tone as even as possible. 'And there's a witness, Tina Runham. She is a bedder at St Eldith's and she saw Jodie's injuries.'

DCI Beetham showed no surprise.

'But you knew that already, didn't you?' And her anger ignited after all. 'We are waiting for DNA results that might identify her rapist. That's the urgency. Why would you even suggest that I would lie about what happened to Jodie?'

'It was still a possibility. I wanted to test for cracks. I want to know if somebody is playing games, Ronnie.'

'And you thought it might be me?'

'Look, we finally have a major breakthrough, and it's all linked to you and your sister. How many people could have sent that tip off? How many people could link Jodie, Kirsten and St Eldith's?'

Ronnie mulled it over, tried to find more than one other possibility but finally had to agree. 'I can see how I might make the shortlist. Just me and the killer,' she conceded.

'Correct.'

'And now I'm in the clear?'

'You're the same longshot as you were before,' he told her. 'My money is elsewhere, though. And what are you hoping to learn from me?'

'I'd like to know more about the rape investigation.'

She expected a blanket 'no', but instead he said, 'Ask me and I'll decide what I can share. It's confidential, of course, but you know much of the sensitive information already.'

'Is it true that Jodie's might be the first known case?'

He nodded. 'Correct again.'

'And how many have there been since?'

'That we know of? Fourteen including Kirsten.'

Fourteen. Fourteen terrified women and one dead in the years after Jodie's attack. She didn't know whether her sister could have made a difference, whether Jodie could have remembered enough to change the course of anything. 'It was months after the attack when she told me, and I tried to make her report it. She wouldn't or couldn't, and I should have respected that. Instead, I really pushed her.'

'And you feel bad about that?'

'I do, but I'm not sure that I wouldn't do the same again. I think it was too much for her to even contemplate.' Ronnie turned her thoughts away from her sister. 'Is there a pattern?'

He wavered one hand in the kind-of gesture. 'The attacks themselves all have similar traits; the victim is drugged, assaulted, and left bound in the bath with the water running. Beyond that, it's vague. The attacks occurred within a forty- or fifty-mile radius of Cambridge, an hour's drive at the most. All the women were under thirty but there's a spread of ages: seventeen is the youngest, right up to twenty-eight. Most in their late teens, early twenties, like your sister. They are women who live alone. Your sister's attack bucked that trend, but perhaps he realised that it was too high risk and adapted.'

'Any idea how they're being selected?'

'None. We looked at their social media, shopping habits, employment, family and hobbies. Pretty much every angle possible. There's just nothing that stands out. The most common denominators were "shopped at Tesco" and "owned a cat",' he said without humour.

'When was the most recent?'

'This January.' He pre-empted Ronnie's next question. 'There have been three assaults since Kirsten's murder, and the women all survived.'

'But you don't think Kirsten's death was an accident?'

'Absolutely not. There was no sign of disturbance in her flat and no sign she had fought either. Therefore, I don't believe the killer lost control while trying to restrain her. She'd been heavily sedated and strangled before she was moved to the bath.

'We have a criminal psychologist attached to the investigation; he was convinced that the rapist would kill on each subsequent occasion.'

'And what does he say now?'

'That it's just a matter of time.'

CHAPTER 43

Fenton spoke little on the way back from Huntingdon. It suited Ronnie: the meeting with DCI Beetham had given her plenty to think about. She waited to speak until they left the main road, and she knew they had a couple of miles and less than ten minutes before he dropped her home. 'Why did they want to see you?' she asked.

'They're running analysis on our blackmail victims to find any link with their rape victims.'

'Is that a problem?'

'Not at all, if it works. But we've already tried to find a link between our victims and I'm guessing they won't find anything. They are no further ahead with their case than we are.'

'We need those DNA results.'

'Tomorrow, Ronnie, I'm sure of it.' He dropped her at her door. 'Make the most of the evening. Say hi to Noah.'

Noah's room was about ten feet by eight with a window overlooking the street at the front of the house. Ronnie had glanced up from the car, but no lights were on. It was only seven and she would have expected it to be too early for bed, but Alex pointed at the ceiling and made the sleep gesture. He mouthed the words, 'He's knackered.'

She went to his room first. Noah lay on top of his bedcovers, and on his side with his back to the door.

'Noah,' Ronnie whispered. 'Are you awake?'

A couple of puddles of discarded clothes lay on the floor and the only other sign of the little boy's presence was a Lego model of some kind of truck that stood on the windowsill. It was rugged with over-sized wheels, and she couldn't tell whether it was part of a kit or whether Noah had just put it together from spare parts.

'I'm sorry I'm back late.'

She didn't expect a reply. She was pleased to spend time with him, even if he wasn't awake. She gently opened the wardrobe door. Some of his clothes were on hangers, the rest were heaped at the bottom. There were a few spare hangers, which she filled from the pile. She made a mental note to buy some more. Most of the clothes were dark and the light was too poor to attempt to sort them by colour, so she tried by garment instead, with T-shirts on the left followed by trousers and jeans, then hoodies and jackets. Jacket to be precise. He just had one, a dark blue school coat.

When she'd finished, she leaned over the bed and planted a kiss in his hair.

'Goodnight,' she whispered again.

Ronnie was almost at the door when he spoke. 'I'm awake.'

'You shouldn't be.'

'I've been awake each time you've come up.' His voice was small.

She turned back to look at him, puzzled. 'Why didn't you say anything?'

'You said you'd come and say goodnight, and I wanted to know if you still would if you thought I was asleep.'

'I promised, didn't I?' Ronnie managed to say the words but was shocked to feel tightness at the back of her throat and the sudden surge of sadness. 'I'm sorry I haven't seen much of you yet.'

'It's fine,' he said. 'Uncle Alex said it would be like that. He said we could spend most time together at weekends although sometimes you have to work those too. Is that right?'

'Yes, and sometimes I have to do extra. Like today.'

He sat up in bed and stared at her. 'Can you turn the light on?'

'I shouldn't really, should I? It's going to make you even more awake.'

'I can't see you properly.'

She realised then that the light from the landing would be falling on Noah and causing her to be in silhouette.

'I'm scarier with the light on, you know?' she quipped, and reached back and flicked the switch. He grinned and stretched out his arms, and they embraced for several seconds.

Ronnie sat on the edge of the bed. 'How's school?'

His shoulders gave a swift up and down. 'Okay, I suppose. A bit boring but I like my friends. Apart from Kieran Jenkins.' Noah screwed up his face. 'He's always got to be the best at everything. Well, he's not the best at keeping quiet. Every single lesson it's *I've done this, and I've done that.* He's the other side of the room to me. Thank goodness.' Noah stressed each of the last two words and rolled his eyes. 'I get to sit next to Molly. That's almost as bad. She talks all the time, but I just ignore her.'

'Who do you like then?'

'Billy. Billy and Liam. They are good mates.' He nodded, agreeing with himself. 'Who do you work with?'

'I don't really know them yet.'

'Which ones do you like, though? I knew straight away I'd like Billy.' He stared into her face, waiting for an answer and ready to give his approval.

It was her turn to shrug.

'I think they'll be pleased that you've come once they get to know you. I said that to Uncle Alex, and he said they'd be thrilled.' Noah tried to suppress a grin.

'Thrilled? Do you know what the word sarcastic means, Noah?'

'No,' he said, in a way that showed that he did. 'Alex says you've never liked anybody you work with. But you need to try. And that way you'll be happy to stay in Cambridge because we need you here.'

'Well, I'm absolutely not leaving Cambridge, not as long as you're here. But I don't know how well I'll get on with my colleagues. I will wait to see.'

He was out of bed and over by the windowsill before she'd had time to register that he'd even moved. Children were alien creatures.

'Look at this,' he said. He put the truck on the floor, pulled it back and let go. It rattled forward, not making much progress against the pile of the carpet. 'It's better downstairs,' he said, 'where the floor is hard and shiny. And look at this.' He picked it up and waved it under her nose. Ronnie had to lean back to get her eyes to focus.

'It's Lego Technics. That's like the Lego that older kids have, and the instructions are really complicated but I've done loads of Lego kits. Not any this difficult but loads of them and what I learned is you have to get each page right before you turn on to the next page. So, you've got to follow the instructions and if it goes wrong you need to pull it apart and go back to the last time when it was working.'

She nodded. 'You've done a really good job of this. I wasn't sure whether it was a kit, though, or one you've made up yourself.'

He snorted. 'I couldn't make up anything like this. It's awesome! It's the Monster Jam Max-D.'

She did her best to look impressed. 'Perhaps we could get a shelf up for some of your models?'

'Maybe.' He waved the truck. 'But I hadn't finished.'

'Oh, I'm sorry,' she said.

'I haven't finished saying that you going to work is like me with the Technics. You think you're not very good at getting to know people, but nobody is good at anything until they work through it one step at a time.'

'I promise I'll do my best.'

His expression was earnest. And suddenly she wanted nothing more than to reassure him. 'I like Malachi,' she said, 'and John Fenton is probably okay. I don't know the rest yet, but that's not a bad start, is it?'

'Nice one,' he said, and fist bumped her.

'Now, are you going to sleep, or coming down for a while?'

'No brainer.' He scuttled towards the stairs. 'Am I allowed hot chocolate?'

He had reached the bottom before she'd reached the landing.

Noah's world was simple, and she wondered how long it would stay that way.

CHAPTER 44

Ronnie woke a few minutes before five, immediately alert with her heart already racing. She hadn't even unpacked her running gear, but she found the right box and ten minutes later she was out on the dew-damp pavement with her breath unfurling in front of her. She walked briskly to warm up and started to jog when she reached the towpath.

She didn't care that it was still more night than day. She could see the dark edge marking the drop from the path to the Cam on one side and the uneven shadows of the grass on the other.

She hadn't come for the scenery.

She had come to clear her mind of uninvited thoughts. Of debris. Of the constant churning.

She picked a slow pace; one she thought her out-of-practice legs and lungs could still maintain. She counted her strides in groups of twenty.

Twenty.

Twenty.

Twenty more.

Half a mile and she found her rhythm. Another half a mile and the first thoughts untangled and floated free.

She'd grown up wondering whether she would inherit her mother's instability. Or her father's indifference. She'd seen other kids turning into their parents with unquestioning inevitability. She wasn't far enough through life to look back and know for sure, but she hoped. She'd also worked with third generation cops. Arrested fourth generation criminals. And heard too many times that the apple never fell that far.

Noah's father was a rapist. When he was older, she would be the one to tell him. The one to disillusion him. She wasn't scared of his genes, but the stigma worried her. People were judgemental. Losing his mum should have been enough. But there was going to be more pain in his life, and it couldn't be avoided.

Ronnie kept running and thought about her sister.

Just stills at first, frozen moments. Young Jodie lying on the window seat, reading. Watching TV. At the kitchen table, her upper body twisting, pretzel-like around her schoolbook, resting her head in the crook of her arm to hide her writing. Jodie with the uncertain smile at the gates of St Eldith's. Jodie carrying baby Noah from the hospital.

And Jodie and Noah again and again.

Jodie had been a private person and she had told no one the identity of Noah's father. Not even Ronnie and Alex. But someone knew.

She replied to her own thought, *Or did they?*

The darkness had lifted to grey. The dark hulks of the canal boats were beginning to morph into benign floating homes and the rowing clubs had launched the first sculls of the day.

Ronnie kept running. Her stride didn't break.

The link between Jodie and Kirsten's murder was the assault, not Noah. And the rapist would have known both women's names. And if the rapist didn't send the note, someone else knew too.

The phrase *testing for cracks* came to her and pushed the other thoughts aside.

DCI Beetham had said it.

It conjured a flattened hand running across a sheet of glass, feeling for a weak spot. Then homing in on an imperfection. Pushing on it, pressing until the fingertips blanched. Until it creaked and fractured, with the flaws spreading like veins.

Or perhaps it was a single crack, a neat fissure that disappeared when the light was right.

She stopped in her tracks, then bent over her knees for a few breaths. The river flowed at a tilted angle, the boathouses seemed skewed, and the only cyclist seemed to be freewheeling uphill, but her head was clear.

She straightened, pulled her mobile from her pocket and headed for home.

CHAPTER 45

DCI Beetham answered on the second ring. 'DS Blake. I wondered when you'd call. But I wasn't expecting to hear from you so soon. You sound out of breath.'

'I was up early, I couldn't sleep, and I kept going back over our conversation. You said that he drugs and assaults his victims. Why did none of them see him? Jodie knew who she had been out with.'

'He broke in and the victim woke to find a man in her room. His face was covered . . .'

'And it was the same every time?'

'Yes.'

'How can you be sure it's the same man?'

'I would bet my career on it, possibly even my pension. There are any number of reasons why it could have been different for your sister. For example, if it was his first attack; he might have taken advantage of an unexpected opportunity. What else?'

Ronnie sometimes took several attempts to phrase questions diplomatically; it was fine when there was time to construct a message, more dangerous when she found herself on the spot. She told herself to just say it, and hoped for the best. 'I can't help thinking that you fudged the picture a couple of times, sir.'

'Only two?' To her relief, she heard a smile in his voice. 'Go on.'

'You told me you were testing for cracks. At the time I thought you were questioning my integrity, and by eliminating me, you

161

were confident that the killer had sent the note. But that isn't the case, is it?'

'You weren't a serious contender, DS Blake; I never thought you wrote that note. When I asked who else could have written it, it was a genuine question.'

'You said your money was elsewhere. Where exactly?'

'Our letter writer knows more about this case than either your team or mine.' He cleared his throat. 'Keep that in mind, DS Blake, and let me know if you find a crack in the picture. I think we both know it's there.'

She ended the call and reached home in time to walk Noah to school.

Ronnie sat in a corner of the DEAD team's office. Malachi had gone to interview Enzo De Santis's former girlfriend Bethany Wiley, but Tess, Will, Jenna and Dimitri were all present.

She zoned them out. She'd been in the building for an hour and now she was alone with the two clear unopened evidence bags, signed out to her and temporarily her responsibility.

One contained the list of three names and the other contained the envelope which had contained it.

They were side by side on the desktop. The stationery looked like common supermarket-grade fare. Both were printed in bog-standard Arial 12-point from an inkjet printer. Narrowing it any further would take a budget that no one was going to authorise, especially for an anonymous note of unproven provenance. Long gone were the days when a damaged typewriter key could provide a vital clue. She slid the bag containing the envelope closer. Personally she found feeding an envelope through a printer a time-consuming and frustrating experience. It read:

Joan Fenton
Special Investigations Team for the Eastern Region
Parkside Police Station
Cambridge
CB 1JG

Thirteen words plus the postcode. She would have found it quicker and easier to write it than type it. Sometimes members of the public had no idea about forensics and investigative techniques. Other times, they imagined the police had every TV-show resource to hand and an endless budget. So, it was conceivable that the effort to print the information had been made just to avoid the scrutiny of a handwriting expert or a graphologist.

But Ronnie was certain the letter was not a hoax from a random member of the public. For one thing, the names on the list had already proven to contain information that only somebody close to the truth would know. Secondly, there was the name and the address on the envelope; although Fenton's name was incorrect and the rank hadn't been included, everything else had been accurate. The chance that the envelope wouldn't find its way to the right desk had been reduced to practically zero. Ronnie looked across the office but didn't catch anyone's eye, so she addressed the room instead. 'I have a question.'

Tess looked up first, closely followed by Jenna and Will. Only Dimitri remained oblivious.

'This envelope is addressed to the Special Investigations Team for the Eastern Region. How widely known is that title?'

Will replied first. 'Well, it's been the name since the start, so it's been around for a while.'

Then Tess. 'Yes, but most people just call us the DEAD team.'

'But,' Jenna added, 'they would probably know the right name If they stopped to think about it.'

'Depends who they were,' Tess added and glanced in the direction of the envelope. 'No one's going to put DEAD team on an envelope. It might never make it through the post system. It will be way too tempting for somebody to get nosey and open it up.'

Will grinned. 'Tess's devious brain strikes again. And they could have just written the boss's name on it, and it would have turned up.'

'They misspelled his name and missed his rank,' Ronnie pointed out.

'Perhaps it's a dig at him,' Jenna mused. 'They went to the effort of getting the rest of it right. I think it's as likely to be a slight as it is to be a typo. Just my opinion.'

163

'That would make it personal.'

'I guess it would,' Jenna said, then laughed and added, 'Do you want me to bring his current wife in for questioning?'

Dimitri was the next to speak. 'Since the team formed, the DI has been quoted fourteen times in local papers and three times in nationals. Twelve have mentioned the investigation but not the department, five have attributed him to Cambridgeshire Constabulary and only two have mentioned our team by name. His rank has been correct in every case, and there's been no instance where either his first or last name has been misspelled.'

He swivelled back to his computer screen and the conversation died. Ronnie made some notes, then turned to the letter itself. Aside from Jodie's name, Nigel Beckett's and Zoe Richardson's were now familiar to her, but until today she hadn't seen the words that introduced them,

There's more than just blackmail and these three people know it.

And then at the bottom, in half-size font that was somehow more sinister than black capitals would have been,

Hurry, before someone else has to die.

'Melodramatic, isn't it?' She looked up to see that it was Jenna who had spoken and was now standing a couple of feet from her desk. 'Fenton said it was the sentence at the bottom that made him check. He gave the names to Dimitri and me. It took us minutes to find out that two, Jodie and Zoe Richardson, were already dead, and a couple more phone calls by Fenton to determine that Nigel Beckett was living in a state of constant fear.'

'So yes, it was melodramatic,' Ronnie agreed, 'but also effective at getting attention.'

Ronnie moved the two evidence bags to one side, put her mobile phone on the desk and used her mug and a coaster to make the three points of an equilateral triangle. It caught Will's attention and Tess turned to see what he was staring at. Ronnie put her hand on the mug.

'Imagine this is the murder of Kirsten McLeod.' She tapped her fingers on the phone. 'This represents the rape investigation, and finally this,' she nudged the coaster, 'that's the blackmail investigation. The link between the rapes and Kirsten McLeod's is clear, the same MO.'

Will moved closer and Tess shimmied her chair across the floor. Ronnie moved her hands, one on the mug, one on the coaster. 'So, what's the link between the murder and the blackmail?'

'Nigel Beckett,' Will answered. 'He's terrified, right? He's living under threat from the person who blackmailed him, who also killed Kirsten McLeod. He's scared that what happened to Kirsten McLeod could happen to his own family, maybe his daughter, and that's why he's refused to explain about the blackmail. So we have a link, but that link has only been made because of that letter.'

'And what about these two?' Ronnie continued. She moved her right hand from the mug to the phone. 'The rapes and blackmail offences occur in a similar timeframe with a similar geographical spread, but we have no proof that the rapist and the blackmailer are the same person.'

Jenna answered this time, her voice sharp. 'We've already estab-lished that the rapist and the killer are the same person,' she glared at Ronnie, 'and it's the same person who blackmailed Beckett.'

'Is it though?' Ronnie moved the coaster to the middle of the desk, put the mug on top and the phone on top of that. 'It stacks up very neatly, doesn't it?' She picked up the two evidence bags. 'It's a lot of faith to put in one letter.'

Tess looked defiant and was the first to respond. 'Not when it's given us the best leads of the investigation so far,' she snapped.

'And doesn't that ring alarm bells with any of you?' Ronnie snapped back.

Jenna was studying the pile of objects. 'I understand what you're saying.' Her tone was more even, but there was still resentment. 'Fenton asked us to look at the names on the list, not the source of the letter. Perhaps he has reasons to trust it that we don't know about?'

Well, Ronnie thought, there was only one way to find out.

She left the items stacked on the desk and the office was silent as she left.

CHAPTER 46

Ronnie knocked on Fenton's door and pushed it open when she didn't get a reply. He was facing his computer, on a video call. He waved for her to sit in the chair on the opposite side of his desk. He was using headphones so she could only hear his side of the conversation.

'They're not back,' he said. 'Yeah, this afternoon at the earliest. Yeah, of course we fast-tracked it. Absolutely. As soon as we get it, I'll call you first.'

Her guess that he was talking about Noah's DNA sample was confirmed when Fenton referred to NDNAD, the abbreviation for the National DNA Database. He ended the call and apologised to her, although she wasn't sure why. He looked weary, but not in his usual no-sleep kind of way.

'I think your team is pissed off with me already.'

She placed the two evidence bags side by side on his desk, turning them round so that the letter and the envelope were the both the right way up for him.

'I have a couple of questions.'

'Go on,' he said.

'Quite simply, who and why?'

He stood up.

'And for that,' he said, 'I'm buying you coffee. Get your jacket, it's cold out there.'

He had an overcoat hanging by the door and was pulling it on before she'd even moved.

'Ronnie, has nobody ever offered you coffee before? I'll be down-stairs,' he said and left his office ahead of her. She retrieved her own jacket from the back of her chair and her phone from on top of the mug. It could have been an early lunch, but Dimitri still tore his attention away from his computer and frowned at her, as though she was bunking off.

Fenton was on the ground floor, halfway between the lift and the bottom of the stairs. He was sending a text and continued to stare at his phone for about thirty seconds after pressing send.

'Everything okay?' she asked.

He nodded but didn't turn his attention away from it for several seconds more.

'I think so,' he added, then kept the phone in his hand as they walked outside. 'We'll go to Thrive, it's the vegan place around the corner. You'll only get soya milk in your coffee, but they do a good carrot cake if you like that kind of thing.'

It was a short walk, and it was good to arrive before the lunchtime rush; the place was empty, and it looked as though they could be the first two customers of the day. Fenton chose a table at the opposite end to the counter.

'I had needed to get out of there for a while and when you came in with those two questions, I thought the timing was perfect. They are the very ones that keep me awake at two a.m. If we knew who sent that letter, I guess we would know why that person has so much infor-mation. I wish they would come forward, but there's absolutely no way to reach out to them, unless you have any thoughts?'

Two coffees arrived then, accompanied by two slices of carrot cake. Ronnie hadn't felt hungry up to that point. There was too much going on in her head and the less she ate, the less she wanted to. But her appetite returned on the first bite.

'It's good,' she said, but then immediately set it to one side. They were out of earshot of the staff, but she was still careful with her phras-ing. 'It doesn't seem as though the letter writer was guessing at anything. They knew exactly what happened to Jodie, making them either the perpetrator or somebody he confided in. Firstly, why would he?'

'He might have had enough, but doesn't have the balls to hand himself in?' Fenton shrugged. 'We could guess on that till the cows come home.'

'Okay, so if it's not him . . .'

He nodded. 'Perhaps Jodie confided in someone?'

'No,' she shook her head. 'Absolutely not.'

'Then it could be someone close to the rapist who wants him caught.' Fenton's lack of curiosity irritated her. 'It could be a wife or a girlfriend,' he finished with another shrug.

'Then why not identify him? Why leave us breadcrumbs that could leave him free for longer?'

'They could be scared to name him, scared to have us coming along and questioning him before we've got all the evidence together. It could leave them very exposed. Perhaps they have doubts about his guilt and want us to get all the evidence together and make an arrest once there's no room to argue.' They were both fair points and Ronnie hadn't considered either of them.

'So, what's your theory?' he asked.

She stirred her coffee, and again checked that they had complete privacy before she spoke. 'I think the blackmail is separate to the Kirsten McLeod case and the rapes. They only seem to link together because of that letter.'

Fenton shook his head. He leaned closer, speaking firmly but quietly. 'No, Nigel Beckett was blackmailed by someone who knew details of Kirsten McLeod's murder. Details that weren't made public. That's compelling. Your questions are bang on, Ronnie; finding out who sent it will be a major step, but if we find the why first, that's going to open it right up.'

'Don't you think there's something else at play? What if the investigation is being manipulated, that the killer is playing with you and not the other way around?'

He smirked. 'Let's just stick to what's already on our hands.' He pushed her plate back towards her. 'Don't you like it?'

'It's great, thanks.' She broke the cake in two with her fork. 'And I have a third question, too. Why now?'

She finished her cake in silence. Neither of them had the answer.

CHAPTER 47

Newmarket was to horseracing what Cambridge was to university education; both world leaders. Beyond that, there was little in common. In Newmarket, the horse walk looped the town centre, and in the mornings and afternoons strings of racehorses were ridden from their yards to the gallops.

One of the Suffolk officers had told Malachi that a road traffic collision with a horse in Newmarket was the driver's fault even if the car was stationary, and swore it was a local by-law designed to protect the town's main industry. Malachi suspected urban myth but never checked. Each of the few visits he had made to Newmarket had been linked to racing. Stables, betting shops, pubs and hotels existed for race days.

Bethany Wiley had moved to a racing yard on the edge of town and agreed to meet him at 10 a.m. Cadogan Stables was on a different scale to Cormac Halloran's estate. The gravelled car park was accessed through a gap between a veterinarian's practice and a care home. The stable blocks stood in a horseshoe facing the car park with just a short strip of grass between. She'd phoned at ten-to, telling him she would be waiting by her car and checking he was on his way. When he arrived five minutes later, there was only one person in the car park, a young woman with jet black hair, in full make-up and leaning against a blue Fiat 500, watching the entrance.

She was next to his car by the time he opened his door. 'I can't be long,' she told him.

He glanced towards the stables, hoping there'd be an office of some kind. 'Is there somewhere we can sit?'

She followed his gaze. 'There's nothing here. And I don't have time to go off site.' She was tall but lightly built, wearing dark blue jodhpurs and a matching gilet. Her eyelashes were layered with enough mascara to make her eyes look disproportionally large. She was pretty, in a Tim Burton corpse-bride kind of way. 'Here's fine. Just ask me whatever.'

'Sure?'

'Why not. I've only got ten minutes anyway.'

Malachi took out his notebook. 'Can you confirm you had a relationship with Enzo De Santis?'

'We did that on the phone.'

'I know. There are just a couple of opening questions.' He checked her personal details before asking, 'Who knew about the relationship?'

'It wasn't one, not at first. I think people thought we were just mates.'

'People?'

'Other staff. Nobody cares anyway until the shit hits the fan and then it's everyone's business.'

'Did Mr De Santis tell you that he'd received a blackmail demand?'

Her eyes were bright blue and pinned him each time he spoke, then flicking back to the yard each time she replied.

'Yeah, it wound him up. He thought she'd done it to get at him. And I asked him what he meant and that's when I found out that his wife knew, and it was all going tits up between them.'

'Did you have any idea who might have sent it?'

'He said it was her, and so I thought it was. But I didn't get into it; I didn't want to be in the middle of their mess, did I?' She looked at him, waiting for an answer.

'It must have been difficult for you,' he managed.

'I was angry, course I was. Fucking furious actually.' She flashed an expression to match. 'I had a perfectly decent job. Look at this place compared to the other one. I look like an idiot now, don't I? He told me that him and his missus were together for the kids and that

170

there wouldn't be any fallout. What a load of bollocks. I found out later he'd said that to pretty much every new girl that came in the yard.'

She wasn't looking anywhere else now, just at Malachi. She needn't have worried; she had his full attention.

'It just started off as a bit of a laugh,' she continued, 'a bit of fun, really. There's always somebody banging someone at every yard. It's just the way it goes. He's a good-looking bloke and he said he wasn't getting any at home. I didn't want anything serious, not at my age. And I thought it was quite handy, you know, him being married and everything.' She kicked at the gravel with the toe of her boot. 'Course she found out and dumped him and then I was stuck. He got all clingy, and I would have looked like a right tart if I'd just dumped him, wouldn't I?'

Malachi made sure he didn't move his head; neither a nod nor a shake seemed the right thing to do.

'He's a proper liar too. Told me he could use the cars whenever he wanted. We did it in the Aston one night. Bit cramped. But toilets on a plane are cramped and everybody does it up there. It's like one of those rites-of-passage things.'

Malachi's pen hovered above his notebook, rewinding her last couple of sentences. 'Hold on, are you saying he didn't have permission to use the vehicles?'

'I'd seen him driving them on his own, sunglasses on, looking like the business, and I thought he had permission. Turns out it was all work related, picking up owners, using the cars to impress people.' She snorted as though the idea was beneath her. 'We took the Ferrari out one night, that was cool. Said it was his favourite, something to do with his first name as well. I mean, him being Italian and everything. Ferraris are Italian, right?'

'They are, and you're saying that Mr Halloran didn't know that Mr De Santis was making personal use of them?'

'Right. I think that's what got Enz the sack in the end. That and everyone siding with the wife.' Again, the snort. 'And Mr Halloran went ballistic.' She split the word into its individual syllables and accented each with an upwards flick of her hand. 'Ball-iss-tic. Me and my ex, not this ex, the last ex, we did it in the car plenty of times and had no idea it was a problem. It's some sort of public thing . . .'

'Public decency.'

'Right. We were in a layby, not the town centre. How's that public?'

Malachi reminded himself that the best answer might be another question. 'I need to make a list of the places you went together.'

'When?'

'Up to the time he received the blackmail message.'

'When do you want the list?'

'Now, please. I can speak to your employer if we need more time.'

She hesitated, looking at the yard again, then shook her head. 'It won't take long anyway. We went to 'Spoons twice . . .'

'Which one?'

'The Regal in Cambridge. We had drinks.'

'What dates?'

'Fridays both times. I don't know dates.' She pursed her lips. 'Actually, I kind of do. The Friday before he got that message and the Friday before that.'

'Okay. Where else?'

'Milton Country Park,' she replied.

'When was that?'

He expected to be noting another date, instead she said, 'Both times after 'Spoons. Then a couple of times in the park-and-ride car park and once by the airport.'

CHAPTER 48

Malachi was back in the office just after one. The others had taken lunch a few minutes before, and it was just him and Ronnie. He dropped into the chair opposite her. His notebook was in his hand, with the cover folded back and his thumb holding a pen to the open page and looking as though he needed to get something off his chest.

'You saw Bethany Wiley?' she asked.

'And then Cormac Halloran.'

'And?'

'Enzo De Santis had been using Mr Halloran's cars while he was away. He found out and sacked them both. Mr Halloran isn't the forgiving kind.'

'What did he say?'

Malachi glanced at his notes and then back at Ronnie, ' "Fucking liberty after every fucking opportunity I gave that arrogant little . . ." ' Malachi stayed deadpan, 'Then my ink is a bit smudgy.'

'I read the rest from here. He's a character. How did he find out?'

'He received a fine from the speed camera in Barnwell Drive and said that the only person getting speeding tickets in his 812 should be him.'

'Which car is that?'

'The Ferrari,' he added. 'I didn't know that either; he told me, otherwise I would have googled it.' He turned to a different page in his notebook. 'It tallies with the date that Bethany Wiley said she and De

Santis first went to Cambridge together. He drove her round town, revving the engine and generally showing off. Then they spent an hour or so at the park-and-ride car park.'

'Waiting for a bus, I suppose?'

'Exactly my guess, although when you read her statement, you'll see that it was even less romantic than that. But what she did provide was a list of dates when they were out together. All were in one or another of Cormac Halloran's cars, which, by the way, are registered to his company, Cormac Halloran Racing.'

'And? More speeding tickets?'

'No, just that first one,' Malachi raised an eyebrow, 'but it was a good thing Halloran was sitting when he discovered that his DBX had been left in a multi-storey car park.' Then he added, 'That's an Aston Martin.'

'I did know that, but spit it out, the suspense . . .'

'I know, I'm sorry.' Malachi pulled his chair closer to the desk. 'Bethany Wiley mentioned public decency and claimed that she didn't realise that sex in a public place could be an offence.' He paused to pull a face. 'She didn't really know the definition of a public place either . . . but then she admitted that she and De Santis had been given words of advice for being intimate in a layby.'

'Where was this?'

'Up by the airport.'

Ronnie wasn't familiar with its location beyond noticing small planes flying low and coming in to land when they'd driven from the east side of the city towards Newmarket.

'And in a Range Rover Overfinch,' he added. He glanced at his notebook. 'More wiggle room apparently. That was on Sunday, the tenth of October 2021.'

'And the blackmail WhatsApp appeared on the fifteenth, so the timings fit . . . Any officer would run a PNC check in that situation.'

'That's what I thought. Enzo De Santis was driving his boss's car, but it was registered to the stables, rather than personally to Cormac Halloran.' According to Bethany Wiley, he explained that he was a director of the company.'

'I bet he'd had that line pre-prepared.'

'Not just for the police either. She still thought at that point he was more important than he was. I made a note of her comment too.'

He passed Ronnie his pocket notebook and it was her turn to raise an eyebrow. 'She also has a way with words. Any idea who the officer was who stopped her?'

'No,' Malachi took back his pocket notebook, 'I've drawn a blank, but I'm also—'

Their phones both pinged, with a millisecond gap between the tones. Ronnie read hers first, 'Fenton wants us now.'

'No,' he held his message for her to see, 'he wants you first.'

John Fenton sat squarely at his desk with his hands loosely clasped and resting on his closed laptop. He'd positioned a single chair across from him and Ronnie knew it was meant for her.

'Has something happened?' she asked.

'I've just had a phone call from the forensics lab, and there's an update on the DNA sample. I will be briefing the team, but I wanted to speak to you first.'

Ronnie drew a breath then exhaled slowly. 'Thank you, I appreciate it.'

'When I was notified that the results were on the way, I put myself in your shoes and thought about my own kids. For me, it's the unforeseen that's terrifying. All kinds of threat from illness to accident to the one in a million chance they'll be snatched from their beds. I know you're new to having a child, but has that hit you yet?'

'It has.'

'In my experience, the more you know about most problems, the more likely they are to go away.' He opened the laptop, and it began to quietly hum. 'As you know, these DNA results can determine whether another sample comes from a blood relative of Noah's. Can you try to see that acquiring that information will be a good thing?'

It was easy for Fenton to say those things. No doubt he had good intentions, but Ronnie's life was littered with unforeseen events and their consequences.

'You have a match, don't you?'

175

'Not directly, but there is a partial from a historic common assault arrest. Michael Richardson, now deceased.'

'So, Matthew and Owen are . . . ?'

'His sons. And one of them is Noah's father.'

Ronnie was still trying to absorb the information as she followed Fenton to the main office. Everyone was present and they all turned to Fenton as soon as he took up position at the front of the room.

'Update,' he began and gave them the details, as before, in very few words. Those few words covered it, though.

'Jenna, can you and Will interview Matthew, I will interview Owen. We'll ask them to come in and aim to conduct both simultaneously. We can request DNA from them but cannot demand samples without any substantive evidence of an offence.' His gaze brushed over Ronnie. 'In situations such as this, the child's guardians can request a court order to establish paternity, and that would be our next avenue.'

Will raised his hand. 'Does DCI Beetham also have the results?'

'Yes, we were both copied in.'

'Will his team be taking over this investigation?'

Fenton's expression clouded. 'Honestly, I don't know yet. I will keep you all informed of any decisions. For now, this links to both investigations, so we will proceed.'

Ronnie's thoughts drifted; she needed to speak to Alex as soon as possible. Michael Richardson and Zoe Richardson would have been Noah's grandparents; it was a lot for both her and Alex to get their heads around. Better to do it together. She also wanted to speak to Malachi alone; he had met both Richardson brothers and had filled her in, but there had to be more he could tell her.

She pulled up a photo of Noah and texted it to Malachi, *Does he look like either of the brothers?*

Malachi turned his phone over in his hand, clicked the message and studied the screen. *I can't tell.*

Fenton wrapped up and was about to leave the room when he turned back at the doorway. 'Malachi,' he hooked his head in the direction of his own office, 'you're coming with me.'

The instruction caught Malachi off guard, and he scrambled to his feet, shooting a questioning glance at Ronnie. 'It's fine,' she mouthed, then added quickly, 'What was it you were going to say to me?'

'When?'

'When that text arrived from him.'

Malachi shook his head, looking blank. 'I don't remember.'

'Malachi,' Fenton barked.

In all the time he'd been with the team, Ronnie guessed that this might be the first time the boss had singled him out. Malachi practically threw his chair back under his desk and hurried towards the closing door.

God, the lad needed to toughen up.

At the last second, he turned back towards her: 'It was the PNC check. There's a note on my desk.'

'I'll do it,' she nodded and gave him a thumbs up.

CHAPTER 49

Every police station Ronnie had ever visited had mugs that advertised chocolate brands. Creme Egg mugs were a favourite, the KitKat mug came in a close second, and Malachi had one on his desk which he'd filled with pens, pencils and a six-inch ruler. A Post-it note was stuck to the front. He'd written '10/10/21 Range Rover Overfinch' followed by the registration number.

'Hey, Ronnie.' It was Tess. The office was empty apart from the two of them and Dimitri. 'Are you okay? It's a lot for you to take in.'

Ronnie held up the Post-it note. 'It's not even a full sentence.'

'Seriously though, I thought it was good of John not to kick you out once he had the DNA results. He could have shut the door on your involvement at that point.' She paused and seemed to consider what she'd just said. 'I suppose he would have given you the information anyway, but it's better to have the support of the team while you're working through it.'

Ronnie wasn't aware that she had support from anyone in the team, apart from possibly Malachi. Perhaps this was Tess's way of broaching it. Then Tess added, 'I'm going out for some fresh air. Do you want to come?'

Ronnie glanced at the window; it was a bright day, but it looked as though the full winter sun had done nothing to warm the air. 'Yes, I do actually,' she replied, then asked, 'I need to pull up the record of a PNC check on this, who's the best person?'

'I'd ask Jenna. Or Dimitri, as he's here.'

Ronnie had seen more of the back of Dimitri's head than she had of his face, but he turned at the mention of his name. He held out his hand and she passed him the note. 'No problem,' he said. 'Give me ten minutes.' Then he looked across at Tess, 'Are you walking her around the Piece?'

'I reckon.'

'Okay then, see you in twenty-five,' he said and turned his back again.

Ronnie had already concluded that conversations with Dimitri finished when Dimitri ended them. 'Does he always hear everything that goes on in the office?' she asked Tess as they left Parkside.

She laughed. 'Yes, his brain's in stereo; his ears do one thing, his eyes do another. Actually, it's probably more than stereo, it's like multitasking plus.'

'As long as there's a computer involved?'

'Yes, exactly.' Tess pointed across the road. 'I like to walk around the perimeter of Parker's Piece; does that suit you?'

Ronnie nodded, then asked, 'What do you want to know?'

'I'm sorry . . .'

'I have some questions, that's why I agreed to come on your walk, and you have some questions, because that's why you asked me. You go first.'

'Wow, that's cynical,' she cocked an eyebrow, 'but fair I guess. It's heading for a mile around the perimeter of Parker's Piece. If I'm in the office I try to do it once in the morning, and again in the afternoon. If I smoked, I'd spend at least that long outside, so I take the time and don't feel guilty. Besides, I'm usually working.' She tapped her temple, 'Thinking time counts and Byron has been a thorn in our side. There's been some movement since you arrived. I wanted some insight, nothing more.'

'Is that it? The list of names opened it up, not me.'

'Don't you think that's strange?'

'I do,' Ronnie agreed.

They were walking anti-clockwise. Diagonal footpaths intersected the grass. They'd been silent for several minutes before Tess spoke, 'Most people cut across,' then added, 'Your question for me then.'

'From the case file, it looks as though you were the officer who dealt with Valerie Douglas when her husband reported the blackmail.'

'That's right.'

'And you interviewed the two lads, Harry Lee and Ethan Laird?'

'That's right. It was a while after the assault, and so they'd already made statements. I was following up after Mrs Douglas had been identified.'

'Were you surprised she hadn't been identified sooner?'

'Yes and no. Mostly there will be witnesses when there's an incident in broad daylight, and the only security camera covering that corner was angled towards the other side of the junction. Luck wasn't on our side. Then no, because it's so difficult when kids are that age and they're the only witnesses. Ethan was quite traumatised, but also desperate to help us. So much so that he embellished.'

'How?'

'Small things really. For example, he added some details to the car, sports wheels and metallic paint. And he described Mrs Douglas as a blonde lady in high heels, even though her hair was grey and she owned nothing higher than loafers. The story was soon all over the papers, but with enough incorrect details that our suspect list started looking like who's who of Cougarville.' Tess paused and reconsidered, 'Actually, embellished is the wrong word. It was hard for him to admit he didn't know some of the details, and I think he was worried that he wouldn't be believed.' She tutted. 'He had fourteen stitches, so of course we believed him.'

Tess talked Ronnie through her interviews with both boys and the interactions with their parents.

'When victims have angry family members, it adds pressure doesn't it?'

'Tenfold,' Ronnie agreed.

By the time Tess finished explaining, they were on the far side of the park, the furthest distance from the police station.

'I asked Fenton for background on you all,' Ronnie told her.

Tess shot a sideways glance, 'And?'

'You spent over ten years in a sexual offences unit; how many times did you encounter a rapist who was also a blackmailer?'

'In sextortion cases, yes. Stranger-rape cases, no.' She slowed as she considered. 'Many sexual offenders are known to us for other crimes, but most often it's violent or volume crime. Nothing this sophisticated.'

'Tess, do you really believe the two investigations are linked?'

'Do you have reason I shouldn't? We have two rape suspects now, and unless they have unknown siblings, one of the two will be your nephew's father. DCI Beetham's team will be all over them for the other rapes and Kirsten McLeod's murder. Jenna and Dimitri will be raking through their finances and their personal data. We are finally close, Ronnie. My gut feeling? The rapist committed Kirsten's murder and blackmailed Nigel Beckett. We're looking for one person, Ronnie.'

CHAPTER 50

When Ronnie returned to the office, Dimitri was sitting with his back to her, staring at the computer screen. He was the only one in the room and everything seemed normal. 'I have the information for you,' he said. 'Like I promised.'

She expected him to hand her a printout, and, at most, to have added a sentence or two; Dimitri Horvat was certainly a man of very few words.

But not today.

She noticed then that he had moved a second chair alongside his. 'Take the seat,' he said. And as she did so she saw a single sheet of A4 paper on the desk in front of him. He had marked it with three parallel lines, drawn from left to right across the page. Approximately two-thirds of the way along, he had added a vertical bar to link the three. 'I will show you something,' he said, 'But for now it is just between the two of us.'

'Okay.' She didn't understand why, but okay, she would see where this was leading and then decide.

'The top line is the blackmail, the middle line is the rape investigation and the bottom line is the investigation into the murder of Kirsten McLeod. He wrote B, R and M against them. 'You have been concerned about the way they are linked, and I understand why.' He pointed to the vertical bar. 'There's only been this connection.' He wrote 'NB' against it, 'Nigel Beckett, right?'

She nodded. So far this aligned with Tess's instincts but Ronnie guessed it wouldn't stay that way.

'And you want to find other proof that this blackmailer is connected to the rape and murder investigations? Well, I have a link, but not one you're expecting.' He drew an X on the blackmail line, spaced between the start and the mark for Nigel Beckett, then pointed to it with his pen. 'Here is Enzo De Santis. The man who likes riding in many cars,' he added, with a rare glint of amusement. He made two or three keystrokes; his computer unlocked. 'Look at your PNC check,' he said.

He didn't need to point out what he had discovered. She spotted the name so fast that it might as well have been the only two words on the screen. 'Shit,' she muttered. 'Kirsten McLeod ran the PNC check?'

They were still the only people in the room, but he shushed her in any case. 'There's more.' He drew a second X next to the first and tapped it with the tip of his pen, 'Here is where Val Douglas assaults the two boys. Now look here.' Then he returned to the computer and clicked across to another screen.

A resident returning home had found the boys in distress on the pavement and had called the police and an ambulance. 'This is the report of the initial response written up by PC Craig Vincent.'

Ronnie started scanning the document from the top, but Dimitri jumped ahead and pointed further down the page.

Also in attendance PC Kirsten McLeod.

'Why wasn't this picked up?' she asked. She didn't expect an answer; they both knew the murder investigation would not go through every single crime or callout Kirsten McLeod had attended without a specific reason, and there had been nothing to suggest Kirsten McLeod had been linked to anything she'd encountered on shift. Especially so long before her death. There would have been hundreds in a year.

Ronnie took Dimitri's pen and added another X. This time at the very start of the blackmail line. 'St Eldith's. What about that one? Can you link Kirsten McLeod to the college?'

He shook his head. 'I couldn't find anything.'

Ronnie stared at the paper and the three lines, willing herself to find some sort of explanation. Kirsten McLeod cautioning Enzo De

Santis and being present when the police and ambulance had been called out to the two injured boys couldn't be a coincidence.

'What about the suspected blackmail cases?'

'I looked at the first one already. I haven't had time to look at any others.'

Ronnie went back to staring at the page, Dimitri at his computer screen.

If Kirsten McLeod hadn't checked the vehicle details, there would have been nothing on record. 'What if she had had contact with St Eldith's, but there had been no further action?'

'Yes,' he replied. 'But if it was a callout, we'd have that initial contact logged even if she decided it was NFA when she got there.'

'Okay, so it's either not under St Eldith's or it never came in through the call centre.'

'Then we need to request her pocket notebooks from document storage, unless DCI Beetham's team already has them.'

'I doubt it,' Ronnie replied. 'There's been no indication that they have connected her death to the job at all. I can ask the DI to request it.'

'No.' Dimitri's voice was low but firm.

'Dimitri, why don't you want to tell anybody?'

'Can we just find a little bit more, just to be sure? I can request the pocket notebooks; they will let me have them. And you can look through yourself and be sure that nothing's been missed about St Eldith's.'

Ronnie should have said no. Should have gone to Fenton with the update.

She hesitated before replying, but in her head she'd already decided. If there was anything in Kirsten McLeod's pocket notebook that might tell Ronnie what had happened to her sister, then she would find it. If she left it to anybody else, she would never be sure that something hadn't been missed.

'Okay,' she sighed. 'You get me the pocket notebooks and it will be between us until we find out more.'

CHAPTER 51

Owen Richardson was dressed as before, down to the same dark green hoodie. It now had a smear of white paint on the left shoulder.

Malachi sat alongside DI Fenton, who had told him that it would be useful for him to be there. But had followed it up with a comment about not getting in the way. Malachi told himself not to overthink it.

Fenton hadn't given any indication of how he planned to structure the interview. Fenton was often very direct, but Malachi wasn't prepared for the bluntness of his opening gambit. He dropped two eight-by-ten photographs of Jodie on to the table.

They landed simultaneously and just as Owen bent forward to take a closer look, Fenton said, 'She killed herself. Fell one hundred feet on to concrete.'

Owen blanched instantly. 'Matthew told me she died, but not how . . .' He didn't make eye contact with either of them at first; he struggled to drag his gaze away from the images. 'Why?' he asked it quietly the first time, as though addressing Jodie's photo. Then repeated it when he finally looked up at Fenton.

'One theory is that it might be connected with what happened to her at St Eldith's.'

'Which was what? No one has even told me.'

'Now isn't the time for pissing around with your answers, Mr Richardson.' Fenton tilted his head. 'Her family needs information.'

'I don't need to piss around with anything, detective.' Owen picked up the more recent of the two pictures. 'I liked her. I don't know anything, I just heard rumours, and only after she'd gone. I don't like rumours, they're meaningless, but if that's what you want, then fine.'

'Go ahead.'

'Other students said she was beaten up. Or that someone had tried to murder her. Or that she had fought off a rapist. The most common were the hazing stories, but no one was ever suspended. I don't have a favourite theory, just a bunch of hearsay.'

'But you say you liked her?'

'I did.'

'But not enough to find out what had really happened to her.'

'It wasn't like that.' He still held the photo. 'What do you want from me?'

Fenton picked up the other photo. It was Jodie at the gates of St Eldith's. 'Apparently, this is her at the start of her university journey. By the end of it she was pregnant.'

The words took a few seconds to hit home.

Malachi was curious about Fenton's approach; starting with Jodie's death and working around to her pregnancy via St Eldith's had been confrontational and risked Owen just clamming up, but Owen seemed so blindsided that it had gone in the opposite direction and his guard had dropped completely,

'Did she keep the baby?' he said at last.

'She did.'

He thought about that for a few seconds. 'Did someone rape her?'

'We believe so.'

'And she still continued with the pregnancy.' He nodded to himself. 'That is a leap of faith.'

'In your previous statement to DC Henry here you claim you never had intercourse with Miss Blake, but I am going to ask you for a sample for DNA analysis. It is voluntary at this point; however, if you refuse, the child's family will request a paternity test through the court.'

Owen shook his head. 'I didn't . . .' he began, then fell silent.

Malachi didn't plan to speak; the words just came out. 'Why was your brother so angry if all you did was go to the cinema?'

He and Owen stared at one another but, in the end, Owen had no appetite for lying. 'We kissed, nothing more.' He closed his eyes. 'I'm not the child's father and I'll take the test to prove it. I didn't hurt her either, but I can't prove that, can I?'

CHAPTER 52

'They both agreed to the DNA test,' Fenton was on a video call to DCI Beetham, updating him with the latest. 'Matthew Richardson admitted having intercourse with her. Owen claimed he didn't, but we'll see.'

DCI Beetham gave a humourless laugh. 'It's interesting how Matthew had an about-turn when faced with the possibility of an irrefutable paternity test. And if he is the father, no doubt he'll claim it was consensual sex.'

'Of course. It'll be his best defence.'

'Well, I appreciate you picking that up for us.' Beetham seemed pleased with himself.

Fenton wanted to tell him that any progress had been a biproduct of the DEAD team's investigation and not because they were a free resource for Beetham's team. But Fenton couldn't think of a way to respond that didn't sound petty. He just grunted before realising that Beetham had moved on and was waiting for a reply to a question he'd missed. 'Sorry, go again,' Fenton muttered.

'I asked, are Matthew and Owen aware that we're making links to a rape and murder investigation?'

'Not murder, no. But Jodie Blake left St Eldith's in the wake of a scandal, both brothers knew that. And we're requesting DNA for a paternity test, but we're the police, not child support or Ancestry.com; I think the fact that there's a criminal investigation involved is implicit, don't you?' Fenton managed to keep his tone just short of full sarcasm. 'And in answer to your questions: Owen asked outright, Matthew didn't.'

'Assuming they speak to one another, they'll both have time to prepare answers before the results arrive.' Beetham's disembodied face blinked at him. 'Give me your opinion.'

Fenton blinked back. 'I haven't considered it.'

'You have,' he insisted, then waited.

Fenton took a moment to corral his thoughts, again swallowing the urge to tell Beetham what he thought of him and his bloody satellite. 'Matthew looks more likely,' he said at last. 'His involvement with Jodie Blake matches the detail she shared with her sister about the rapist. But Owen claims not to have had intercourse with Jodie, and if he does turn out to be Noah's father, it will raise some significant questions.'

Beetham nodded. 'Agreed. Why don't you concentrate on the job at hand and forget that you have the arse with me?'

Fenton lied. 'I don't.'

'You do, massively. Operation Byron's finally showing some progress and now you're worried it's going to be swallowed up by a larger, higher profile case.'

'Is it?'

DCI Beetham looked suddenly cheerful. 'I have requested that Operation Byron transfers to my team, and Superintendent Cooper is in support, but not yet. We have agreed that, for now, the DEAD team carries on with its lines of enquiry, and my team continues with theirs.' Beetham said it with no preamble and no apology. 'Think of your-selves as a satellite, and therefore I do want your cooperation.' He smiled. 'Aside from Operation Byron, I can't comment on the future of the DEAD team.'

'What does that mean?'

'Let's see how this case goes, shall we?' Beetham was now on the cusp of smugness.

Fenton understood the subtext: *toe the line.*

John Fenton's emotional range was limited. His first wife had said so and his second wife had independently confirmed it. But, when he ended the call with DCI Beetham, he was quite confident that both women were wrong. *Family first, job second* had been his mantra since messing up his first marriage, but second place in Fenton's world was still huge and he felt proud and protective of the DEAD team in equal measures. DCI Beetham was a threat to that.

Fenton, and Jenna, Dimitri and Tess had been the original detectives, brought together to identify and apprehend a kidnapper and killer. They'd started out as a satellite to the main investigation. That now felt like an insult, but back then it had been an opportunity.

The four of them had been a powerhouse. The other three left him behind when it came to data and technology but, somehow, he became the glue that made them work, and after several weeks of persistence they had recovered the victim and caught the perpetrator when the public had expected a body at most.

The four of them were the DEAD team and the idea that DCI Beetham might mess with that was unconscionable. Will had joined later and Malachi later still; the jury was still out on them, but Fenton swore he would fight for the rest of them to continue.

He was still cogitating when Jenna knocked and opened the door. 'Do you have a minute?'

'Of course.'

She came further into the room, then frowned at him. 'Has something happened?' she asked. 'You look . . . wiped or something.'

His instinct was to claim he was fine, but instead he shook his head; they had worked together too long for that. 'We're going to lose this investigation, Jenna; we're going to be nothing but an offshoot of DCI Beetham's team. A satellite office.'

She looked stunned. 'What about our team?'

'That remains to be seen.' He shrugged. 'I didn't welcome the idea; I could have handled it better.'

Jenna narrowed her eyes. 'I'm not going to ask what you said, but Dimitri and I have come up with an idea . . .'

'Go on.'

'I know the Richardson brothers are under investigation, but there's also little evidence against them.'

'We don't know what Beetham has. And we are investigating blackmail, not the other crimes.'

190

Jenna gave her hand a dismissive flick. 'If they had anything, they'd be all over it. Even a positive ID from one of the victims would be torn apart by the defence; he wore a mask, barely spoke, no forensics and so on.'

Fenton didn't know where she was headed, but he agreed with the observations so far. 'I'm listening.'

'As you know, we have been monitoring internet sites looking for him in relation to blackmail victims. Dimitri and I want to set up some new profiles, but this time to look for him as a rapist.'

Fenton shook his head. 'Beetham's team will be all over that. The rape MO is so specific . . .'

'They won't have the skills we have.'

It felt too much like one short ladder for a tall burning building, and he could feel it beginning to crumble around him. 'Slim odds, Red.'

She glared, 'I know, but why not?'

'Is that what you came in to ask?'

'It was.'

He picked up his mobile again, signalling the end of the discussion. He wanted to call home.

Jenna turned to go, but Fenton suddenly changed his mind. How many times had he told his kids not to give up? 'Okay.'

She glanced back, not sure if he was speaking to her.

'Just try it, Jenna.'

She grinned, a moment of relief that reached him from the other side of the room, but for him it faded when she closed the door behind her. Who were they both kidding? He could feel it all going wrong.

His call went straight to voicemail. Typical.

He forced an upbeat message.

CHAPTER 53

Ronnie had left the DEAD team office and found a vacant meeting room on the first floor. She had Kirsten McLeod's pocket notebooks, plus a notepad and pens of her own. She didn't start with the earliest, but selected the notebook that started on 12 August 2015, weeks before Jodie had arrived at St Eldith's.

PC McLeod's handwriting had been small and uniform at the start and end of entries. When she had rushed, the letters had grown looped tails and the words slanted across the page.

To Ronnie it looked like the handwriting of a teenage girl, and it conveyed so much more than a typed log could have done. As with all pocket notebooks, the ink was black, and corrections were completed by striking words with a single line. But personal details slipped in elsewhere. Like the way every capital K and capital M was slightly more ornate than the other letters because she had developed them in her signature. The notes mostly had the desired factual tone, but in the places where it looked as though she had hurried, the sentences were constructed less logically, and the descriptions less succinct.

Ronnie read from the start for the first dozen or so pages, listening in her head for Kirsten McLeod's voice to come through. There were occasional spelling mistakes and punctuation errors, but not in the way that implied Kirsten had been slapdash. Even when the sentences were a little muddled, her intention to record the information correctly was clear. How had Linda Beckett described her? Ronnie cast her mind back to their conversation. *Keen and steady*. The contents of the pocket notebook echoed it.

When Ronnie had finished with the opening sample, she skipped through, scanning each page in case anything familiar jumped out. Michaelmas term had started in October.

There was no precise date for Jodie's assault, but she'd narrowed it down with the combination of her own memory, Noah's birth date, and the comments made when she'd visited Professor Knox and Tina Runham. A check with St Eldith's student records department had shown a leaving date of 8 December that year, but the administrator had explained that they never used the actual date, but the Monday following notification of a student's departure. It gave Ronnie an end date but left the timeline slightly fuzzy.

Ronnie slowed through the dates from the start of Michaelmas to 8 December. Kirsten had spent much of the time in the city centre, dealing with shoplifters and day drinkers and incidents of minor public disturbance, and then all the usual nonsense that came with a late turn and the night-time economy.

There was plenty of detail but nothing for Ronnie.

Dimitri had requisitioned every pocket notebook of Kirsten McLeod 's career and Ronnie had calculated that the first date range she'd looked at had the highest odds of bearing fruit. Police work rarely panned out that way.

She grabbed a coffee and settled down for the long haul.

The type of entries in December were familiar to her; these could have been her own notes from her first couple of years in the job. The build-up to Christmas: more money being spent, more debt to go with it, more alcohol and a different pattern of socialising. And all the crimes and incidents that went with that.

Then the Christmas break itself. Domestic abuse, accidents and sudden deaths. Relentless page after relentless page. Kirsten had been thorough with her notes, but new officers often started that way, their notes becoming sparse as workload increased and their fresh enthusiasm wore off.

Ronnie waded into new year and the season of the nation's collective hangover. Debt, divorce, depression . . . she turned page after page.

6 January 2016. Stopped for advice by woman identifying herself as Tina Runham.

Became tearful and asked advice about reporting a suspected violent assault on a student. Had witnessed injures on possible victim consistent with sexual assault but unwilling to provide further details. Advice given.

Ronnie drew the book closer and reread the notes.

She texted Malachi first. *Can you free yourself up for an hour?*

Then she called Dimitri, 'Tear yourself away from your computer and come down here.'

He hung up without replying and arrived in the meeting room a couple of minutes later with a laptop case slung over his shoulder and his mobile phone in his hand. He saw the open notebook in front of her. 'You found something. I thought the odds were good.'

She showed him the entry. 'I am going over now. Malachi can lead, as I'm not supposed to be there.'

'Be careful, it would be a shame to lose you from the case.' He nodded to himself and put his hand on top of Kirsten McLeod's pocket notebooks. 'And I will read these,' he added and turned away.

CHAPTER 54

'So how do you want to play this?' Malichi asked.

Ronnie had told him that Tina Runham had spoken to the police in January 2016. She said it had come to light through double-checking some old records, which wasn't entirely untrue.

They walked across to St Eldith's and made themselves known at the porters' lodge. Tina Runham appeared a few minutes later.

'Back again?' she said. She sounded welcoming but looked puzzled.

'We just have a couple more questions, if you don't mind,' Ronnie told her. 'Is there somewhere we could go?'

Tina took them through to a side room, nothing more than a stone corridor. It was private, although unheated and bitterly cold.

Ronnie left it to Malachi to ask the questions.

'We've been crosschecking old information and discovered that you had another conversation with a police officer back in January 2016. Do you remember that?'

Tina hesitated. 'Do you mean the policewoman I spoke to in the street?'

'That's right.'

'Oh.' Tina flushed slightly. 'I didn't think to mention it. That student, Jodie Blake, went home and I didn't hear anything about her again. Then, when all the other students went down for Christmas, and I was catching up on some of the housekeeping jobs that I'd left until the holidays, I found myself opening doors to empty rooms. It made me think about that morning when I found her.' Tina frowned at the memory. 'Like I said, it proper shook me up. And each time I went to a new room I thought of it again. By the time I stopped for Christmas and was spending time with my kids, I couldn't help but wonder how she was getting on and what had happened to her.

'Then I saw that policewoman. I'm not sure what made me speak to her really. It was a kind of spur-of-the-moment decision.' Tina bit her lip. 'It was a bit embarrassing in a way because I didn't mean to turn it into a big drama or anything, but I just burst into tears. She was only young, but she was genuinely nice. She took time to talk to me.'

'Do you remember how much you told her?'

Tina shook her head and shrugged. 'Not really, I just garbled a load of stuff out about a student being injured. And distressed. That I didn't know what happened and she was naked.' Tina's arms flapped up from her sides. 'I don't know what else I said. Anyhow she pulled some information out of her pocket. She had a rape advice line leaflet, and another one on domestic abuse, and then another one that was a suicide hotline.

'She was just really kind. And I guess because I'd been so emotional and then calmed down again and I felt better after speaking to her, I started to wonder if I'd turned it into something bigger than it was. You know, having too much time to think over Christmas.'

Malachi had been nodding and encouraging her to continue talking. Now she reached a natural break, and he spoke: 'Did you see her again?'

'Not that I'm aware of. In passing maybe . . .'

'Sorry,' Malachi said. 'I meant, did she come here?'

'She did, she followed up, but I missed her. She spoke to Dr Zoe.' Tina frowned and looked away. 'There was something strange actually. I'd completely forgotten. Well, not forgotten, I just haven't thought about it for years and certainly never connected it.

'I'd slipped over on one of these tiled floors and hurt my back. So, I'd been off for a couple of weeks recovering. Dr Zoe seemed really quiet when I returned, you know in that washed-out way people get when they've had a bereavement or shock. All the colour had drained out of her and she was a bit of a zombie to be honest.

'I asked Professor Knox. It felt like I was stepping over the line. I normally only speak to the senior staff when it's something to do with the rooms or a student's welfare. Anyhow, he was good about it, but that's when I found out that the policewoman had been back again. He said that it had upset Dr Zoe so badly that she hadn't been able to eat or sleep. He wanted to know who'd got the police involved.' She frowned at the memory.

'Did you tell him?' Malachi asked.

'No, I just didn't want to get in trouble, so I said I couldn't imagine who had, or something like that. It was like walking on eggshells for weeks.'

'Why didn't you mention this before?'

'I was only thinking about what happened when Jodie was still here, not afterwards. And it's only 'cause you brought this up today that I remembered the other bit. You know, the part I said I'd forgotten.'

'There was something else that happened?'

'Yes,' she said slowly, 'I didn't put the two things together at the time, and I can't explain why they're connected now, except I know they are. It might be nothing,' she began.

In Ronnie's experience *it might be nothing* preceded as many important statements as it did irrelevant ones.

'They had an argument. In his office it was.'

'Professor Knox and Dr Richardson?'

'Yes. I only caught it because they had the door open, and I happened to be in the corridor. "How can I pay it?" she said, and he said, "Look, what will happen if you don't? It could turn out to be a lie, but the scandal would still wreck the university's reputation." All they were talking about was money and I assumed it was fees or bills or something.'

Ronnie finally spoke: 'But now you don't think it was?'

'No.'

'Why have you changed your mind?'

'Like I said . . .' Tina began, but then stopped. 'Actually yes, I do know. I disappeared back up the corridor and they didn't know I'd heard anything, but I saw Dr Zoe later in the day and she had that same expression. The one where it looks as though someone's died, or you've had really bad news, never because your employer has forgotten to pay a bill.'

CHAPTER 55

They waited half an hour outside the rooms of Professor Colin Knox.

He was with a student, a bookish undergraduate with a downy moustache and a beige V-neck pullover that he might have inherited from his grandad.

The student opened the door, thanked the professor, and scurried past Ronnie and Malachi and away along the corridor.

Colin Knox invited them in. 'I had that lad down as making it to the end of the first year, but not coming back for the second. Unless he discovers a decent work ethic in the next twenty-four hours, I think he'll be sent down before Christmas.'

He looked down the corridor for a few more seconds before closing his door. 'Let's hope I put the fear of God into him.' He turned to Ronnie and Malachi. 'Please sit. I take it you have some follow-up questions?'

Ronnie had intended to let Malachi ask the questions, but she jumped straight in. She wanted to employ a little bit of bullshit, and she guessed that Malachi would have a straighter approach. 'I've reviewed our case files and discovered that there was a further visit to St Eldith's in January 2016.'

Knox pushed down the corners of his mouth and shook his head, as though mystified. 'I don't think so.'

'Sorry, no, the visit was to your wife. But she spoke to you about it afterwards and was quite distressed. Now do you remember?'

He didn't answer immediately, and it was the kind of pause that should have included the slow tick of an antique clock.

'I had forgotten.'

'Can you explain what part of the interaction had upset her so much?'

Malachi had brought his laptop, and she took a gamble that he was switched on enough to play along. 'Pull up the report, would you, and pass it to me?'

She smiled at Knox. 'Professor, please don't rush. It takes most people a few minutes to remember a conversation from that far back.' Ronnie hadn't particularly warmed to Professor Knox or his ego and she guessed that he wouldn't want to perform less well than 'most people'.

Malachi passed her his laptop. She had no idea what document he'd brought up on the screen, but she pretended to consult it. 'I think your wife was upset about the assault?' Ronnie prompted.

Professor Knox gathered himself. 'Yes, but Zoe didn't realise at first. A policewoman arrived and said she was making some initial enquiries about the safety of our students. Zoe answered her questions, truthfully of course. But she didn't mention anything about the Jodie Blake incident. What could she say when we really didn't know what had happened. But that was exactly what the policewoman brought the conversation around to. She'd had some kind of tip off that it wasn't hazing at all.'

'You're the only one who's mentioned hazing, Professor Knox.'

'It was just the first thing that came to mind. We know it goes on at colleges. I felt it was a possibility.'

Ronnie didn't reply but made a point of studying the computer screen and pretending to read a few lines. She was confident that Tina Runham had told her the truth. 'What in particular caused your wife so much distress during that visit?' And before he could answer, she continued, 'Did your wife discuss blackmail with you at this point? Or was it later?'

He shook his head and said nothing.

'Why did she pay a blackmail demand? We know that you advised her she should.' He was still stalling. 'Have you spoken to your stepsons, Professor Knox?' Ronnie asked him. 'Did they tell you they've been asked to provide DNA samples?'

'Matthew called me, told me you'd spoken to him, but never mentioned the DNA.' He closed his eyes then and sighed. 'She paid because of her boys. It was all because of them.'

'Zoe was a good woman. She cared about me. She cared about this university. But most of all she cared about her sons.' Colin Knox had finally dropped the pretence and had started talking. It seemed like a cathartic release.

'I'm sorry if I've given you conflicting information, but now I know you've asked for the boys' DNA, I think I need to be completely candid with you.

'As I told you before, Jodie stopped attending my tutorials and at first I just thought she was ill, but eventually Zoe told me that she'd been subjected to some kind of assault. A nasty assault. But she hadn't wanted to report it to the police and for some reason, which only became clear later, Zoe did as she was asked and helped the girl move back home.'

Referring to Jodie as *the girl* grated with Ronnie. Malachi knew it and fixed her with a steady eye.

Knox continued, 'Zoe seemed preoccupied and agitated at first. But that settled and from what I can remember we had a good Christmas. Normal. Just us and the boys popping in. Then, in the new year, Zoe had that visit from the policewoman and it was clear that somebody knew what had happened to Jodie Blake. Zoe rang her then.'

'Rang Jodie?' Ronnie was startled. She'd always imagined that the day Jodie had left St Eldith's was the day she had last contact with the place.

'I think it's that phone call that really upset her. She told Zoe she'd been on a date, and it had gone wrong, badly wrong. She said she hadn't reported it and she just wanted to forget about it.'

'Did she identify the man?'

'She refused, said she just needed to get on with her life.'

They had been the words Jodie had used when she'd spoken to Ronnie, and they still echoed in her ears.

'We lived in the accommodation here at the time, and Zoe took to pacing the corridors. She couldn't sleep. I kept asking her what she wanted to do, but she said there was nothing. And then she stopped wanting to talk to me about it. Started drinking more, saying that it helped her to relax, and then that it helped her to sleep. She wouldn't go to the doctor. Didn't want to do anything except stay here and fret.'

He stopped abruptly and stared out of his window. Across the quadrangle. His expression was pinched, as though his thoughts were hurting him.

'I never had the full picture. I wanted to be supportive, but I was really getting to the end of my tether. Then moving on, maybe a couple of months, she told me she was being blackmailed. She'd received a threatening message. I asked her to show me, but she said she couldn't. It had disappeared as soon as she had read it.'

He turned and gestured at the wider room. 'I'm not exactly Mr Twenty-First Century and disappearing messages sounded fanciful to me. And that's when she told me that the blackmailer would reveal the identity of the St Eldith's rapist. A threat to one of her sons and a threat to her precious college – both in the same breath. She paid it and I'm embarrassed to say I encouraged her.'

'Even though one of your stepsons could have been a rapist?'

'And when at least one of them definitely wasn't. If the black-mailer had carried out their threat, everything could have been destroyed. All our lives would have been ruined. On the flip side, if we stopped the blackmailer, then the police would have no proof that anybody had committed a crime . . .' His sentence trailed away. 'I'm sorry, I know that sounds heartless.'

His voice was softer as he continued to speak. 'Paying the money was Zoe's decision, but I supported it. And I'm standing by it now.'

CHAPTER 56

St Eldith's to Parkside Police Station was a ten-minute walk, but Malachi didn't even waste the first thirty seconds before he said to Ronnie, 'I just accepted it when you said old documents had led you to need to speak to Mrs Runham again, but there was nothing in that conversation that would have generated paperwork. No crime was logged, and she never made a witness statement. Am I allowed to know what's going on?'

Ronnie had no intention of keeping Malachi in the dark the way that Fenton and the rest of the team had done. But she couldn't share this just yet. 'I'm not shutting you out, Malachi, but I need to get a bit more information together before I can give you details.'

Malachi considered what she'd said. 'And I suppose it would put me in a difficult position if I knew something before Fenton.'

'If that was the case, I suppose it would,' she agreed. 'Look, there will be something to show Fenton, just not yet.'

They turned on to Parker's Piece and took one of the diagonal foot-paths across it, heading towards the police station, and ending within yards of the spot where Ronnie had first set foot in Cambridge.

So much had happened since she stepped from that bus. She'd barely heard of St Eldith's then. She had also had no idea that the place where she'd come to live, this beautiful city, was also where her sister's life had been destroyed.

She blinked a couple of times and came back to the present. 'What Knox said today matches Tina Runham's account, but there's still so much to come straight. If one of the Richardson brothers is the rapist, does that mean he was also blackmailing his mother?'

'Why not?'

'I'm not sure. It just takes me back round to thinking that the rapist and the blackmailer are two separate people.'

'Perhaps they are,' Malachi mused. 'Perhaps one is Owen, and the other is Matthew.'

Ronnie groaned at the prospect. 'Look, the bottom line is that we just don't have enough go on.'

'Yet.'

'We're going to send ourselves round in circles until we get further with this.'

Malachi agreed. 'My aunt says, when it starts to look like Escher, something's wrong with the picture.'

Despite everything, she smiled. 'I quite like Escher.'

'Me too, but it's not real life, is it?'

'No,' Ronnie agreed. 'That would actually be worse.'

They were about the meet the point where the diagonal paths crossed, so just two or three minutes' walk from Parkside. Before anything else, Ronnie planned to find Dimitri, to see how much progress he had made with Kirsten's pocket notebooks. She wasn't sure why he'd picked her to confide in or, more importantly, why he'd kept his ideas from Fenton.

Dimitri's parting words came back to her, *it would be a shame to lose you from the case.* She hadn't paid much attention before, but now they struck her as strange. 'What do you know about Dimitri?' she asked.

'He's been in for about nine or ten years, less time than Jenna and Tess, I suppose, but he'd only ever worked in digital intelligence until he joined the DEAD team.'

'What made him move?'

'I think it was who. Superintendent Cooper sent him to the DI for their first case, and he just never went back.'

'Did he want to?'

'No idea. He doesn't give away much.' Then a few seconds later he added, 'But he sees and hears everything.'

CHAPTER 57

Dimitri was in the first-floor meeting room, exactly where Ronnie had left him. He had one pocket notebook open in front of him; the rest were still in a pile but turned upside down. He'd set up his laptop on the table, with a notepad and pens to one side, and his mobile to the other; he looked at home.

'This is the last one,' he said.

'Have you found anything else?'

He didn't reply, but raised a single finger indicating she should wait.

She drew up a chair and, by then, he had placed his free hand on top of the pile, preventing her from doing anything but watch him read. He was a few pages from the end when he stopped, tore a strip of paper from his notepad and slotted it in between the pages. He carried on without comment and took a few more minutes to reach the end of the notebook. He placed it face down on the top of the pile, then turned them all over and straightened them.

'Well?' she asked.

'Everything,' he replied.

'What do you mean, everything?'

'I mean all. We had three confirmed cases and two suspected cases up to October 2021, and all five of them are there. In addition to that, you already found the Tina Runham connection, then finally, that last entry, Baz Collins.'

Ronnie struggled to place the name.

'Nigel Beckett's bookie,' he prompted her. 'Some teenagers went round to his betting shop and kicked the window in. They were trying to steal cash from the till. There was none, but Kirsten McLeod was the officer who responded. There are a few more pages, then the notebook finishes the week before she died.'

Ronnie nodded. 'Did you see anything about her visiting St Eldith's?'

'No, but you have your link between the blackmail and the rape and murder now, don't you?' he said.

'It's time to take this to Fenton.'

'No, not yet.'

'Why not? We can't hold on to things.'

'Listen to me.' He lowered his voice. 'All the known cases came before Kirsten McLeod's death, and they are all in these books,' he slapped the pile, 'so Kirsten fed information to the blackmailer.'

'Or inadvertently gave it away?'

His irises were such a deep brown that they were almost black. That, or his pupils were dilated to almost the width of his eye; Ronnie couldn't be sure. 'Ronnie,' he whispered, 'you know what this means, don't you?'

She did, and it was an unpleasant truth. 'The information used for blackmail came from police incidents. Someone inside is either the blackmailer or is feeding information to them.'

'And until her death that information came from Kirsten McLeod. Then in July 2023 there were the first of six suspected cases.' Dimitri's expression quickly soured. 'Let me prove there's a link.'

'How? You cannot search through every pocket notebook of every officer, and those suspected victims are adamant they haven't been blackmailed.'

'I believe them.'

Ronnie slumped back in her chair and stared at him, looking for any clue in his impassive expression. The only thing she could decipher was his willingness to wait while she worked it through. 'Are you saying that the cases before Kirsten's death might be the only genuine ones?'

'I am.'

'And the others are what? A smokescreen?'

'Maybe. And the link is the person who pulled them together. The person who brought them to the DEAD team.'

'And who is that?'

He shrugged. 'Not you, me or the new kid.'

'How long have you thought this?'

He shrugged, held his thumb and forefinger a millimetre apart. 'Just a seed of a thought until now. But today convinced me.' He dropped his hand to the pocket notebooks again, clearly possessive of them. 'We have great skills, and yet we have made so little progress.'

And finally, she understood. 'You think it's someone in the team, don't you? And you trust me because I joined too late.'

'And because you didn't come here through choice,' then added, 'the DEAD team was thrust upon you.' He was momentarily amused by his own paraphrasing and it was the first sign of humour she'd seen from him.

'What now?' she asked.

'Two things. Number one, you need to know that I agree with you: in my opinion, the rapist is not the blackmailer. But I suggest we hold that information back right now. The DNA results will come back and maybe we can catch our blackmailer off guard. Do you agree?'

'Okay, and we'll review then?'

He nodded.

'And number two?' she asked.

'There's more I can tell you, but it involves your sister. Are you prepared for that?'

It wasn't a question she could answer with any certainty. 'I need to be,' she told him. Her voice faltered as a wave of apprehension swept through her.

'Yes, or no?'

'Yes,' she replied. 'Yes, I am.'

Dimitri moved his chair closer to Ronnie's and pulled his laptop nearer but looked directly at Ronnie when he spoke. 'Stop me if you have questions. I know my accent is strong, so tell me if I need to repeat myself. It is not a problem.'

'I will. Go ahead.'

'Jenna and I both come from intelligence backgrounds; that's why we are together on this team. Different skills, though. Mine is the computer, obviously. Hers was community intelligence. But both of us have seen how people let their guard down online, especially when they think they are anonymous.' He spoke slowly, careful to make sure that she was understanding everything she was being told. 'Sometimes they brag, other times they want validation.'

He waited for her to nod her understanding.

'Did DI Fenton tell you that we had the idea of searching for the rapist online?'

'Yes, he told me, and he expected that DCI Beetham's team would already be on it.'

'We were not planning to follow in their footsteps . . . keystrokes. Jenna suggested we targeted rape-fantasy chatrooms. She thought of it as soon as she heard how your sister and Kirsten McLeod were connected to this case. We had several days' head start before Jenna asked Fenton if we could.'

'Is it the norm to keep things from him?' she asked.

'He always knows in the end.' Dimitri shrugged. 'But sometimes we test ideas first.'

'Like this time?'

'We were vague, we did not give him the full details, so you are the first to know. Jenna and I set up fake accounts for a number of sites. We had certain parameters we were looking for. Most related to the usernames. People set up these accounts and pick a username which makes some kind of statement, rather than being as anonymous as, say, a random text string. I was in one of these sites and found a file posted on an associated page. This part of the site was full of short stories; fanfiction for rape if you like.' There was a flash of pain in his eyes. 'There are worst sites, but it is not a recommended experience.'

Ronnie didn't trust herself to reply but willed him to keep talking.

'We both read through a lot,' he told her, 'looking for a connection. Most read like audio descriptions for porn movies. But one was different. It isn't a story but the conversation between two of the site's anonymous users. We haven't shown it to anyone yet, but I'm going to send it to you now.'

She nodded.

'I want you to read it, while I document these.' He patted Kirstin's notebooks.

He sent the email, and she felt her phone vibrate with the incoming message. Goosebumps rippled across her skin, and she shivered, suddenly cold. 'I can't here,' she managed to say. She needed to be on her own, and somewhere she felt secure. 'I'll call you,' she muttered and rose from the chair.

Her discomfort must have been clear as the enormity of what he was expecting suddenly dawned on him. 'I'm sorry, don't read it. I didn't think.'

'It's fine,' she told him. It was too late now, she had Pandora's box and wouldn't hand it back no matter what evils it contained.

'You can change your mind.' He stood too, his bony frame awkwardly towering over her. 'I should not have asked.'

'It's fine,' she repeated and managed a smile, then left without another word.

All the way home she clutched her phone, as tightly as Dimitri had clutched Kirsten McLeod's pocket notebooks.

CHAPTER 58

Ronnie made pasta bake for dinner. It wasn't exactly created from scratch, but it wasn't straight from a jar either and, as cooking wasn't her strong point, she was pleased with the result.

Both Noah and Alex went back for seconds, which she took as a compliment until Alex announced that he'd been hungry enough to eat absolutely any old crap.

No wonder he was single.

Alex did the washing up, while she sat with Noah and checked his spellings. She was sure she hadn't had words like necessitation, thermal and articulate at his age. He managed eight out of ten and three pages of his reading book before Alex returned. From then on, the odds of keeping Noah focused on homework quickly diminished.

Ronnie hadn't wanted to fall into the habit of being the one chasing all the schoolwork while Alex became the fun one, but she enjoyed it far more than she expected, and she had a feeling that Noah did too. There was structure to it and it was less daunting than challenging herself with spontaneity. And in between the spellings, the snippets of conversation flowed naturally.

She slipped away after about twenty minutes and shut herself into the box room that had been converted to a tiny study. She opened her laptop so she could read the email on a full-sized screen.

Dimitri probably expected her to have done this the moment she arrived home, but she'd needed to give herself space first. Enough time to feel grounded and ready.

She took a breath and opened the file.

Just as Dimitri had said, the document was the conversation between two chatroom users, MoonLake69 and DrownXHer, and the extract started part way through the conversation.

MoonLake69: It's not the desire to do it that makes me special. It's the feeling of achievement once it's done.

DrownXHer: That makes sense, but I don't know where to start.

MoonLake69: Think about what you want. Do you want to hunt her down? Or trap her? Or have her come to you willing until she changes her mind. Use your imagination. Everything in the world is possible in your mind if you train it.

DrownXHer: Okay. I like it when her heels are too high and when she's drunk and her ankles wobble. It reminds me of a baby deer.

MoonLake69: What else?

DrownXHer: And when it's night-time and her arms are bare, they flap around trying to help her balance. And she squeals because it's half fun and half scary. And it's that squeal I like.

MoonLake69: Why?

DrownXHer: She wouldn't make that noise if she was sober. From the very first drink she knows she will be vulnerable. Do you mean something like that?

MoonLake69: Yes, that's good, very good. Mine is more specific; I've worked on it a long time. And it's okay not to rush. I choose the careful ones. By being careful they think they have everything under their control. They're busy worrying about the small things; their little modern first-world problems.

DrownXHer: So, what do you do?

MoonLake69: I dismantle her. I take everything she thinks she controls and break it apart. By the time I have finished, she has stopped fighting. People only fight to try to get back to

211

some version of where they were before it began. I show
her that all the safe building blocks that made up her life
were brittle illusions. That nothing she could go back to
would be the same again. I violate her home, her body, her
mind. I build up to it. The expectation, that is half the joy. I
watch her as she flounders, then as she is spread out and
ready for me. If she is lucid enough, she will realise that she
can do nothing but wait for me to take what I want.
Entering her when the resistance is gone, is the other half of
the pleasure. It is sublime.

DrownXHer: You're better at this than me.

MoonLake69: Every time, hone it. Make it the best for you.
Keep an open mind and develop what you do. I took risks
the first couple of times because the opportunity to fulfil my
fantasy presented itself. Learn the thrill of planning. I wash
mine down afterwards and then they start again.

DrownXHer: What do you mean?

MoonLake69: Naked skin and cold water. Washes away any
trace of me.

DrownXHer: How do they start again?

MoonLake69: It's a refresh, thanks to me. They will never see
sex the same way again. Remember, they've been dismantled
and whatever they rebuild it will be thanks to what I did to
them. Planning it is pleasure. The sex is pleasure. But thinking
of the women out there who think of me before, during and
after having intercourse with any other man; that's ecstasy.

Ronnie stopped reading but couldn't drag her eyes away from the
screen. Alex and Noah were downstairs shouting at each other, laugh-
ing raucously.

She couldn't go down there. She felt contaminated.

She closed the lid on her laptop so she wouldn't look at it any
more, folded her arms on to the desk and buried her head. She stayed
like that for several minutes then drew herself upright again, picked
up her mobile, and phoned DCI Beetham.

CHAPTER 59

It was a fifteen-minute journey north on the A14 to Cambridge Services; seven and a half miles of bullet-straight road before it curved into the services' slip road and round to a car park indistinguishable from any other major truck stop.

DCI Beetham hadn't been able to meet her until 9.30 p.m., but he was waiting for her in an unoccupied section of the food court by the time she arrived. Many of the concessions had closed, but there were two takeaway cups of coffee standing on the table in front of him. 'I hope you have something good for me,' he said.

'Well, I found the crack in the picture.'

She explained how the identification of Cormack Halloran's Range Rover Overfinch had led them to pull the record relating to the PNC check. Which in turn had led to Kirsten McLeod's pocket notebook entries. Dimitri had photographed every relevant example he'd found and had forwarded the images to Ronnie, who had downloaded them on to her phone. She passed it over to Beetham and he moved through them slowly. He reached the end and passed the phone back to her. 'Every time I think I've heard it all, there's something else.'

She sipped her coffee; it was still hot but tasted as though it had been made from yesterday's dregs. 'You must have gained plenty of insight into Kirsten McLeod; does this tally with what you know of her?'

'I worked out of Parkside for a while, so I knew Kirsten a little.'

Ronnie must have looked surprised.

213

Beetham looked amused. 'It's not like the Met,' he told her. 'It's a small force and everybody would know everybody at Parkside. It's only newcomers like Malachi and you who wouldn't.' He tried his coffee and then looked at the cup in disgust, as though the label might own up to its deficiencies. 'Fresh brewed, apparently.' He kept drinking. 'I would have pegged her as honest. No high-flyer, mind you. But keen to get things right. At least that would have been my opinion before reading those.' He tipped his head at her phone. 'One way or another, she was providing the blackmailer with information, and it now has to be our primary hypothesis that it was the motivation for her murder.'

'There's more you need to know,' Ronnie told him, and explained how Dimitri had found the chatroom file.

'What does Fenton say?'

'He doesn't know yet. Dimitri wants to talk to you first, and I promised I would phone him when I was with you. Would you start by reading this chatroom exchange?' She opened it then passed her phone to Beetham again, and again he took his time.

It was impossible to second guess his thoughts or emotions as he studied it, but he had grown grave by the time he reached the end.

'Dimitri is waiting for your call, but there's something I want to ask first. Would you agree to me interviewing one of the rape victims?'

'Why?'

'Either Owen or Matthew Richardson is Noah's father; that makes them a person of interest in the rape investigation, but there will be no chance for arrest without us building the case. I will be in a unique position to interview one or more of the victims.' And she knew what she was about to say next was either going to convince Beetham or close the door on the idea. 'I heard Jodie's account first hand. I know it was a long time ago but what if that means I can spot something that no one else can?'

'I'll need to think on that one, Ronnie.'

'I hope you know you can trust me?'

Before he could reply she tapped her phone with her index finger and asked, 'Do you think that discussion is genuine? Does it ring true to you?'

214

He looked puzzled at the sudden change in topic, but answered without hesitation, 'Hard to tell, but if I had to put money on it, I would say yes.'

She nodded. 'Please speak to Dimitri. Hear what he has to say.'

She unlocked her phone and found Dimitri in her contacts; she offered it to DCI Beetham, but he shook his head. 'No, just send me the details. I'll call him when I'm somewhere private.' Then he reached for her coffee. 'Are you finishing it?'

She screwed up her face. 'No, but I did try.'

He drained her cup with a look of abject disgust. 'I hope that's my worst decision of the day.' His phone buzzed in his hand as it received Dimitri's contact details from Ronnie, and he took his car keys from his pocket. 'I'll call him from my car.' He picked up the empty cups but paused before leaving. 'There is one victim who I think will speak to you. Her name is Olivia Hall. I'll call her before I speak to Dimitri and let you know.'

'Thank you.'

'And Ronnie, I do trust you.'

CHAPTER 60

The frost was heavy, and the ice had formed on Alex's car in thick layers that looked like ferns and feathers. The fog was doing an excellent job of impeding the morning light. Without looking at her watch, Ronnie would have struggled to guess the time.

She just needed to be at Ely for 8.30. It was less than twenty miles, but she allowed an hour. She headed along the A10; the first few miles were on the same straight flat road through farmland that she'd taken when she first visited Linda Beckett. The fog began to break up when she was halfway there. It remained in the fields to her left and right but ahead of her she caught the first glimpse of the grand Romanesque elevations of Ely Cathedral.

Ely was a cathedral city and had been an island until the Fens had been drained in the 1600s. That was the sum of everything she could remember from her sparse secondary school geography lessons, but it was easy to see why the Church had chosen it as the location for the cathedral; it must have seemed like a miracle rising up out of the water.

Olivia Hall lived in a newer part of town, a development of houses and flats with neat black iron railings surrounding their small front gardens. The properties bounded all four sides of a modern-day village green.

Ronnie drove slowly, peering at the property numbers. Number 43 was one of the smaller properties, a mid-terrace house with a navy-blue front door, a window to one side and two above.

The morning remained gloomy. At number 43 the downstairs lights were shining, glowing golden through the curtains. There was parking immediately outside the front door and Olivia Hall stood in the doorway to greet her. Her hair was short and dark, styled with a pixie cut and complemented by small sharp features. The effect was elf-like. She couldn't have been over five foot two either.

'Thank you for seeing me.' Ronnie shook her hand. It was cold.

'I don't doubt you're still working on my case, but every time I have a call from DCI Beetham or one of his team, it's a positive. Even when there's nothing to report.' She waved Ronnie inside and closed the door behind them. 'Please, have a seat.'

The room was small and square, with the stairs rising from one corner and the kitchen door in the middle of the opposite wall. Olivia wore a chunky-knit sweater, thick leggings and sheepskin thermal slipper boots. Despite her outfit, the central heating was still turned up high.

Ronnie removed her jacket straight away, draped it over the back of the closest armchair and sat down. Olivia sat cross-legged at the nearest end of the settee. There were two photos next to the television: a photo of Olivia and a dark-haired man of about her age. They were in a restaurant, snapped as they chinked their glasses together; the other was of a family group of almost a dozen people, with Olivia second from the right-hand end and the same man next to her.

Ronnie pointed to the photos. 'Is that your husband?'

'Chris, yes, it is. We've been married two years but together since sixth form.'

Olivia had been twenty-two when she'd been assaulted, and she nodded at Ronnie as though she understood the unspoken question. 'Yes, it was very difficult. But it was us against him and what he'd done, and we promised ourselves from the start that we'd stick together, and we have.'

Ronnie introduced herself and explained her involvement with the team. 'So, you see, I'm new to the area and new to the investigation, but I asked DCI Beetham for special permission to speak to you. I received a first-hand account of a similar attack and I'm hoping that by speaking to you directly I can learn something that isn't obvious from reading your statement alone. But,' she emphasised, 'there's no pressure on you.'

Olivia shook her head. 'It's seven years ago and it's not as raw as it was. I haven't given up hope that there will be an arrest and that I will have an opportunity to say everything I'm going to say to you in front of a court. You can ask me anything you like, and it will help me prepare.'

Olivia's victim statements had been shared with Ronnie and she already knew the answer to her opening question, but she needed to start somewhere. 'Where were you living at the time?'

'I had a little flat in the centre of Ely. It was above a charity shop in the High Street. I loved that flat at the time; the building was old, and everything was a bit wonky. The front door was right next to the shop door. I lived in Witchford before, it's a village just up the road, and I would come into Ely because it was lively and had my favourite bookshop and my favourite café. I decided I wanted a flat and I thought I had found the perfect one. It was a few doors from the bookshop and in the liveliest part of town. Witchford had been too quiet for me.'

She took a breath. 'Anyway,' she said, and gave a small apologetic smile, 'Ely High Street is different at night. Most of the shops don't have flats upstairs, they have offices or storage. Even before this happened, it reminded me of an empty theatre or a fairground after closing time. It has energy in the daytime. Vibrancy. I didn't particularly like Ely at night-time, but I loved my flat. I'd come home from work, shut the door at pretty much the same time as the shops closed, and that would be me. Tucked away till morning like the rest of the town.'

Olivia pulled her jumper sleeves over her fingers then hugged herself.

'My old cat Blotto had moved with me, and he would come in and out through the back. There was a metal fire escape and in the warmer weather I would leave the kitchen window unlatched and he would nose it open and come inside. The police think that's how the man got in.

'I'd gone to bed at about ten, and I have no idea what time I was attacked. I used to fall asleep quickly, so for all I know it could have been quite soon afterwards. The first I knew was when he grabbed my ankles. He'd already pulled the duvet off me. It was on the floor by then, but it was him grabbing my ankles that woke me. He pulled me really fast.' She chewed her bottom lip and her gaze slanted past Ronnie. 'I think if I'd woken sooner, maybe if I'd heard him, then I might have got away, but from the second he held my ankles like that, there was nothing I could do. I came off the end of the bed and banged on to the floor. I remember flailing around, but between the bed and the hallway there was nothing to grab on to apart from the doorframe. But he was pulling me so hard that it barely slowed me.'

She took a couple of slow breaths.

'Are you okay?'

She nodded, 'Fine. I just need a second.'

'Can I get you a drink?'

Olivia closed her eyes and continued her controlled breathing. Ronnie knew the technique; she'd tried it herself but without Olivia's focus or poise.

After several minutes Olivia's eyes opened. 'He'd switched the bathroom light on and everything else was dark.' Her voice was steady again. 'It was behind him, so he was pretty much in silhouette. He was wearing dark clothes and a ski mask. I couldn't even see his eyes although I knew he could see me because the light from the bathroom was hitting one half of my face.'

'Did he speak?'

'All I remember him saying at that point was "No." I struggled a bit and that's when he said it. And when I didn't stop, he slapped me. I cried out, but I don't know how loudly, and then he hit me again harder. I don't think he had to worry. I don't think there was any chance anybody could have heard.

'He cable-tied my wrists in front. I think I struggled a little, but every bit of him was covered and I couldn't have left a scratch on him. But within a few seconds, I couldn't even try. He used what's called a spreader bar on my legs.' She paused and her face flushed. 'It's a sex toy. I didn't even know there was such a thing. It was explained to me afterwards and they kept asking me questions until they had a full description and I think they knew the type.' She frowned. 'I know I blushed then, and I know it's stupid. It's part of the ongoing humiliation, you know?'

'I understand.'

'The hallway floor was tiled, and I'd been wearing nightshirt and knickers. He cut my underwear off me and stuffed the knickers in his pocket. And then . . .' her voice wavered and one of her covered hands pressed her throat, 'he had a little bottle. He forced my mouth open and squeezed this liquid in. I didn't know what it was, but it tasted foul. He pinched my nose and held my mouth shut until I swallowed. It burned and I cried out and asked him what the hell he'd given me. He slapped me again but never replied.'

Ronnie had seen it in the notes. GBL, gamma-butyrolactone, converted by the body into GHB, which was probably the best-known date-rape drug. It would have left Olivia drowsy and certainly subdued.

'He gagged me then and I had to wait like that,' Olivia continued. 'It wasn't hard to guess what was coming. He'd been frenzied up to that point, but he suddenly stopped. He stood by the bathroom door watching me.'

Ronnie had no doubt that he'd been getting off on the thrill of watching her as well as waiting for the drug to take effect.

'I swear I never took my eyes off him. I thought that even if I could spot the smallest clue to his identity, it would be worth it. Although, I also remember thinking that I would be dead if he thought I'd seen his face.

'He didn't move until I started shivering. It was cold by then, but I suppose the adrenaline was running out and the drugs were kicking in. He went into the bathroom, and I heard him washing his hands. The water stopped running and there was silence and stillness for what felt like ages. I was listening for his breathing, but I couldn't hear it over mine. I kept making a whimpering sound and couldn't stop myself.

'Then he came out of that bathroom in a fury. He was back to being the man who dragged me from my bed. He hauled me over on to my front. My hands were crushed under my body, and I was crushed under him. He had his fingers twisted in my hair and was banging my head against the floor.' Olivia's face had become pinched and there was panic in her eyes, but she kept going. 'The sex did damage; I had external bruising and internal bleeding. Maybe it was over quickly, I don't think so, but I don't know.

'My face was against the floor and there was nothing to see, and yes, I did close my eyes then. When he was done, he released my legs, and dragged me by the ankles again, this time through to the bathroom. He switched the hall light on, and the bathroom light off.

'There was a second or two at most when I could see his clothes and see his build. His jacket and trousers were some kind of waterproof fabric, the kind that doesn't shed anything. He was turned away from me as he adjusted the lighting so, again, I didn't even get a glimpse of his eyes. His jacket rode up, though, and underneath I think he was wearing a blue disposable decorators' overall, like a PPE suit.'

Ronnie nodded.

Olivia continued, 'So I didn't manage to see anything of value. I couldn't even describe how big or tall he was, just somewhere in the range of average.' Her hands slid out from her jumper sleeves and she touched one wrist with the fingertips of the other hand. 'I can still feel the way he gripped me, though, and I would be able to identify his hands even now just by the way they wrapped around my ankles.

'He put me in the bath, sat me up against the taps. I was scared he was going to kill me and leave me there. Instead, he tied me so I couldn't move. I was bound under my armpits and across my chest. Then he turned on the shower and, before he left, he cut through my gag and took it with him. He shut the door behind him and all the shouting in the world wasn't going to bring anybody. I was drowned out by the shower, muffled by the walls and at the back of the building with no one around.

'It was Chris's mum's birthday the next day thankfully. We were taking her to lunch at the Cutter – it's a pub down by the river. And when I didn't turn up and I wasn't answering my phone, Chris came up to get me.'

'You weren't living together then?'

'No, he didn't even have a key, but when he didn't get an answer from the front door, he was smart enough to come around the back. The man had unlocked the door when he left and that's how Chris found me.' By now, Olivia had pulled the cuffs of her jumper back over her fingers and wrapped her arms around herself again. 'I wonder if it had been winter, or if the flat had been colder, whether I would have died.'

Ronnie had wondered the same.

'I know he's done it again since, but I don't suppose somebody who's wired that way does it just once. And it seemed too practised for me to have been the first. That's why I'm happy to speak to you or anyone who has a chance of stopping him.'

Ronnie had to try to listen and not think about her sister, but it had been impossible. There were differences: for one, the attack on Olivia seemed more premeditated. He'd even used a condom and he had been meticulous at not leaving a trace; something which even the forensically educated frequently failed to achieve.

'And you stayed in Ely?' Ronnie commented.

'Yes, I love it here. But not that flat. We could have moved away, but why should we? He knows who I am, and I haven't got a clue who he is, and that will remain the same wherever I go.'

Olivia Hall was tiny and, Ronnie guessed, perpetually shivering against the fear of cold, but there was no doubting her strength and Ronnie hoped that one day she would be able to appear in court on the same list of witnesses.

She generally struggled to give compliments; to her ears they always sounded too awkward and potentially insincere, even though she only offered them when they were genuinely deserved, but this time it was easy. 'Thank you for your time, Olivia. I'm hugely grateful for your openness and really admire your determination.'

'Thanks, but I don't feel I have a choice. There's a quote that says the greatest crime is to do nothing and another which says that avoiding the truth only prolongs the pain.'

Olivia had no way of knowing how hard the words hit Ronnie. However similar Jodie and Olivia's experiences had been, their choices and outcomes had been dramatically different.

'Proving, if nothing else,' Olivia continued, 'that I practically lived in that bookshop.'

Ronnie told herself to stop making comparisons between the two young women, but in her head Olivia's account was already starting to overlap with her memory of Jodie's, and her image of Olivia's flat threw up pictures of the little bathtub in Room 22 at St Eldith's.

She didn't plan to ask her next question; the words found their own way. 'Do you know of a college called St Eldith's?'

For a fleeting moment Olivia's smile was spontaneous. 'I thought about studying criminology there . . .' Her words faltered suddenly. 'I went for an open day.'

Ronnie froze too. 'When?'

'I'm not sure, but it was before.' Her eyes grew wide. 'Not long before.'

CHAPTER 61

DCI Paul Beetham had arrived at Parkside Police Station at 7.30 a.m. and headed straight up to the budget-eating offices of the DEAD team. Everyone was present apart from Ronnie, but she would be visiting Olivia Hall around about now.

They sat in their usual pairings, Dimitri and Jenna, Tess and Will, and then Malachi on his own. When Beetham had first met them, they'd had real promise but that had been before they'd fallen into the rut of Operation Byron.

It had been departmental suicide.

He was hooking his jacket on a coat peg as he had that thought, and he froze with one hand suspended in the air. Of course, it wasn't departmental suicide.

He snapped out of it, turned to the room and wished them all good morning. He was greeted with polite nods and less polite mutters. 'Cheer up,' he said. 'This case won't last forever.'

Of the few times he had visited Fenton, Beetham couldn't remember a single one where the DI hadn't been firmly planted behind his expansive desk, but today he was standing close to the window. His mobile was in his hand, and he was glancing between it and the view outside.

There was a listless energy about him. It wasn't surprising.

'Who allocated Op Byron to the DEAD team, John? Was it Superintendent Cooper?'

'I guess so; it feels an age ago.' Fenton dragged his attention away from the view. 'I know they came straight to you.'

'We need to talk,' Beetham told him. 'There have been developments . . .'

DS Jenna Reynolds cared what happened to the DEAD team. Fenton was in charge, but he sat in his office and she was the one at the heart of it.

It was time for Operation Byron to wrap up. They were throwing everything they had at it, and when Dimitri found the file from the rape chatroom, it had felt like progress. She wasn't sure what had happened since then; for some reason, he hadn't handed it to Fenton and had dipped into one of his less communicative moods. And then this morning, DCI Beetham had arrived.

Nobody in the room was pleased to see him, except for Will, whose mission in life was to tread water until he could switch to Beetham's camp.

Fenton still thought that Operation Byron would stay his, but under Beetham's control. Jenna knew that might change, and maybe the whole investigation would be snatched from them. Or perhaps DCI Beetham's involvement was a good opportunity. She had set her heart on being the one to close the case and now, if she moved quickly, he might see her potential.

It was almost 10 a.m., and they'd all been in since seven. Fenton hadn't given an explanation for the early call, but it was safe to assume that was because of DCI Beetham coming. Yet, apart from walking across their office and being overly chirpy, Beetham hadn't spoken to any of them.

She called across to Tess. 'What is it we're waiting for?'

'I don't know, but I'm happy to do a coffee run, if anyone wants one. Maybe sitting here and looking busy was all Fenton needed from us.' She had no response from the first mention of drinks, so she tried again, 'Who wants a coffee then?' Everyone did. 'Jenna, do you fancy the walk?'

Fresh air in the working day was Tess's regular escape, Jenna's was to disappear further into her computer, but a fresh perspective might do her good. 'Okay.'

Just as they were about to leave, DCI Beetham came through. 'Right, can we have your attention please?'

Tess and Jenna settled back; Beetham wasn't known for his short addresses.

He managed to write off the next forty minutes and was only interrupted when Fenton finally joined them and asked after Ronnie.

Tess took Beetham and Fenton's drink orders, too, and then she and Jenna left the building.

'Is anything wrong?' Tess asked as soon as they were outside. 'You looked like you needed to escape.'

'Did I?'

Tess shrugged. 'I thought so.'

'I am frustrated,' Jenna conceded. 'We're making progress now and DCI Beetham's lot are going to swoop in and take the credit.'

'Are they really, though?' Tess started walking, immediately falling into her usual quick and even stride. 'We have the blackmail case and if Kirsten was killed because she'd been feeding information to the blackmailer, then we can find the blackmailer and catch the killer.'

'Kirsten was killed by the rapist. Look at the MO. That's a win for Beetham.'

'But Kirsten's connected to the blackmail.'

Jenna flashed her palms skywards. 'So we are looking for one person who is responsible for all of it. I want our team to take the credit for the arrest.'

Tess gave her a side-eye glance and smirked. 'Isn't the point that they are caught?'

'Hey, why the look, Tess?'

She shrugged. 'You want *our team* to take the credit?'

'I do.'

'You want this more than any case we've worked on.'

It was true but Jenna didn't know it had been so obvious. 'Do I?'

Tess didn't reply but stopped in her tracks. She turned to face her but scanned a full 360 degrees before she spoke. 'I have a theory,' she said, her voice barely above a whisper. 'I think someone in our team is playing with us.'

Jenna's eyes widened, 'Who?'

226

Tess shook her head slowly. 'I don't think it's Fenton, but I need to be sure, so that's why I haven't said anything to him yet. Aside from him, I have narrowed it down to Dimitri or Will. I'm certain one of them is involved . . . I have more to check out first.'

'Like what?'

'It's about that rape-fantasy chat . . .' Tess fell silent as a couple of pedestrians approached. She glanced behind her and then back at Jenna. 'I'm not sure. I know something's off. It's not a five-minute chat. My digital skills are a bit out of date, but I'll work it out.'

'Do you want help?'

'No, I'll be fine.' Tess hesitated. 'Maybe. Can I see how I go? Just keep quiet about, it can you?'

'Of course,' Jenna replied and managed a smile.

CHAPTER 62

Ronnie called DCI Beetham as she headed back to Cambridge. 'I think I have found the connection to St Eldith's. Olivia Hall went there for an open day shortly before she was assaulted.'

She immediately realised how sparse it sounded without Olivia's visceral reaction to give it credibility, and Beetham was silent as he waited for her to add more.

'Is that it?' he asked when he realised that she'd finished speaking.

She slowed as the traffic thickened. 'I'm heading to St Eldith's now to ask them for a list of open-day invitees. There must be one for the rapist to know their home addresses.'

'By all means, check it out, Ronnie, but that's a bit thin to base a whole theory on. At the risk of sounding like my old dad, one swallow doesn't make a summer.'

'Yes,' she countered, 'but it's enough to tell you what the rest of the pint's going to taste like.' She pulled up at a set of lights and glanced at her phone in its dashboard cradle, ready for his reply.

'Good point, well-presented,' he conceded, and she smiled. 'And,' he added, 'I will get it followed up with each of the victims. I also wanted to put the brothers under surveillance, but I couldn't get authority. We're keeping a subtle eye on them, and it will be easier once we get the DNA results through today.'

Today.

The word hung in the air for Ronnie. Today wasn't some vague time in the future. Today was going to send Noah's life in an as yet unknown direction.

'They had a spat yesterday, though. We know that much.'

'Owen and Matthew?'

'Yes, a neighbour of Matthew's called it in. Owen turned up at his brother's house shouting. They had a row in the street, but by the time the patrol arrived, it hadn't gone further than shouting and a bit of pushing. I have their names flagged and it was reported straight back to me,' Beetham explained.

The traffic moved again.

'What were they fighting about?'

'We don't know, but it looks as though there's tension building in that corner of the family. The DEAD team also has a list of blackmail victims and suspected victims. What do you know about it?'

'Yes, the names fall in two periods, one before and one after Kirsten's death. I only saw it for the first time this week, so it's new to me too.'

'Right, well DC Horvat is totally convinced that the cases which fall after Kirsten's death are all unconnected. I don't know what evidence he has, though. Any ideas?'

'You've spoken to him more recently than I have.'

'Look, I need to go. Can you get the St Eldith's idea checked out? And I'll catch up with Horvat?'

Ronnie agreed, but there was somewhere else to visit first.

CHAPTER 63

If the DNA results were coming back today, Ronnie wanted the chance to see Noah's father on her terms. To face the man most likely to have destroyed her sister's life. She didn't know which brother that would be, so she planned to see them both.

Her route back to Cambridge would take her past the Science Park and within a stone's throw of the offices of MRH Ltd. She hadn't planned what she would say to Matthew Richardson; in fact, she wasn't sure if she wanted to speak to him at all. She just wanted him to be standing in front of her and to be able to look him in the eye. She wanted to see the answers to some of her questions written on his face before the merry-go-round of science, media, arrests and the criminal justice system took away the chance.

She gave her name and waited. It wasn't long before Matthew Richardson opened the door at the far end of the foyer. He eyed her warily and invited her to follow him to a meeting room.

He didn't offer her a seat, and she was pleased. He didn't sit either and she placed herself so that she was almost toe to toe with him.

'I don't appreciate the constant interruptions at work. I would prefer to visit Parkside,' he said.

'I'm not here as a police officer, I'm here as Jodie's sister.' Her words dried up.

There was a long pause before he spoke. They glared at one

another, and she wondered who she was looking at. A rapist, perhaps. A killer, possibly. Noah's father, maybe. Or all three.

'What do you want?' he asked at last.

He had the face of someone not used to smiling and she couldn't tell whether he was sweating or whether it was normal for his skin to have an unhealthy sheen.

More than anything else, he looked scared. But scared people can be desperate, and desperate people do terrible things. 'I wanted to see you before the results came through. We're going to find out whether you are Noah's uncle or Noah's father. One way or another, your family is going to be linked to mine.'

'Genetically, yes. But whoever fathered the kid did so a long time ago.' He blinked. 'We don't have a connection to him; Owen and I agree on practically nothing, but we do agree on that.'

Ronnie shouldn't have been surprised; she'd seen it over and again during her career. There was a smugness in the way he thought he could just brush away Noah's existence.

'And,' he continued, 'you should know we don't have money.'

The burst of rage that rose in Ronnie was sudden and brutal. 'I don't want your money.' While her brain rallied round for the right words, she heard herself repeat the same phrase again, but louder this time. 'I want the truth.'

Finally, she caught hold of herself and took a step closer. 'I thought it might be a possibility for my nephew to have a relationship with his uncle. But whoever turns out to be the father is the person who raped my sister. I know that because she told me.'

He leaned away from her but didn't step back. 'She was off her face drunk.'

'Meaning what? Rape doesn't count?' Ronnie ploughed on, 'And my relationship with that person boils down to two things; they're going to prison and I'm helping them get there.'

He held up his hands, ready to repel her.

'Don't be ridiculous, I'm not going to hit you.' She spat the words, convincing herself, even though slapping him had suddenly become an almost irresistible urge.

'You're a psycho, like him.'

'Like who?'

'Owen. Just get out before the police come for you too.'

Clarity returned as fast as it had deserted her. She backed away, then turned and hurried back to the car. What a mess. What a goddamn mess. At least she hadn't hit him; there would have been no return from that.

She leaned against Alex's Ford but didn't get in. She abandoned the idea of visiting Owen, but she still needed to get to St Eldith's and wanted to arrive as soon as possible. She wasn't going to drive while her temper still flared.

Ronnie knew she had been signed off by occupational health for a reason; her peaks and troughs of emotion were too spiky. Too near the surface. But she hadn't accepted the decision until now.

She was supposed to stay calm under pressure, not flare up. Brute force didn't get results in this job, and yet that was exactly the way she'd wanted to behave. She had wanted to give control and rational feeling a joint day off. Wanted to raise her hands and surrender to a red mist had been the mental equivalent of aiming for a quick drink after work and ending up slaughtered.

Succumbing to the urge to go and see either one of the Richardson brothers had been equally inexcusable.

'Shit,' she muttered. She closed her eyes and didn't move, ignoring the cold morning air and the dampness of the car's bodywork against her back. She should walk away from the case but knew she couldn't.

A man's voice startled her, but even so, she opened her eyes slowly.

'Sunbathing?' His tone was light but there was concern in there too. He was about Ronnie's age, and scruffy, but he carried it as though it was a style choice.

'Contemplating a career change.'

'Off to join the circus?' He folded and unfolded the car key in his hand. 'I'm often tempted.'

She blinked and studied him properly, then pushed herself away from the car so that she was standing straight. 'Are you Owen Richardson?'

'I am. And you?'

'DS Ronnie Blake.'

'Ah, Jodie's sister?'

'I'm not here officially, I shouldn't be here at all.' She shrugged. 'I had this daft idea that I needed to see you both before . . .'

'Before the DNA results?'

She nodded. 'It seems stupid now.'

'Careerwise, I'd imagine so. But from a personal point of view, why not? You're trying to make sense of what happened.' He shoved his keys into his hoodie pockets. 'I'm going to see Matty now, but I'm sure you worked that out.'

'With my detective skills.'

'Yes.' He smiled at her. 'I'll tell Matty we've spoken. He won't make a complaint.'

'He probably should.'

Owen shook his head. 'Get back to work and forget the circus. And don't worry about the results.'

He started to walk away, but she called after him, 'How can you be so calm about them?'

He kept moving, walking backwards for a few steps as he replied, 'Because my brother's a miserable sod, but he wouldn't hurt anyone.' Then he turned away and was gone.

Ronnie liked the sentiment, but nobody had misplaced faith like family.

CHAPTER 64

She dumped Alex's car back at their house and walked to St Eldith's; she'd already learned that it was quicker than driving and trying to park.

From her experience, people who manned reception desks and service centres had either been employed for their customer-facing skills or to repel all enquiries.

Bob Murgatroyd fell into the second category. He was, by his own description, the master of the St Eldith's open day. He was approaching forty, adenoidal and proud, he told her, of setting up the right processes and sticking to them. He was also stubborn and the personification of the jobsworth mentality.

She was patient. 'I'm not asking for the information; I'm asking if you have the information.'

'What you are asking falls under the general data protection regulations.'

'I know what GDPR is; I'm a police officer.'

'Then you must know that I cannot share that information with you.'

'I'm asking you to let me know what the list is called, I'm not asking to look at it today.'

'Yes, and I'm explaining to you that access to the list, if we have it, falls under GDPR and therefore I cannot disclose any of its details.'

'The title of the list is not personal information.' She smiled at him. 'I'm sorry, Mr Murgatroyd, I think I haven't explained myself very well. We are putting in a request for the information you have on prospective students. We just need to know what you call that document so that I can fill out the form correctly.'

His supercilious expression didn't budge, and she guessed he was about to come back at her with a repeat claim that simply telling her whether the information existed and what the file was called might be in breach of data protection regulations.

She scanned the room, hoping for inspiration. The office was an equivalent size to Knox's and a floor above. It had a view of the court-yard and by the window was a lectern bearing a leather-bound volume, open in the middle.

She moved a little closer to it. The pages were handwritten in copperplate script and from the way that Murgatroyd suddenly puffed himself up, she guessed that the hand was his.

'It's stunning,' she told him.

'That's the register of graduates, handwritten as it has always been.'

'You just told me its name.'

'It's not a computerised document.'

'And there's another myth, Mr Murgatroyd.' She ran a finger along the front of the lectern. 'I suppose the other option would be to request everything. Documents like this,' she said, 'can be scooped up with everything else. A job lot if it's easier.'

His mouth opened and closed a few times before he found the words to go with it, 'It's just called "Open Days for Prospective Students". It's an Excel file,' he added.

'In the meantime, don't touch it. I will expect to see a last saved date earlier than today and the formal information request will be with you this afternoon.' She tapped the lectern once more. 'And your book is beautiful,' she told him as she left.

CHAPTER 65

Ronnie had no laptop with her, so when she returned to Parkside she sat at Malachi's desk with him and asked him to pull up the documents she wanted to see. She checked the time; it was barely noon. 'I wish those DNA results would hurry up,' she said to Malachi.

'Is that what's making you twitchy?'

'Twitchy?'

'Sorry, that's the wrong word . . .'

'It's okay, Malachi, it's probably not.'

'Can I get you a coffee?'

She smiled and shook her head. 'Not unless it comes with milk and a bright idea.'

Malachi frowned. 'I do have something, but it's more of a question than an idea, if you have a minute?'

'Go for it.'

'Or do you want the coffee first?'

'Idea, then coffee.'

'Well,' he began and leaned closer, his voice low. Tess and Dimitri were across the room, at desks either side of Fenton's office, and she doubted whether either could hear. 'I know the consensus from almost everyone is that the blackmailer and rapist are the same person, but can I tell you what puzzles me?' He didn't wait for an answer. 'Why has our blackmailer gone to huge lengths not to be identified, while the rapist gave himself a name in the chatroom?

'The disappearing WhatsApp messages take it to an extreme; they were sent from burner phones, which were purchased from multiple locations. The phones weren't used until they were several months old and the possibility of identifying the buyer on CCTV or through witnesses had diminished. Then, when the message finally comes through, it's typed on paper and photographed. I don't see how they could be more anonymous, but then there's the chatroom conversation. Let me show you.'

Instead of pulling it up on the screen, he had a printed copy. She'd been at home when she'd read it, sitting in the little office within earshot of Alex and Noah. She had read so far, and then she'd stopped. It had been the wrong environment. She'd scanned the rest of it the following day, but nowhere to the depth that Malachi had. He'd written notes and annotations.

'The rapist is the opposite,' he said. 'He hasn't stuck to the bare minimum. He's volunteered information and embellished, and then are the three sections I've highlighted in orange. There might be more, but I haven't found them yet. In each case, it's when he's describing leaving the women under the shower. Here's the first, *there's no such thing as too much of water.*'

'I saw that,' she said, 'and I assumed it was a typo.'

'No, it rang a bell with me as soon as I saw it. It's from *Hamlet*. It was our Shakespeare text.'

'How did you remember that?'

'I knew I'd seen it before. It was on the bottom half of a left-hand page and formatted like a play. It narrowed it right down.'

She had meant it as a rhetorical question.

'And here,' he pointed further down the page, '*drowning is a quiet, desperate thing* and finally *gasping for air underwater, is like giving love to someone who doesn't want it.* You see, he's showing off. It's nothing like the other mindset; they are complete opposites.'

'And these are also quotes?'

'They are.'

Ronnie read and reread the document. 'I can see that now,' she agreed, 'the blackmailer is avoiding taking any risks with their identity, whereas the rapist is . . .'

'Too arrogant,' Malachi finished for her.

Ronnie stared down at the page with the first highlighted quote *too much of water*. She tapped the desk with the tip of one finger, making a pulse.

She didn't consciously make a plan, but let her mind go where it needed to. 'Have you shown this to anyone?'

'No, I was waiting for you.'

'Fenton needs this,' she told him.

'It doesn't mean anything on its own.'

'Malachi, trust me, this is great work.'

'I think he's busy.'

'So, interrupt him.'

Malachi wasn't convinced. He didn't even stand up. This, Ronnie knew, was what happened when people's ideas were sidelined. Malachi had learned quickly that his input didn't count for much. 'I'll come with you,' she told him. 'You'll tell him, and I'll make sure he listens.'

He gathered up his highlighted papers.

Neither Tess nor Dimitri looked up as they reached Fenton's office door. This time she knocked, and they waited.

CHAPTER 66

Malachi's printouts were spread across Fenton's desk. Three small blocks of orange highlighted text among five pages of conversation didn't seem much, and Malachi looked as though he felt the scrutiny was being aimed at him personally. 'Plenty of people read books.' Fenton shuffled the pages back into a pile. 'Wishful thinking clouds everyone's judgement from time to time.' He passed the sheaf to Malachi, 'Yes, it's a few quotes, but perhaps that's our guy's shtick. He's hung up on women half-drowning and reads up on it; that doesn't give us any clue to his identity. And quoting lyrics doesn't make someone a musician, does it?'

'It's more than that,' Ronnie insisted. 'Malachi's logic about the rapist and blackmailer being two separate people is sound.'

'And fits yours and now Dimitri's preferred theory.'

'It needs investigating.'

'Absolutely,' Fenton agreed. 'But not in the place of other more likely leads.' Fenton seemed to have made up his mind to disregard the papers, no matter what she or Malachi said, and Ronnie could feel her anger rising again. Malachi had already taken a step towards the door, but she planted herself more stubbornly.

'The rape investigation is Beetham's,' Fenton continued, 'so, in line with your theory, he can prioritise this. You've given him the St Eldith's open-day lead, Ronnie; contacting every woman on that list will keep them busy. I doubt this is going to be in his top ten.'

'Enough,' Ronnie spat. She didn't know where the word had come from, but it seemed to encapsulate her every frustration. It sounded as though it should have been the start of a sentence, but it was everything she had to say.

Fenton waved Malachi away and only turned his attention to her once they were totally alone. 'We are waiting for DNA results because you . . .' he stopped to make air quotes around his next three words, 'reliably informed us that your nephew's father is the rapist. Now what? Malachi practises his secondary-school English lit skills and all that's forgotten?'

'It's not forgotten at all. They all lived there. They all had opportunity; Matthew Richardson studied literature, and maybe Owen is just a keen reader, but I want Knox in the mix too.'

'It feels mucky in the bottom of the barrel, Ronnie; you need to be careful what you fish out.'

'I'm not scraping; if the women were targeted because they visited St Eldith's then Knox is in the frame.' She jabbed the air between them. 'And why are you being a shit about it?'

'I'll ignore that comment, and I don't know what you expect; we don't have enough for a search warrant. And there's certainly not enough to arrest him on suspicion either,' he added.

'I wasn't suggesting either,' Ronnie countered. 'But what Malachi has identified is valid.' She snorted. 'I'm not stupid. I'm also not invested in this team or Operation Byron beyond finding answers, so I can see what's at the bottom of the barrel better than you can.'

'You're not stupid, no.' He closed his eyes and pressed a hand across his mouth. Ronnie waited as the silence extended out.

She had no idea where his thoughts took him, but knew not to interrupt; there was a struggle going on in the man's head.

Eventually he spoke. 'Sit down, Ronnie,' he said. And there was pain in his voice. 'This is not to leave this room. Do you understand?'

Ronnie nodded and took the closest chair.

'Honestly? I don't want to risk doing anything that sets us back. Operation Byron has gone nowhere; Beetham now has ultimate responsibility for the operation and, beyond that, I don't know whether our team will exist. I'm not sure I'm making good decisions any more.'

'Maybe you don't have the full picture,' she said quietly. 'DCI Beetham told you about Kirsten's pocket notebook entries, but Dimitri also has a theory; that someone in this team used them.'

Fenton held up a hand to stop her. 'No, stay away from that idea, Ronnie. If the blackmailer was fed information by anyone, it was by Kirsten McLeod; unless we can show any new cases after her death, then that's where it ends.' He glanced at his computer as an email pinged in. 'One person, three crimes. You'll see.'

He opened the message, read it, and then turned the screen to Ronnie.

The DNA results had arrived.

CHAPTER 67

Owen and Matthew Richardson arrived together. When Ronnie saw them side by side she could see a resemblance, but only just. Nose and eyebrows, she decided. Matthew looked a lot like the photos Ronnie had seen of his mother, Zoe. Perhaps Owen resembled his father, but she had no way to compare. The point was, neither of them particularly resembled Noah, but one of them might resemble the man he would one day become.

DCI Beetham had returned to Parkside, and he and Fenton had taken the brothers one at a time to an interview room. Owen first, and now it was Matthew's turn.

DCI Beetham led, 'Before I show you the results, Mr Richardson, is there anything you would like to tell us?'

Matthew pursed his lips. Then shook his head, 'No.'

He was sitting but hunched over with his hands clasped between his knees. His shoulders were at desk height and rounded over. He looked one step away from curling into a ball.

'What do you think the results will say, Mr Richardson?'

'I don't know.'

But he did know, Beetham was sure of it. He took the printout from its folder and passed it across to Matthew Richardson. Richardson didn't reach for it, so Beetham placed it directly in front of him.

242

'You will see that there are columns representing the child, and others representing the alleged father, being you. The columns of information are compared and that produces the probability of paternity score below.'

Richardson was staring blankly at the page, so Beetham leaned across and pointed to the figure in the box: 99.9998%. 'You are the father of Noah Blake.'

Still no response.

Owen had known with complete certainty that he wasn't the father; by that token, Matthew should have realised that he was.

'Matthew? Matthew, you are Noah Blake's father, do you understand?'

Only Richardson's eyes moved, his gaze flashed across the desk and met Beetham's, 'It's a lie,' he growled. 'I think it's a set up. I think you're all playing games, trying to get me to admit to something . . .' he drew a quick breath then raised his voice, 'something I never did.' He sat up, suddenly straightening in his chair.

'You have already admitted to an intimate relationship with Miss Blake . . .'

'Not that night I didn't. I'd seen her a couple of days before, we did it then.'

'When do you think the baby was conceived?'

'That's what I'm saying, the time before.'

'Do you understand that the child is yours?'

'Not if it makes me the rapist. I didn't force myself on her.'

DCI Beetham took a breath and adopted what he considered to be his most patient tone, 'You were intimate with Miss Blake? Yes, or no?'

'Yes, but not on the night we fought.'

'You understand you are the biological father of her son Noah? Yes, or no?'

Matthew folded his arms and glared, 'Yes.'

'And what do you know about Kirsten McLeod?'

Matthew's gaze darted from Beetham to Fenton and back again, and the colour drained from his face. 'No comment,' he managed to say, and stuck with the same answer for the remainder of the interview.

It took Matthew Richardson a while to understand that he was free to go. People often made that mistake; they agreed to an interview and seemed to think they needed to stay until the police were ready to dismiss them. Perhaps it was a sign of good manners, and sometimes of innocence; the ones who knew the score, stood up and walked – they were often the ones who needed to stay behind.

Beetham and Fenton stood in the foyer of Parkside and watched the two brothers leave. 'We'll never get a conviction for Jodie Blake's assault,' Fenton reminded him.

'I know, but if he'd cracked and admitted it, we would have been able to look at him for the other assaults.'

'And his reaction to Kirsten McLeod?'

'Maybe something in it, or perhaps he's just afraid of being made to take the blame.'

But Fenton didn't comment; instead his attention had diverted to somewhere over Beetham's shoulder. 'Oh good,' Fenton muttered, looking as jaded as Beetham felt.

Beetham followed Fenton's gaze and turned to see Ronnie striding towards them. 'Do you think she watched them walk out of here?'

'I reckon she did.'

CHAPTER 68

Just like micro expressions, plans could form in a fraction of a second. It was rare for them to arrive that quickly and in Ronnie's experience they turned out to be polarised between the particularly good and the much regretted.

She'd been sitting at an upstairs window, drinking coffee and waiting for the Richardson brothers to leave, wanting to catch up with Fenton and Beetham. She'd hurried down for an update, and the plan had arrived between landings.

She didn't bother with any preamble. 'I have an idea,' she told them. 'It's not complicated; but if it works, it will give us enough for the search warrant and arrest on suspicion.'

Fenton looked resigned. 'Tell me then,' he said without enthusiasm.

She shot him a frustrated glare. 'You can tell me it's crap after you've heard it.' She switched her attention to Beetham, who motioned for her to proceed.

'Owen Richardson, Matthew Richardson, Professor Colin Knox. Obviously, they are all linked to St Eldith's. Explicit details of the rapes have been shared by the person using the screen name MoonLake69 ...' She paused, making sure she had their full attention.

Fenton fluttered his hands with a *get on with it* gesture. DCI Beetham's expression was thoughtful.

Ronnie continued, 'Kirsten McLeod was killed because she knew too much about the blackmail scam, and her killer was either also the rapist or someone who knew the rapist's MO.'

DCI Beetham had already begun to nod, 'And if the blackmailer knew it, it's safe to assume they were already blackmailing them.'

'Yes, yes,' Fenton kept on with the impatient hands, 'and?'

'The name MoonLake69 will resonate with the rapist and, if they are two separate people, possibly the blackmailer too . . .'

Finally, Fenton caught up. 'But it will mean nothing to anyone unconnected to the crimes?'

'Exactly.' Ronnie nodded. 'All we have to do is find out who takes the bait.'

'And I suppose you've thought of that too?' Beetham asked.

And Ronnie grinned.

Now DCI Beetham sat to one side while Fenton stood in front of the team and outlined the plan, finally summing up. 'Remember, the golden egg here is probable cause. If the outcome is enough for a search warrant, then the job's a good 'un.'

Ronnie whispered to Malachi, 'Does he always say that?'

'It's a favourite.'

Fenton continued, 'Jenna, Dimitri. How long to set this up?'

Jenna replied first, 'We need time to get the brothers on site and make sure that Knox is available.'

Dimitri turned to his computer, his fingers dancing over the keys, and he turned back to Fenton in seconds. 'Knox will be at a lecture hall right next to St Eldith's; he's giving a lecture at four. Should we use it, or delay?'

'No, this will work in our favour and better than observing him from the quad. We will need to have someone in the lecture theatre.' Fenton glanced around, and his gaze settled on Malachi, 'You're up.'

'He knows me.'

Fenton brushed the concern aside. 'You're the only one of us who can pass for a non-mature student; as long as you're not in his face, it should be fine. Dimitri, how big is the venue?'

'It seats two hundred. Horseshoe arrangement; tiered. The lecture is for first-year undergraduates and classed as mandatory.'

'So, half will turn up,' Tess said. 'That's still a decent number.'

'We can be ready in one hour,' Dimitri added, finally answering Fenton's original question.

'I want someone on each person. Will, you'll have Owen Richardson. Tess and Jenna, take Matthew Richardson. And then you, Malachi, will stick with Colin Knox. Body-worn video from all of you, please. The rest of us will be on site but at a distance.'

'How's this going to work? I have visited him twice; he's going to recognise me,' Malachi muttered to Ronnie.

'It's freezing weather, go and buy yourself a Cambridge University hoodie, sit at the back. Chances are he won't look up there, and if he does, he'll just notice a typical hoodie and you'll just be another student. Keep your head down.'

Dimitri spun his chair to talk to them, 'I ordered one in blue from Giles and Co. this minute, coming by taxi by quarter past.' He spun back to his computer.

'See?' Ronnie nudged Malachi with her elbow.

'Better than making the drinks,' he admitted.

'It's all under control,' she added, though she doubted it was true.

The lecture theatre was just to the rear of the college and called the Rodin Room, perhaps in an attempt to encourage deeper rumination. It was a new building, and Malachi's camera's view of Professor Knox was via the central aisle and unobscured. Malachi was seated behind enough students to conceal him but, just to be sure, he was sporting his new blue hoodie, courtesy of Dimitri, and hiding behind an extra-large hot chocolate, courtesy of Ronnie.

Malachi had realised that the other risk of being spotted was directly prior to the lecture. He'd waited for Dimitri to confirm that Knox was still in his office and had then hidden among the other students waiting to be admitted. He needn't have worried; Knox must have come through a different entrance and appeared at the front of the hall five minutes after the students had settled.

His style was detached, not the more collaborative approach Malachi had experienced when he had been at college.

'As you will be aware, today's topic is "Narrative and Self-Concept" and, as Donald E. Polkinghorne espoused, "When the self is thought of as a narrative or story, rather than a substance or thing, the temporal and dramatic dimension of human existence is emphasized." That was in 1991, and I will discuss today how the views of narrative and self-concept have evolved since then.'

Plenty of the students were ready to make notes and leaned forward, clearly engaged. Malachi was lost already. If this had been his class, he would be slipping a little lower behind his double-chocolate with whipped cream.

Tess and Jenna located Matthew Richardson with ease. As expected, he was in his office. They had been sent as a pair and told to expect resistance, if only the verbal kind.

Tess showed her warrant card at the reception desk and asked for directions to his office. The security guard had all the hallmarks of being ex-job and didn't question either of them.

They found Matthew Richardson in a fifteen-foot-square office located between the lifts and the toilets. Whatever MRH Ltd had once been, it was now two desks, one printer and Matthew Richardson.

They introduced themselves. 'We need you to accompany us to St Eldith's.'

'As always.'

'What does that mean?' Jenna asked.

He gave a weary smile. 'Personal joke; it's not somewhere I have ever really left.' He closed his laptop and didn't argue. 'No point asking why you want me, I suppose?'

'We have some documents we'd like you to look through and identify if possible.' Tess could see his mind working, trying to fathom what the documents might be and what they would have to do with him. His mind could ponder it all the way into town; it was nothing but the cover story they'd concocted on the way over. Tess figured that any college as old as St Eldith's would have accumulated untold quantities of paperwork and it would be enough to give the smokescreen needed.

They'd both expected more of a battle, though. He stared out of the side window of the vehicle throughout, and only spoke as they were within sight of the college. 'Where do you need me?'

'It's up on the first; I'll take you through,' Jenna told him.

He nodded. 'I'll be glad when this is all over.'

She asked him what he meant, but he shook his head and didn't reply.

Will Green brought Owen Richardson in. Ronnie had arranged for him to be in the dining hall with Tina Runham. Nothing formal, just the two of them waiting for some *routine follow-up questions* about Dr Zoe Richardson's tenure. Ronnie was confident that Tina would keep them both occupied with a mix of curiosity about now and reminiscence about then.

All Ronnie needed was for each of the men to be present and occupied in some way.

She had sent Tess, Jenna and Matthew Richardson to Bob Murgatroyd's office; she was sure that would do the trick.

She dropped back as Will and Owen passed by. She recognised the porters from her previous visit. The younger of the two was called Jeff and the other was Brian. They had the rapport of colleagues who spent a great deal of time in the same space.

'Full set today, Brian.'

'That's right.'

Jeff turned to Ronnie. 'Both the Richardson lads are familiar faces, you know. You probably didn't need to call them in; they would have come anyway.'

'Would they?'

Brian replied, 'Definitely Matthew, he's close with the professor.'

'That's right,' Jeff chipped in, 'Owen is the odd one out, walks round sometimes and then back out again. Friendly enough, mind you.'

'Yes, but less at home here than the other two, he is. Feels like it's been the same forever.'

Not after today, Ronnie hoped. Ronnie had everything she needed; phone numbers, printouts and a mental note of everything she planned to say. Fenton, Jenna and Dimitri were positioned around the college.

249

'Do you have a public address system?' she asked the porters.

'Yes, we do. We can contact every communal area in the buildings,' said Brian with a touch of pride.

'And does it cover the new lecture hall?'

'Well, yes,' Jeff answered cautiously, 'because technically it's on our grounds, so it comes under our security remit, but we wouldn't usually—'

'I will need to use your public address system,' she said.

That silenced them. They looked at one another. 'You can't.'

Dimitri had already established that it was located in their lodge. 'What's wrong with it?'

'It's only for staff,' Jeff told her.

Ronnie smiled, doing her best to be disarming, 'Well then, one of you can do the honours.' She slid her first sheet of paper across to them, 'I need one of you to read this.'

Jeff read it, frowned but then nodded, 'Will do.'

Ronnie's smile vanished, and she took a breath. This was all she had; the simple plan that might hurt Noah, but could also see justice for Jodie, Kirsten, Olivia Hall and the other victims.

If it worked.

CHAPTER 69

Professor Knox used the full width of Rodin Room; he paced, he was animated and articulate. He used the area in front of the first row as though it was his stage. He wore a radio mic, and his voice filled the auditorium to the very back. Knox debated, but mostly with himself, Malachi noted. But he knew exactly when to throw a question to the audience, to grab a keen student and either reward their answer with his approval or throw dismissal back at them.

Malachi could not follow the subject but was a little awed by the control Knox had over his class. He spiced the narrative with anecdotes of past student glories and slides into ignominy.

He used the word ignominy; Malachi had searched it.

His slide deck was sparse, and he clicked through only a few key points. The rest was Knox, and the students' ability to stay alert, make notes and keep up.

Knox was over to the far side of his stage, to the right-hand side from Malachi's perspective, where his view was most obscured by those sitting in front of him and he was watching Knox through the gap between the backs of people's heads. He heard the muted crackle of the central PA system before Knox seemed to notice. Knox kept speaking, only stopping when the first two words had drowned him out.

'Attention please.'

*   *   *

Will strained to hear Owen and Tina's conversation. They hadn't asked who they were waiting for, or why they were there.

'I've seen you here when it's been a weekday,' she said, 'but I never like to interrupt.'

'You should.' Owen leaned towards her with his elbows on his knees.

He was, Will decided, one of those people who were comfortable anywhere. The kind that slept standing up on trains, or across four seats in the departure lounge. No wonder the guy lived out of a couple of bags.

Will wasn't convinced that was even possible. He hoped the search warrant would be against Owen Richardson and they'd uncover an undeclared house rammed with evidence.

The PA crackled into life then and a voice he didn't recognise asked for their attention.

'As long as it's not a fire alarm,' Tina laughed, 'I'm not going out in this.'

'Too bloody cold,' Owen agreed.

They both listened to the message that followed.

'Weird,' Tina raised an eyebrow.

'I don't understand students.'

'Wrong place for you to grow up, wasn't it?'

Her smile faded. His too.

'Yes,' he said. 'It really was.'

Some people had a way with words; Bob Murgatroyd didn't. Matthew Richardson seemed to be doing a better job of switching off from the man's bunged-up monotone than Tess. She glanced over to Jenna, who seemed too deep in her own thoughts to notice Murgatroyd either.

There had been countless times when Tess had been in far more unpleasant surroundings, with far less tolerable people. But this situation was new to her, and Ronnie had warned her about the pressure. Tess focused on breathing and staying present in the room.

Richardson looked pained, but had only asked once when he would be seen, and Jenna had assured him that DI Fenton would be with them shortly. Murgatroyd was showing him his entries in the hand-inscribed ledger. 'The correct term,' he wittered, 'is copperplate. People commonly confuse it with English roundhand.'

'Really?' Richardson replied. It didn't sound as though he was listening, just trying to make the right noise at the right time.

'Take the uppercase L, for example, can you see how I have two loops? English roundhand would only have the upper.'

Richardson stared blankly at the ledger, and Tess could see he was also lost in other thoughts and probably not absorbing anything Murgatroyd was saying to him.

Jenna remained detached.

This was a strange kind of limbo. Superficially mundane, but the atmosphere hung with the dead air that preceded a storm.

Richardson proved his disconnection from Murgatroyd's droning when he turned to her, cutting off a description of an uppercase P.

'When your DI gets here—,' he began, but was then interrupted by the PA. He listened and waited for it to finish without reaction. Then he left a couple more seconds to be certain he wouldn't be stopped again. 'When your DI gets here, will he keep me for long?'

In the tiered seating of the Rodin Room, the students watched Professor Knox. Some, Malachi noticed, leaned forward, eager to engage with subject matter. Most appeared less interested, fiddling with phones or playing time killing games on their laptops while they pretended to make notes. All faced the front, though. Knox had torn into the first students he'd seen turn away from facing the front.

It fascinated Malachi. He didn't understand the pretence of just turning up and gaining nothing more than a tick in the register, or whatever these places did. Do it or don't was his view.

When the PA announcement began, he estimated that it had at least double the impact on Knox. 'Attention please. MoonLake69 to St Eldith's porters' lodge immediately please.'

A couple of lads in front of him nudged each other, still not over the mid-teen amusement at the number 69. Beyond that, there was a murmur of confusion, but instead of calling for attention, Knox was silent.

The room settled and the floor was his again. He took a step back, then fought to regain the flow of his lecture. 'Apologies, I lost my thread for a moment.'

He turned to the screen, looking for direction. 'French philosopher Paul Ricœur describes emplotment as—' He stopped speaking as the PA repeated the previous message, emphasising the screen name with more urgency than the first time.

Even from the back row, Malachi could see Knox wobble. The auditorium lights were bright, but the sheen of sweat on Knox's face was new and Malachi doubted that it was heat related.

Malachi texted Ronnie. *Send it now.*

Within a few seconds he saw the bloom of the glow from a phone on the lectern. And again. And again.

'Paul Ricœur . . .' Knox began, and struggled through a couple of disjointed sentences before he was distracted by the fourth message arriving. 'Excuse me a moment.' He muttered and reached for his phone. He stared at the screen for far longer than it would have taken to read the disappearing WhatsApp messages, each displaying the sentence, 'I told the police.'

His mic was still live, and there was only one word from him. It repeated, brewing from a whimper to a sob, and then to a guttural, brutal roar, 'No. No. No, no, no.'

Malachi hurried down the steps and arrived at the same time as Fenton from the left and Ronnie from the right. He removed Knox's radio mic and confirmed that his camera was still recording.

The students sat in stunned silence. Now he had their attention.

CHAPTER 70

Ronnie hung back at the porters' lodge. She watched the others leave. She had statements to write, but she had no plans to go back to Parkside tonight.

Brian was ready to lock up. Jeff was already outside.

'You look done in,' Brian told her.

'Thanks, flattery like that always gives me a lift.' She pulled on her jacket. 'And thanks for your help, both of you.'

'Old Bill's a tough job.' He held the door for her.

She suddenly felt exhausted. 'It has its moments,' she admitted.

'It's been a long day all round,' he agreed.

He was right, and it wasn't finished for the rest of the team. Just for her.

For the first time since arriving in Cambridge, she grabbed a taxi and was halfway home when her phone rang. Fenton's name flashed up. 'I'm calling to make sure you've called it a day?' he asked.

'Don't worry, there's an important conversation I need to have when I get home. And I know I have to steer clear of this investigation now. Thanks for letting me in.'

'It was excellent work, Ronnie. Good luck with your family.'

'Thank you, sir. It will be fine.' She quickly crossed and uncrossed her fingers. She hoped it would be, and she wasn't superstitious, but it couldn't hurt either. 'Can I ask the latest?'

'We're waiting for Knox to be declared fit for interview. We'll have search warrants for his home and office within the hour. Too soon to say more than that.'

'So, can I come back in tomorrow?'

'We'll see.'

It was a good enough response.

Next, she texted Alex, *Two minutes away.*

He replied with a thumbs-up emoji, and then, *The dinner's nearly in the dog.*

Ronnie could smell barbecue chicken as soon as she opened the door. And mash, definitely mash. Most evenings they ate at the breakfast bar, or with plates on their laps. She walked through to the kitchen and was greeted by Noah carrying placemats and cutlery towards the dining room.

'Posh dinner tonight,' he announced. 'Alex says it's your all-time favourite.'

'Cabbage on toast?'

Noah screwed up his nose. 'Eww, no. That sounds like one of your recipes.'

'Cheeky,' she called after him.

Alex poured them each a glass of white and passed hers over. 'Do you know?'

She nodded. 'Matthew,' she mouthed, having learned that kids could hear secrets from two rooms away, while remaining deaf to unwanted instructions.

'And?'

She shrugged and shook her head. 'I don't know.'

He shrugged back at her. 'Take the plates. The food's ready, I'll bring it through.'

They sat at the two long sides of the table, Noah next to Alex and Ronnie across from them.

Noah emptied half his plate, then stopped to consider the next forkful, 'Why's it called hunter's chicken?'

Alex answered, 'I reckon because of the barbecue sauce; the hunter's out all night and cooking by the fire.'

'And has he killed the chicken, or brought it with him?'

'What do you reckon?' Alex asked him.

'Killed it. You can't walk around with a dead chicken and then eat it. You'd get food poisoning.' Noah prodded a strip of bacon. 'But what about the pig, Ronnie?'

'I think . . .' Ronnie stopped and considered, 'I think the man's name was Hunter and he was a chef, and this was his famous special recipe.'

Noah spun in his chair and high-fived Alex. 'That's what you said she'd say. Exactly.'

Ronnie groaned, pretended to be offended, 'Am I that predictable?'

Alex winked at Noah. 'Safer to say reliable.'

Ronnie was the last to finish eating. The timing for speaking to Noah bothered her. Bringing down the conversation when he was having fun seemed wrong. Too close to bed and he might not sleep. But it was already getting late, and she wondered whether tomorrow might be better.

Alex was staring across at her. She wasn't sure how long he'd been trying to catch her attention. He gave her a pointed look. 'Do you remember spelling from school, Ronnie? I bet you had words like procrastinate and postponement.'

She raised an eyebrow. 'Was that the week you had precarious and impudent?'

Noah pitched in, 'Do I have to do spellings tonight?'

'No, not today.' Ronnie leaned forward, her elbows on the table. She wished she was next to him, to put her arm around him if he needed it, but she also wanted to see his expression. 'I have a bit of news actually. I have found out who your dad is.'

She waited for him to respond, but he pressed his lips together and lowered his gaze to his lap.

'He didn't know about you, not until today.' She could see small red patches forming on Noah's cheeks. 'And he's not the bad man that your mum thought he was.'

Noah could be outspoken and great company. Easy to forget how young eight years old really was. Now he looked small as he shrank into Alex's side.

'We don't need to talk about it, Noah, we just wanted you to know.' She looked to Alex for guidance, but he looked blank. 'Is that okay, Noah?'

He nodded, and finally raised his head to look at her, his eyes wide and fearful. 'I want to stay here with both of you.'

'I didn't think ... Of course.' It hadn't occurred to her that he might think he had to live with a father he had never met. 'Noah, you're not going anywhere.'

'Absolutely,' Alex echoed and buried a kiss in his nephew's hair. 'You can't move out until you're at least my age.'

Noah's fear visibly slipped away.

Ronnie gathered the dishes and took them to the kitchen, and by the time she returned Noah was his usual self. They spent twenty minutes on a game of cards.

'Time for bed.'

Noah looked tired. 'If I brush my teeth, please can I come down to say goodnight?'

Ronnie nodded; Alex had told her that it had been the same every bedtime since Noah had arrived. Noah would come back down then request one or both of them to follow him to bed to say another goodnight.

This time Noah stopped at the doorway. 'Do I get to meet him?' he asked.

Ronnie and Alex exchanged a glance, and it was Alex who replied, 'We'll have to see.'

'Because I don't think I want to,' Noah told them. 'Not yet anyway.'

CHAPTER 71

Ronnie slept without dreaming of Jodie. It wasn't the first time, but this time it felt like a release or a turning point, rather than a fluke.

She opened her eyes an hour before the alarm, and idly watched the shadows of clouds against her curtains. The day was going to be bright but cold, and she had nothing to do beyond walking Noah to school.

She planned to spend the day in the city, being a tourist, learning its history. She could take a punt tour or ride the open-top bus. Or visit one of the other attractions that locals probably never bothered with. There was a lot to learn for such a small city. But she'd done okay so far; she'd learned about bedders and porters and seen the clock with the golden cricket. Or was it a locust?

She closed her eyes and spent a few more minutes in semi-consciousness. She would call Fenton later, find out whether they needed her. Or perhaps she'd be allowed to start where she was officially intended to be, as a DS for Superintendent Cooper.

As long as she was working. Hers was the best career.

Old Bill's a tough job.

Brian the porter's words. They ran through her head like an earworm. She could even hear his voice as he said it.

Old Bill's a tough job . . . tough job . . . tough job. His words repeating in a gentle rhythm until she dipped back towards sleep.

It was the only job she'd ever wanted.

And it suited her.

Fragments of the case floated in and out of her thoughts, free flowing, sliding over one another, finding direction and order and . . .

Ronnie drew a sharp breath and struggled on to one elbow, blinking herself awake. 'How did what I just thought make sense?' she wondered. She instantly ditched the idea of open-top buses and guided punts; instead, she scrambled to dress, took Alex's old Ford and headed for Kirton.

At Linda's request, Ronnie made tea and toast, stacked a tray with butter and a variety of jams and joined the former detective inspector in her sparsely furnished sitting room. She placed the tray on a low table between the two high-backed armchairs and, again at Linda's request, spread two slices of toast with thin layers of butter and raspberry jam, cutting each slice in four. She chose the same for herself.

'When I first suffered my stroke,' Linda told her slowly, 'I struggled to swallow even sips of liquid. It was just one of the many mundane activities I had taken for granted.' She held up the square of toast and made a cheers gesture. 'It taught me to acknowledge the small pleasures.'

They ate in companionable silence. When she'd finished eating, Linda returned her side plate to the tray. 'So you caught him then,' she said without preamble.

'It looks that way,' said Ronnie.

Linda studied her and Ronnie corrected herself. 'He's the rapist. I have no doubt about it . . .'

'But?' Linda asked, her attention sharpened now.

'Blackmail, rape and murder. I've never believed they were all committed by the same person. And I have a question for you, if I may?'

'Of course.'

'When I visited your husband, he was clearly terrified. More scared than most men would be when their debts have been paid and they are already serving time for their crimes.'

Linda nodded without comment.

'He only risked giving me the link to Kirsten McLeod once he had worked out I wasn't a threat, and that told me two things. Firstly, he didn't know I wasn't a threat until that moment and therefore didn't know the identity of the person who did pose a risk.' She paused, wondering whether there would be a sign of affirmation.

Linda turned her gaze to the family photos. Ronnie waited for Linda's attention to return, but instead Linda spoke. 'And secondly,' she told Ronnie, 'because he was scared the same thing that happened to Kirsten would happen to our daughter, Monica.'

'Did he tell you that?'

'No, I worked it out after your first visit.' Her eyelids flickered and her gaze alighted on Ronnie again. 'And the man you arrested?'

Ronnie shook her head. 'His name is Professor Colin Knox.' She watched Linda for any sign of recognition but, as she suspected, there was none.

'So what's your question?' asked Linda.

'I'm coming to that.'

In a matter of seconds Linda had taken on a weary expression.

'Are you okay?' Ronnie asked.

'I'd hoped it was over.'

'It's close,' Ronnie assured her. 'The blackmailer was using Kirsten to gather information on potential blackmail victims . . .'

'With her knowledge?' Linda asked sharply.

'We don't think so.'

And Linda nodded as though it was the response she had expected.

'Kirsten was murdered because the blackmailer was covering their tracks,' Ronnie said. 'They were already aware of Knox and his crimes so they tried to make it look as though he had been guilty of it all.'

'Sounds like someone who enjoys playing games, probably proud of their own mental resources.'

'At the same time, the DEAD team's blackmail investigation was going nowhere. They had false leads and dead ends, until an anonymous list started them on the trail to Knox.' Ronnie was aware she still hadn't posed her question, but she had wanted to make sure that Linda had context before she replied. 'I realised something else this morning. The other victims were mostly in a better financial situation than you and your husband. They were blackmailed for painful, but manageable, sums of money . . .'

'Because the parasite rarely kills the host?'

'Exactly so. I want to know why your family was singled out. I want to find out which one of the DEAD team has been pulling the strings of Operation Byron. How well do you know them, Linda? Could one of them hold a grudge against you?'

Linda had been in the act of picking up her mug of tea, but slowly replaced it on the tray. She leaned back in her chair and stared at Ronnie, or possibly through her, focusing on more distant thoughts. Ronnie waited.

Finally, Linda said. 'I know them all, the original members that is. John and Jenna, Dimitri and Tess. Will Green joined a little later. There was a joke in the station when that team formed, that there were two requirements for entry: having a skill and pissing off your boss. They were a bunch of misfits, even Fenton, but he somehow manages to hold them all together. And now you're asking me whether one of them is the blackmailer and a killer.' Linda's focus on Ronnie tightened and, despite her frailty, it was clear that she was still a formidable woman. 'One of them who hated me enough to exploit the opportunity for blackmail.'

Ronnie nodded.

Linda lowered her gaze. She stretched the fingers of one hand while the other lay dead in her lap.

Ronnie knew that Linda was trying to understand what she might have done to wreak such devastation on her life. But they both knew that a killer's logic ran to different parameters to their own.

Linda frowned, then looked bewildered for several seconds before she stared back at Ronnie. 'I never made the connection,' she muttered.

'Connection to what?'

'I received a series of threatening letters. They all said the same. *You made a mistake, you are going to pay.* That was all, there was nothing else. It was investigated, but beyond learning that they had been posted from Cambridge, there was no clue to the sender's identity. They were all delivered to the police station apart from the last one.' She paused, the unpleasantness of the memory clear in her expression and her hushed tone. 'My daughter received a card on her fourteenth birthday, and all it said inside was *I'll get you later.* She was terrified, of course she was, but we never even had a suspect. And after that, they stopped.'

Linda fell silent for a few seconds, clearly in thought. Double checking her logic, Ronnie guessed, before voicing her suspicions. Linda nodded to herself.

'It was just after I had turned down an officer for promotion. It was a panel interview and they came to me for feedback. I told them that the final decision had been mine alone, and I gave my reasons. I told them they weren't ready and they reacted badly. They shouted at me briefly, and there was a short confrontation between us. I wrote it off as their disappointment but I saw flash of something then that I didn't like. It was unprofessional conduct and I knew my decision had been the correct one.'

'And now you think they were the sender of those threatening messages?'

Linda nodded slowly. 'Actually, now I have made the connection, I'm certain. Sometimes the ring of truth is crystal clear, isn't it?'

'As a bell,' Ronnie agreed. And when Linda gave her the name, it all made sense.

Ronnie drove back to Cambridge and pulled into a public car park situated a couple of streets away from Parkside station. *Do the coffee run to Signorelli's,* she texted Malachi, and waited for him to arrive. She had a hot chocolate waiting. 'No cream, no flake. But you know these things are still no good for you?'

He shrugged. 'Better than cocaine and gambling.'

'They aren't the only alternatives.'

'Are you mumming me?'

'Actually no, I'm pumping you for information. And I want you to do something for me. Firstly, Knox: how's it going?'

Malachi hooked his head in the direction of the quietest corner, 'We'll sit there, and chances are we won't be seen. We certainly won't be overheard.'

'And we need to be brief, I don't want you to be missed.'

She chose the side of the table with a view of the café entrance; Malachi faced her. 'Knox's house was a gold mine; he went to extremes to avoid forensics in the attacks, but seemed to think his own home was never going to come under the spotlight. His computer used private browser windows, but he's downloaded the messages from the rape-fantasy chatroom. He'd kept them in a hidden folder, like that would achieve anything. He had a supply of Tyvek suits on hand, and underwear he'd removed from his victims was in a suitcase in the loft.'

'Wow.'

'Exactly.'

'What's he been charged with?' Ronnie could hear the urgency in her own voice, and it seemed to make Malachi hesitant.

'Everything as far as I know,' he told her.

'Kirsten McLeod's murder?' she pressed.

'I think so. There's going to be a press announcement later.'

'Who by?'

'DCI Beetham.'

'Shit, does that mean he's winding up his investigation and ours?'

'I'm not sure.' Malachi stared at the froth on his hot chocolate. 'I'm sorry.'

'Okay, listen. I have some information for Fenton, but I need to speak to him in person, and it needs to be in confidence. I don't want to text or call because I won't see who he'll be with or be sure that he won't comment. I'll be here, can you let him know?'

'He's really tied up.'

She tapped the tabletop with the tips of her fingers. Trying to convey the urgency, but she didn't need to ask again.

'It's okay, Ronnie, I'm on it.'

CHAPTER 72

It had been a long day. The arrest was never the end, far from it. The paperwork was immense and ongoing, but Jenna didn't mind. The DEAD team had made the arrest.

In her mind's eye, she'd wanted the credit. She'd hoped for the opportunity to have the breakthrough. It could have been a career highlight.

But she was splitting hairs. This way the whole team benefited, and she didn't begrudge most of them. Not really.

And at least it was over, and it felt like the end of an era.

She guessed it would be a late finish and had brought the right clothes for the weather: hat, gloves, heavy coat, the works. Even an extra jumper. As she layered up ready to go, she noticed Tess had chosen that same moment to pack up her things. 'It's supposed to be minus three out there.'

'I heard,' Tess replied. 'I just looked out this morning, saw the sun and assumed it would be warmer. I walked once round the Piece and nearly passed out.' She already looked cold.

'Do you want my gloves or jumper or something?'

'No, thanks. I'm just going too; I'll walk down with you.'

Jenna held the door and although they took the first flight of stairs in silence, she could sense that Tess was brewing words. But by the time they reached the bottom, she still hadn't spoken.

'What's on your mind, Tess?'

'Were you in with Knox during his interview?' She pushed open the outer door.

The cold hit Jenna, stinging her face. 'I saw it on the playback,' she said, and followed Tess into the icy wind.

'And?'

Jenna wasn't sure what she was being asked, but whatever the question, there wasn't much to tell. 'It was a no-comment interview. Neither Beetham nor Fenton could get him to stray from it. Is that what you meant?'

'I guess. I wondered about Kirsten McLeod.' Tess sped up, battling the cold.

'What about her?'

'It's another anomaly with the chatroom conversations. They bug me.'

Jenna reached for Tess's arm and slowed her. 'Are you saying there's a problem with the arrest?'

'There might be.' She pulled away and picked up her pace again, 'It's too cold, I need to get inside.'

Jenna followed her, 'Where's your car?'

'It's in for a service. Shit timing.' Tess hurried toward the bus station.

'Come to mine and I'll drop you home.' They walked a few yards further and she asked, 'Who have you told?'

'No one yet. I've just been thinking it over. Then today . . .' she raised her hands and dropped them again, 'I don't know why I didn't say anything. Do you think I should tell him?'

'Fenton?'

'Or Beetham.'

'But tell him what?'

'The chatroom conversation isn't what it seems. No one has found out who is talking to Knox.'

'They're trying to.'

Tess shook her head. 'They will fail. That chat was a set up by someone in our team. Someone who pumped information from Knox, found out the details of what he'd done.'

'How do you know?'

'It's complicated, Jenna. It would take me too long to explain. I'm too cold and I just want to go home.'

Jenna tugged her coat off. The air was bitterly cold, but she would still be more warmly dressed than Tess. 'Take it, just till we reach my car.'

'God, thank you. You're a lifesaver.'

Jenna's house was another ten minutes away. They hurried in silence. She took them around to the back of the property, where garages had replaced the original Georgian stable blocks. One had survived at the house at the furthest end of the street, and had promptly been listed as being of historic interest, but everyone else kept their vehicles in style. She pressed the control on her keyring and the door slid upwards.

'Nice,' Tess nodded as she shivered her way round to the passenger side.

'The garage is the best thing about my place,' Jenna told her. When she started the engine, it blasted frigid air for a couple of minutes, but the heated seat activated right away. 'Any better?' she asked.

'I'm having a hot shower as soon as I'm home,' Tess said. 'This cold is ridiculous.'

Jenna put her hand to the fan. 'Warm air's coming.' She glanced over at Tess. 'Look, do you want me to go over the messages with you? We could go to Fenton together, if there really is a problem.'

'What if it's him?'

'Now you're sounding paranoid. You said the problem's complex; he's simple all the way.'

That made Tess smile. 'You're right there. I'll think it through and take it to him in the morning. Have you read the transcript?'

'Several sections, not from end to end.'

'He references every assault except one. Nothing refers to Kirsten. I'll explain that to him, too.'

Jenna dropped Tess home and arrived back at her own house fifteen minutes later. She'd planned to order in food, to turn up the heating and fall asleep in front of the TV.

It would have been a low-key way to celebrate the success of the case, but she'd been looking forward to it. Instead, she still turned on the TV, but she paced.

CHAPTER 73

Tess stood under the hot shower jets until she felt her blood circulating at its proper rate. It was still relatively early, but she dressed in pyjamas and slippers. She'd left her phone on charge on the kitchen worktop and there was a message waiting when she returned to it.

She read it twice and nodded. 'Okay. Okay. Okay.' Each time she repeated the word it was with a little more conviction. Finally, she texted her reply, 'I'm ready.' She took a microwaveable sweet and sour chicken from the freezer and set it to cook for the required nine minutes. She watched the seconds tick while the kettle boiled. She had no desire for food or drink.

Finally, just when she had started to expect a false alarm, there was a knock at her door. The wall clock read 9.55 p.m.

It was late for an uninvited guest.

She didn't own any flash security device. The closest she had was an outside light and a door with a spyhole. She peered out, then released the door. 'Jenna?'

'Can we talk, is that okay?'

'Of course,' Tess stepped back to let Jenna enter. 'Come on through.'

'I knew I wouldn't sleep without finding out what's wrong.'

'Do you want a drink?'

'Not really. Can you just explain what's going on?'

Tess waved Jenna towards the sofa. 'Part of me hoped you'd come. I wanted to speak to you alone. Please sit.' Tess sat beside her. She drew and then exhaled with a nervous huff. 'Where to start?' She gave a tremulous laugh.

'Start anywhere; it'll work itself out.'

'Okay.' Tess nodded. 'I think it went like this: Kirsten McLeod was a probationer; someone had access to her pocket notebooks and cherrypicked cases where there would be no further police action, but those that still had potential for producing blackmail victims.'

Jenna shifted in her seat. 'We all know this.'

'I keep wondering, was she in on it? Or was she being used?'

Jenna shrugged. 'That's one for Knox to answer.'

'Is it though?' Tess mused. Her nerves had settled; stage fright she called it. 'I think she didn't know, but it began to dawn on her, and it certainly would have done when her boss's husband became a victim. You knew that though.'

Jenna opened her mouth, probably to ask what the hell Tess was talking about. Instead she said nothing. It would have been a pointless exercise; Jenna knew Tess knew, but Jenna still went with the charade of shaking her head.

'The first big opportunity was when Kirsten came across Tina Runham, the bedder. And you made your first mistake; you visited St Eldith's to follow up. That's the first piece of evidence and I only found it today.'

'I'm sure I would have visited St Eldith's, but not about the rape.'

Tess ignored her and carried on. 'You found out what Knox had done, and you blackmailed him and his wife. You manipulated him, you formed an online persona, DrownXHer, and you catfished him.'

Jenna shook her head. 'Not me.'

'And you staged Kirsten's murder to look like a rape gone wrong. Knox never refers to Kirsten in his messages because she was nothing to do with him.'

Jenna scrambled to her feet. 'Tess, you are twisting the facts, no one will believe you. Knox did it all.'

Tess leaned back, unfazed by Jenna glaring down at her. 'I have proof of your online identity, and proof you sent the anonymous messages.'

'You can't have, because I didn't.'

269

'I have enough to stop this investigation in its tracks. Are you confident that everything you have done will stand inspection? You added dead-end cases and probably blocked the DEAD team's progress at every turn. Can you survive the scrutiny of digital forensics, of location mapping and forensic analysis of your spending patterns? I bet you've poured thousands into that bloody house of yours.'

'I inherited the money.'

'Of course you did.' Tess grinned. 'And yet I think I saw you flinch.'

'No. If you had half of that information, you would have given it to Fenton.'

'Knox can go down, and I don't care what he's charged with, but I also want a share of what you've taken. I've added it up, it's a hefty chunk. It would have cost you to run your operation, so I don't want half. I think you've had around two hundred K. Seventy-five would be fine.' Tess fell silent then. She held Jenna's gaze and smiled serenely as she waited. 'That's enough for you to pay me, but not enough for you to kill me.'

'You're not bent.'

'I never have been, but I have debt I need to clear. It's a one-off; we can both carry on with our careers.'

Jenna shook her head, backed up, then turned to leave. She didn't speak until she reached the door.

Tess called after her, 'Sixty Jenna?' then with panic in her voice, 'Please?' A sob caught in her throat, 'Fifty even, I could sort myself out with fifty.'

Jenna double-locked the front door and turned back to Tess. 'No deal,' she said, and Tess saw the glint of a blade in her hand.

CHAPTER 74

It was a classic set up. Tess as the bait and the team in the wings; the DEAD team doing what the DEAD team did best. And Jenna fell for it even though she'd been on the other side of the fence.

Ronnie and Will were closest: in the garden on the other side of an unlocked patio door. Dimitri had the audio and visual in hand, and Malachi and Fenton were at the front of the house.

They were waiting for Fenton's confirmation that they had enough evidence.

Ronnie couldn't hear the exchange, just Fenton telling them to hold back. She watched intently, trying to guess the conversation. Tess looked nervous, then upset. Jenna displayed a narrower range of reactions. She looked composed. Cold. Jenna headed for the door and, for a moment, Ronnie thought she was ready to leave.

Fenton again ordered them to wait.

But then the blade caught the light, and Ronnie and Will both ran.

Ronnie made it through the door first; she hurtled towards Jenna and smacked the knife from her hand. She tried to throw her to the ground, but Jenna's response was automatic. She caught Ronnie's cheekbone with her elbow a moment before Will finally took her down.

She kicked out one last time. 'Pack it in,' Ronnie commanded. Will rolled Jenna into a facedown position to cuff her, but it was Ronnie who read her rights. Jenna pressed her lips into a tight line and glared.

'What happened to my sister?' Ronnie demanded. Then she pulled Jenna upright. 'What happened to Jodie?'

Jenna looked at the room full of people and shrugged. 'I sent her those WhatsApp messages and I told her what she'd done.'

'Tried hard and loved her son?'

Jenna shook her head. 'She could have stopped him, but she wouldn't. And I told her what he did to all the other victims that came after her. I made it clear.'

Ronnie's throat tightened. She felt Fenton's hand on her arm, pulling her away. 'Why?' she managed to say.

Jenna's voice followed her as she backed away, 'It wasn't always about money; sometimes people deserve to be punished.' A small smile bloomed on Jenna's lips. 'She killed herself because she walked on by, because she looked away. She chose her punishment.'

CHAPTER 75

Ronnie returned to St Eldith's the following morning.

Brian and Jeff were both on duty. 'Am I allowed to walk around?' she asked Jeff.

'Of course. And good to see you looking well. We heard about the professor. Shocking,' he said. 'And about your sister.' There was genuine sadness in his expression and she appreciated that more than any spoken words of sympathy, 'You must have mixed feelings about this place.'

It was true, she hated the thought of St Eldith's in so many ways, but the happiest photo of Jodie was here, outside these gates. She'd been bright and excited. Ready to start out in life.

She nodded her thanks to Jeff, but couldn't speak; she had yet to cry, but without warning she was now fighting tears.

She followed the corridor anticlockwise, aimlessly following one hallway after the next but inevitably arriving at a dead end outside Room 22. She touched the door with her fingertips and then leaned on the wall behind her and slid down to the floor.

The tears flowed unchecked then.

She gave into it. Told herself it was okay to cry. Okay to admit how much it hurt.

Knox had been found and stopped.

Jenna would be punished.

Ronnie heard herself sob. The tears so heavy that she could barely see. It didn't matter; she didn't have to hold it in any more. And the sobs grew louder, wracking her body. Releasing a little of her illogical self-recrimination. She could never have saved her mother or her brother.

But Jodie?

She didn't know. Just knew she loved her, and it would always hurt.

Then in the middle of it, she felt someone next to her. Holding her, rocking her, like the child she'd never been allowed to be. She buried her face into Tina Runham's maternal shoulder, and they cried together.

Afterwards she slipped away from St Eldith's and home to Alex and Noah. They had pizza delivered and *Indiana Jones*.

The three of them sat on the floor with their backs to the sofa and the two pizza boxes between them. 'Did you know,' said Noah, 'that Indiana Jones is in Han Solo's imagination?'

Ronnie stopped mid-mouthful. 'You're kidding?'

Noah shook his head. 'No, it's true.'

He turned to Alex for confirmation. 'Apparently so,' her brother confirmed. He pointed at the screen, 'Watch, there's an R2-D2 hieroglyph.'

They continued watching and she smiled sadly. There were, as Jeff had said, mixed feelings. It was all bittersweet, but she was home.

Ronnie arrived at Cambridgeshire Constabulary Headquarters in Huntingdon for a noon meeting. DCI Beetham had called her in and now she sat opposite him and DI Fenton.

Fenton spoke first. 'The DEAD team has received a stay of execution, and I want to thank you for the part you played. The team will stay as is, with DCI Beetham in the background.'

'Not too far in the background, though,' Beetham cautioned. 'Will also helped me decide what to do with the team. He has opted to join me; he's more of a bean counter than an operational detective. He was not in his comfort zone,' he chuckled, 'not at all. And now you have a choice, Ronnie. Do you want to start with Cooper or join my team?'

'Is there an option three?' she asked.

'The DEAD team?' He nodded as though it was no surprise. 'John and I have discussed it. There's one vacancy. Tess is taking Jenna's old role, so you would be in the outside team with Malachi. How does that sound?'

She turned to Fenton. 'May I have a word with you in private, sir?'

Beetham dropped back in his chair, clearly curious, but stopping short of interfering.

Ronnie offered no further explanation, and after a few seconds Beetham said, 'Okay, I'll give you five.'

'I thought we would leave, not him,' she muttered to Fenton.

'Likewise,' he replied. 'So what is it?'

'Don't you wonder why Jenna took such a huge risk?'

Fenton was clearly puzzled, not sure of where she was headed.

'She could have left it alone,' Ronnie continued. 'She had caused so much misdirection within the team that Byron was on the verge of being wound down in any case.' She leaned closer, making sure Fenton couldn't look away when she was ready to make her point. 'Beetham's team were already hunting the rapist and Kirsten's murderer with the theory that they were the same person. She wanted the murder to be wrapped up with the rapes.'

Fenton's brain began to stir, 'But if the connection was made to Kirsten and the blackmail, it would have been too much of a coincidence that she was then killed by one person when another had a motive. Jenna wanted it all tied up in one go.'

'Correct,' Ronnie agreed, feeling pleased to use one of Beetham's stock phrases while sitting in his own office. 'So she sent the anonymous note, tying it all into a neat little package.'

'And?' Fenton flapped his hands, palms upwards. 'She wanted to make the arrest. She wanted to keep control. And it all went horribly wrong for her.'

'Yes, yes, and yes. But she also wanted something else and the clue was on the envelope. Jenna was a perfectionist, planning everything to the last detail. Correct?'

He nodded, 'Absolutely.'

'And yet she addressed you without your rank on that envelope. Called you Joan.'

He frowned and she saw the first sign of a squirm.

'I am guessing that it was no accident. It was her own private, spiteful dig at you. Deliberate disrespect.'

'But why?' Fenton shrugged. 'I thought we had a good working relationship.'

Ronnie smiled at him with more than a hint of condescension. 'I've been here no time, but the station rumours weren't so hard to dig up. Unhappy first marriage, ending suddenly. You had a roving eye.'

'It was years back, nothing serious, and we both knew it.'

Ronnie pinned him with a hard stare. 'You would be wise to give Beetham the full details and, secondly, I want to work in the DEAD team, but nothing happens like that ever again, not just with me, but with anyone. If it comes to my attention, your wife will know too.'

Beetham's return was so well timed that Ronnie wondered whether he had been at the door and listening for them to fall silent. He sat again and seemed oblivious to the change in atmosphere. 'I asked how you felt about a switch to the DEAD team?'

She nodded, 'Thank you, sir, I'd like that very much.'

They firmed up the arrangements, then Fenton stood as she readied to leave, 'Thank you, Ronnie, and I'll see you on Monday.' As the door swung slowly closed behind her, she heard Fenton say, 'I need a word please, sir.' And she smiled.

She arrived back in Cambridge at 2.30. She parked Alex's old Ford in the multistorey and walked the few minutes to the corner of East Road and Parkside. She'd chosen the spot where she'd alighted the bus on her first day in Cambridge.

Owen Richardson was already there, in jeans and a hoodie despite the cold, and with his shoulders hunched against the wind.

She'd imagined them standing right there for a few minutes, getting their awkward new situation introductions out of the way. But it was too cold to do anything but head for a café. 'Do you know Thrive?' she asked. 'It would be warmer in there.'

'Okay,' he said, and they walked in silence. She spent the minutes wondering what she was supposed to say, and what might be going on in his head.

She pushed the door open and they stood at the counter for several seconds before he held out his hand in sudden and slightly awkward formality. 'Thanks for seeing me,' he said. 'I'll get to the point. I'm wondering whether I could meet Noah. I thought it was a bad idea at first, since I'm just an uncle and his dad . . . well, I don't know what will happen there . . . Do you think Noah would want to meet me? Could we talk about it?'

'First off, don't underestimate being an uncle. And second, yes, we can talk.'

He grinned, suddenly lit up and the awkwardness vanished.

'I have heard the carrot cake is worth a try,' she said.

'With hot chocolate?'

'You know, I think I will.' Malachi would be proud, she realised, and simultaneously it occurred to her that she hardly recognised herself. She was no longer Ronnie Blake from London and she was glad.

ACKNOWLEDGEMENTS

Firstly, thank you to Broo Doherty and Krystyna Green. It took a long time to percolate this one and I appreciate your guidance and being told to throw away an early draft; it hurt but it was ultimately the best thing I could have done.

And a word of advice to new writers everywhere . . . having to bin 50,000 words may hurt, but sometimes it's less painful than keeping them.

There are two people who I will thank for every book. Christine Bartram, without whom I would not have finished the first and Claire Tombs who stopped me giving up before the third.

Thank you, Dr William Holstein. Our conversations date back years now . . . usually dark, frequently enlightening, always appreciated.

A plot is like unravelling a twisted puzzle, sometimes the next move is clear, other times I turn it over and over, looking for an answer. Sometimes bouncing possibles around is invaluable. To John Swinfield, Kathryn Roux, Jane Martin, Lisa Sanford, Genevieve Pease and Jonathan Dancer, thank you all for your time.

Heartfelt thanks to the wonderful support I have received from Lana and Will, Dean and Stella.

Thank you to the following people from the Constable team who help to transform a manuscript into the finished article. They say you can't judge a book by its cover, but I think that's the point of having one . . . Thank you so much Sean Garrehy for the stunning artwork

– you have captured the atmosphere of this book. A copy-editor looks at the book from multiple angles, spotting the flaws that might bug or disappoint the reader. This is one of my favourite parts of the process; I hope that there will be some subtle tweaks to give the book a final polish, and hold my breath in case there is a major 'oh no' moment. Thank you, Howard Watson. You are insightful and always a pleasure to work with. And thank you to Amanda Keats for looking after the book between completed manuscript and finished product – beautiful work.

Thank you to the people who have lent their names to some of the characters: Dave Butterworth, John Cookman, Paul Beetham and the wider team who work in police education, including Kat Soame and Debs Davis, from whom I have learned so much about the inner workings of police officers' brains.

And finally, to the group of people to whom this book is dedicated: Amanfi Aggrey, Ben Everly, Bex Kellett, Bhasha Mukherjee, Charlotte Yip, Indie Loader, Ken Cheng, Paul Linton and Scott Sweeney. Meeting you all wasn't just fate, it was genius.